Smoke Bomb

NEW YORK TIMES BESTSELLING AUTHOR

ABBI GLINES

Visit my website at
www.abbiglinesbooks.com

Cover Designer: **Damonza.com**
Editor: Jovana Shirley, Unforeseen Editing
www.unforeseenediting.com
Formatting: Melissa Stevens, The Illustrated Author
www.theillustratedauthor.com

To the librarian who took the Sweet Valley High book I was returning in 1989 and put ***Heaven*** *by V.C. Andrews in my hand. May our libraries be filled with rebels like you.*

Prologue

TRINITY
ELEVEN YEARS OLD

I was hungry. My stomach growled, and I chewed on my bottom lip, trying to decide what to do. Facing Tabitha, my stepmother, each morning was difficult enough, but this week, her son, Roy, was visiting from college. He scared me in ways Tabitha didn't.

The bacon she had cooked for him smelled so good, but I already knew she wouldn't let me have any. I'd be given an apple or a can of peaches if we were out of fresh fruit. Later, when she went to the church's planning meeting for their fall festival, I could sneak in the kitchen and make a sandwich. It would be dinner when my dad was home from work before I got my first real meal of the day. She would make something special for Roy, and I'd get to eat it too. Last night, Dad had worked late and missed dinner, so that meant I had been left locked in my room. If Dad wasn't here to see me eat, then I didn't get to eat.

When he had married Tabitha, she hadn't started off hating me—or maybe she did and hid it. The first time she told me I was fat because my breasts were getting big, she wrapped me in athletic tape to flatten them, then made me drink this awful stuff that caused me to vomit. She said I had demons in me and she had to get them out. I went to Dad and told him.

That had been my first mistake. Tabitha had gotten worse after that.

I swallowed nervously and stood up to walk to my door and listen. I could hear Roy talking and Tabitha's laughter. Perhaps she was in a good mood with her son here.

My stomach rumbled again, and I closed my eyes and prayed. "Lord, please let her be nice today. I really want some of that bacon. I'll be good. I won't make her mad," I whispered, hoping he was listening. Although I had no proof that he ever had before.

Opening the door, I stepped into the hallway and walked toward the kitchen. The delicious smells grew stronger, and my mouth watered.

Yesterday hadn't been a good day for me. Tabitha had come into the bathroom when I was bathing and seen me without the athletic tape around my boobs. She was furious, accusing me of going behind her back and eating. That an eleven-year-old didn't have boobs my size. She claimed I was gluttonous and sinful.

She grabbed my arm and jerked me out of the tub, then made me drink that awful stuff so I would vomit. I did. Several times. Until there was nothing left.

Roy had arrived later that day, and I'd been sent to my room with a warning not to come out.

My boobs were smashed down as tightly as I could get them. Before walking into the kitchen, I looked in the mirror one more time, making sure I appeared as flat-chested as she seemed to think I should be.

The laughter and talking silenced when I entered. Tabitha swung her gaze to me with the disgust and hatred I was accustomed to seeing.

"Good morning," I said, then forced myself to look at Roy, who was looking at me in a weird way that gave me the creeps. "Hello, Roy."

He took a bite of bacon and sneered at me.

"What are you doing out of your room?" Tabitha snapped.

"I, uh … it's, uh, breakfast, and I'm hungry," I replied.

She let out a laugh that chilled me to my bones. I knew that laugh. It didn't mean anything positive. "You're always hungry. You'd eat us out of house and home if I allowed it. Benjamin works hard enough. He doesn't need his selfish daughter making me spend even more on groceries."

Roy chuckled from across the room.

Tabitha took an apple from the bowl on the counter. "This is all you need. You've got enough fat on your body already."

I took the apple and sank my teeth into it before she could change her mind. Nothing had ever tasted so good.

"That's disgusting. Take it to your room and eat it. We don't want to be subjected to your gluttonous behavior," she barked at me.

I hurried from the kitchen, still eating my apple on the way to my room. I didn't mind that she wanted me to leave. Being in the same room with them wasn't something I enjoyed either. Closing my door, I sank to the floor and ate the entire apple—core, stem, and even the seeds. I never knew when she was going to let me eat again. If Roy was here all day, then I wouldn't be able to sneak into the kitchen for a sandwich.

"Please, Lord, let my dad come home for dinner," I prayed.

I

If you cling to the memories that broke you, then you'll miss the beauty in front of you.

Chapter ONE

TRINITY
PRESENT DAY

Perhaps the word I was looking for was *ironic*. It seemed a harsh word and made me feel as if I were looking at this with no emotion. That couldn't be further from the truth. In the past week, I had suffered from every emotion known to man—or at least, it'd felt like it. Regardless, *ironic* was a good word. One that encompassed all that had happened in the past six months.

The soft whispers, hushed voices, even crying that I could hear on the other side of the wall I was leaning against reminded me that I should be out there. People expected me to be. They wanted to tell me how sorry they were, that they were praying for me, what a good man Hayes had been, and best of all, that it was God's plan. I, on the other hand, didn't want to endure listening to it. They knew nothing.

I wasn't sure how long I could stay in this dark prayer room until someone found me. My stepmom, Tabitha, would come looking soon enough. She wouldn't want me to embarrass her in front of the church. There had been no one more thrilled than Tabitha when Hayes proposed to me. The minister's grandson, who would soon be a minister himself. He was loved and respected in town. He should have been. Hayes was one of the most genuine, kindest, warmest people I had ever known. Somehow, he had chosen me.

The door opened, slamming against the wall, and I jumped, startled. My gaze shot up from the handkerchief I had been twisting in my hands, expecting to see Tabitha. My excuses were on the tip of my tongue when I froze. That was not Tabitha.

It was a man. A very large man. A slightly terrifying man. His eyes locked on me, and he studied me. I couldn't tell much in the darkness other than the silhouette of his face was masculine, defined, most likely attractive. Not that it mattered.

"You must be the missing fiancée," he said in a deep voice, letting the door close behind him.

I nodded, but said nothing.

He walked over and sat down on a bench across the room. I watched him, wanting to ask who he was and what he was doing in here. His intimidating presence, however, kept me from speaking. He had to be at least six foot three. The suit coat he was wearing seemed tight across his wide shoulders, as if it were ready to rip apart if he simply flexed.

The man reached into the pocket of his coat and pulled out a flask. My eyes went wide as he opened it and took a long drink from it. When he lowered the flask, his eyes met mine again.

"You want a drink? Might help you face that out there," he said, holding it out to me.

I looked at it for a moment and considered it. The fact that I was even thinking about it reminded me of all that Hayes had never truly known about me.

Finally, I shook my head. "I can't have the Baptist folks smelling spirits on my breath," I said softly.

He nodded, then twisted the top back on it before putting it in his pocket. I found myself wishing there were more light in here. The only window was small and made of stained glass. With the dreary day outside, it didn't shine much light into the room. I was curious about what he looked like. His voice was deep, and there was a drawl to it that was oddly familiar.

"Got to fucking go out there sometime," he said, shifting his gaze from the colorful window to me.

I knew that. I was going to. As soon as I convinced myself I could survive it.

"He ever tell you about the time he shot the window out of the parsonage?" the man asked with a hint of amusement in his voice.

Was he talking about Hayes?

I shook my head.

The man smirked then, and even in the shadows, I could see the way it curled his lips. I dropped my gaze back to my lap. This was Hayes's funeral. I would not sit here and appreciate another man's good looks.

What was wrong with me? Scratch that. I knew what was wrong with me. So much that I didn't have enough time to list it all.

"He was seven. Damn, he was a strong-willed hothead. Thought he knew it all." The man chuckled. "Fucker didn't know shit."

I was officially intrigued. How did this man know Hayes? They weren't friends. I had met all his friends. Yet something about him made it clear he was struggling with Hayes's death as much as I was. He sighed then and stood back up.

The door opened again, and light filled the room. This time, it was Tabitha. Her red hair was styled and sprayed so much that it wouldn't budge in a windstorm. Her frantic eyes met mine, and then there it was. The fury, the resentment—all the things she had always felt for me were once again bursting wide open. Hayes was no longer here, and she had no use for me. Except for today, and I was letting her down. I wasn't out there for all the church people to see.

"What do you think you're doing? Being a selfish brat, like you always are. Get out there right this instant, Trinity. I will not let you embarrass this family," she spit at me with the disgust and hate in her eyes that I hadn't seen since the day Hayes had met me at my car after church and asked me out.

I started to stand up.

"She's not going anywhere until she's damn well ready to."

The deep voice startled Tabitha. She hadn't seen the man in the darkness.

She opened the door further so that the light filled the room and shot her angry glare toward him. "Excuse me, sir," she said in her haughty voice. "You do not have a say in what she does or does not do. She will go to the sanctuary and stand there like her fiancé would have wanted her to."

The man stood up, and Tabitha had to tilt her head back to look up at him. "She's a grown-ass woman. She can do what she wants to do. And you, lady," he said, nodding his head toward Tabitha, "don't know shit about what Hayes would have wanted."

Tabitha's eyes flared, and her lips thinned. She wasn't one to be talked down to. Even before she'd married the mayor, my father, when I was ten, she had looked down her nose at the world. Tabitha felt important, but I had no idea why.

"You don't belong here," she stated. "I have never laid eyes on you in my life, and I've known the minister's family for over ten years. I'm going to go get Officer Randal to escort you out. You shouldn't have been in a room alone with a young girl, and language such as yours is not accepted in these walls."

I wanted to groan and cover my face. I didn't know this man, but Tabitha was embarrassing me anyway. Being connected to her was just another one of the things to add to why my life had been hell. Bad luck had struck on the day I was born when my entrance into this world had killed my mom, and it never stopped.

"Damn, I sure hope you try," the man replied with amusement in his voice rather than anger.

I lifted my gaze up to look at him now that the light was illuminating his face. Although I immediately wished I hadn't. I hadn't expected him to look like that. Sure, I had noticed the defined angles of his features in the darkness, but good Lord, that man looked like sin. I swallowed hard and thought about praying for forgiveness, then remembered I wasn't praying anymore. I had given up my belief in God when I got the call that Hayes was dead.

He didn't look back at me though, and I found myself relieved. I wasn't sure I could handle seeing his eyes. Not if the rest of him looked like that.

"Trinity, now." Tabitha's voice was sharp and clearly near hysterics.

She wasn't used to being spoken to that way. I, however, would pay money for this to continue.

Hayes wouldn't want this though, and I knew it. He had wanted me to try and find peace with my stepmom. I stood up and walked over to her, not looking at the stranger, for fear I'd see disappointment in his eyes. He didn't take orders. He was his own person, and he'd just witnessed how weak I was.

Tabitha grabbed my bare arm so hard that her nails bit into my skin. I winced, but said nothing as I went with her out of the room. Perhaps if she squeezed hard enough, it would hurt bad enough that I could go into the sanctuary with tears in my eyes. Because they would want me crying. They would want to see me completely broken and devastated.

What none of them understood was, I had been broken and devastated so many times in my life that it took more than the death of someone I cared deeply for to make me cry. Tears didn't come for me anymore. I was twisted inside. Hayes had seen something else in me that I wanted. I truly wanted to be the girl he had thought I was.

Unfortunately, I never had been. There was a darkness in me that I couldn't flush out. It wouldn't go away. It called to me and made me think things. Terrible, sinful things. It was no wonder God had never once answered one of my prayers. Hayes had been the only break I'd ever gotten, and God had only allowed me to have that for six months before snatching it away too.

"You are a disgrace," Tabitha said through her teeth as she dragged me toward the entrance of the church.

I didn't argue with her because I probably was. She stopped when she saw Officer Randal and dropped her death grip on my arm.

"Officer," she said in her fake voice. The one she used here at church and in town. The one that made everyone think she was a God-fearing, churchgoing woman who loved the Lord. "There is a man here who doesn't belong. He went into the prayer room, where Trinity was trying to be alone to grieve. The profanity out of his mouth and disregard for the house of the Lord were awful. You need to get that man out of here. I fear he is dangerous."

It took every ounce of self-control I had not to roll my eyes. She sounded ridiculous.

"What man? Did you get a name?" Randal asked with concern in his tone.

She opened her mouth, then shut it again. Neither of us knew his name, but even if I had, I wouldn't have shared it with her. I was a fantastic liar. Her gaze swung to me, and I shrugged. Then, I saw her eyes narrow, as if she thought I was lying, but she wouldn't treat me bad in front of witnesses that mattered. The man in the prayer room did not matter to her.

"There!" She pointed, and I turned my head to see him walking down toward the sanctuary.

His dark hair was cut short, and I could see from here that his eyes were a lighter color. Not boring brown, like mine. I wasn't sure though since he wasn't looking at me. His entire body seemed to flex with each move he made. I wondered if he was one of those built guys that had muscles all over. Hayes's body had been that of a runner's, and had been nothing like this man's.

"Oh," Randal replied, and his tone dropped. "I'm, uh, sorry, Mrs. Bennett. Uh, I can't ask him to leave."

I studied Officer Randal as he shifted on his feet nervously. The large Adam's apple in his throat bobbed.

"Who is he? Surely, Reverend Darren and his family do not know this man," Tabitha said, sounding close to losing her cool.

She rarely lost a battle. If she didn't get the massive, good-looking man kicked out of the church, she'd have lost in her eyes, and that would not sit well with her.

Randal ran a hand over his slightly balding head. "He, uh, does indeed know the family," Officer Randal said. "That's Huck Kingston, Hayes's older brother."

Chapter TWO

HUCK

Tugging on the damn neck of the button-up shirt I had worn for Hayes's sake, I felt like I was suffocating. "I hope you're watching this shit show," I whispered under my breath.

I wasn't sure what I believed about the afterlife, but if we did have souls and my little brother was here, watching his funeral, then I was going to at least have on a damn suit coat and button-up. I drew the line there. My jeans and boots weren't going anywhere. Hayes would understand that.

I stood at the back of the church, watching people come in and speak to my mother's parents up front. They had seen me walk in, but neither of them would approach me. I'd made my choice years ago, and although the old man preached about forgiveness and acceptance, he'd never been able to give that to my father. Judgment was clear in his gaze when his eyes met mine. He saw my father when he looked at me. I fucking saw my father every time I looked in a mirror, and

I was proud of it. Creed Kingston had been a hell of a man. Loyal, honest, and proud.

My jaw clenched as I thought of the things he'd said to Hayes and me about my father the day he came to take us away from the only life we'd known.

He had blamed my father for our mother's death when he'd died, trying to save her life. He said that their deaths were God's punishment for the evil my father had done. Carbon monoxide poisoning hadn't been from God; it had been from a fucking faulty detector. I was fourteen years old and fucking furious. Hayes was six years old and wanted to go with his grandparents. Losing our mother was harder on him. He needed that comfort. He was softer, like she had been. Having a grandmother was something he clung to once our mother was gone.

I wanted to stay with the Hughes family, and I told them that. I knew Garrett would make it happen. I hadn't factored in my little brother though. He hugged me tightly with tears in his eyes that day, begging me to go with him. Not to leave him too. My heart fucking twisted so damn tightly that I didn't think I could breathe. So, I went with them to fucking Alabama. It lasted three years. The day I turned seventeen, I couldn't take it anymore. Even though I escaped to Ocala, Florida every chance I got, I was done with this life. I called Garrett, told him I was coming home. I packed my things and left Hayes a note, explaining why I had to leave, because I couldn't fucking face him. Then, I'd gotten on the motorcycle I'd bought with the money I'd made from working at a bike repair shop in town.

"She's not even crying," an older lady said in a hushed tone but loud enough for others around her to hear.

I turned my attention to the two women who were walking in.

"Poor Tabitha. She looks so exhausted with having to deal with her."

The other woman nodded her head. "I know, but it could just be the shock. They were gonna be married in a few months. It couldn't be easy for her after he suddenly dropped dead from a brain aneurysm."

The first woman smiled tightly. "You're right. Here I am, in the house of our Lord, being judgmental. Lord, forgive me."

My eyes shifted then and locked on the woman being whispered about as she entered the room.

I hadn't let myself look at her in that room after the lights came on, but just the once. When I'd gotten a look, I had forced myself not to go there. Because fuck if my little brother hadn't been engaged to a stunner. Long, dark brown hair hung down her back as she walked down the middle aisle toward my grandparents. The black dress she wore had long sleeves, hit at her knees, and had a respectable fucking neckline. However, it clung to her body.

Her waist was small, but she had a flare to her hips. That round ass should be illegal. I wasn't going to even let myself think about her breast size because big tits were my thing, and, Jesus Christ, she had a fucking rack on her.

"You did good, little brother," I muttered. "Real damn good."

Hayes had chosen religion over the family. He'd told me that he loved me, but that the life I lived—that our father had lived—wasn't for him. That he wanted to serve the Lord. Save souls and do good. I hadn't expected him to get engaged to a woman with the body of a porn star. Maybe there had been some Kingston blood in him after all.

She hugged my grandmother, then stood beside her like a statue. Stiff, uncomfortable with this shit, and fucking gorgeous. I watched her as people came up to pay their respects. She gave them a small smile that didn't meet her almond-shaped brown eyes. Those lips of hers were so fucking full that I wondered if they were real. I studied her far longer than I should have and knew this wasn't why I was here.

Shifting my gaze to the casket to the right of the three standing up there as people arrived, I swallowed the fucking lump that swelled in my throat.

Dammit, Hayes, it was supposed to be me that went first. Not you. You were the safe one. The good one. Why the hell did you have to go?

"Walked into a damn nightmare."

The deep voice surprised me, but I didn't flinch.

I hadn't told anyone Hayes was dead, simply because I couldn't say the words. When I had tried, the words wouldn't come out of my damn mouth.

This fucker had found out anyway and driven up to the Alabama-Florida line to be here with me.

"How'd you find out?" I asked Blaise Hughes. The future boss of the family.

"Tracked your fucking ass," he replied. "Then made a call. You'd been strange all week. I could feel it. Knew something bad had you fucked up. Shouldn't be alone with this."

This was what a real family was. This was what my father had been a part of. It was what I had wanted for Hayes. Not the fake shit all around me. People expecting stuff from others. Judging them for not fucking crying. It was sickening. The family was different. Hayes had been born into it, just like I had been and our father before us. The man who had raised Hayes considered me evil, didn't understand what this life was about. What we were about. Well, I'd trust my Mafia family all fucking day instead of these people.

"Who is she?" Blaise asked.

I'd been looking at her again. Fuck, my eyes just seemed to keep going in that direction on their own. She looked so damn lost and hopeless, yet there was some fire there. I'd seen a spark of it in her eyes when that horrible woman came to get her.

"My brother's fiancée," I replied, still finding it hard to believe Hayes had been about to marry her.

She was not minister's wife material. Unless he wanted the men in his congregation to go home and beat off every Sunday after looking at her all during the service.

"Hmm," he said, but nothing more.

The redheaded bitch who had come to get her walked past me, then snapped her head to look in my direction. She glared at me as she walked over to sit on a pew with some other equally awful-looking women. With their floral dresses that went to their ankles and their helmet hair. Could they be any more unfuckable if they tried?

"Looks like you already made a friend," Blaise said with amusement in his tone.

"That bitch is the fiancée's mom, I think. Not sure," I grumbled.

"Wouldn't have guessed that one. No resemblance at all." Blaise pointed out something I'd already noticed myself.

I shrugged and crossed my arms over my chest, feeling the stupid suit coat I was wearing stretch even tighter. "Not my business," I said more for my benefit than anything.

Blaise said nothing, but we'd been friends our entire lives. I could read his thoughts in the silence, and I felt like planting my fist in his face for thinking it. He was right, of course. The girl made me fucking hard. She was sexy as hell. But she had been my brother's fiancée, and she was one of these people. Not for me.

"It should be me in that fucking casket," I muttered. "He was the safe one. Where was that God he wanted to serve?"

My heart constricted in my chest. I'd never see his face again. Never hear his laugh. Fuck, this hurt.

"Fucking wish he'd been with us," Blaise said beside me. "Not here with these people. But he was happy. You got that to hold on to. Even if it hurts like a son of a bitch."

Chapter THREE

TRINITY
SIX MONTHS LATER

This house was much bigger than I'd anticipated. I wasn't sure I could continue cleaning the local library and the other two businesses I currently cleaned for. As much as I liked my evenings alone in the library, the grand I made a month from cleaning it six nights a week didn't compare to the five grand a month I was going to get for cleaning this house three days a week.

With that kind of money and extra time, I could not only pay all my bills, but there was also a possibility I could go to the junior college in town. My future was starting to have some hope. There was a chance for a real life if I could keep this job. It would take me cleaning the library, bank, preschool, and at least four more businesses a month to make this kind of money. Even then, I wouldn't have a moment to do anything other than work.

Smiling for the first time since Hayes's death, I began to dust the furniture in the room that the house manager,

Ms. Hottel, had brought me to. She wasn't the friendliest person, but I wasn't here to make friends. I was here to make money. This was an opportunity that I wasn't going to lose. Good things always seemed to get snatched away from me. I hoped I got to keep this one. It was time the universe gave me a break.

The next few hours, I cleaned several rooms, being sure to clean every square inch even though this house was as clean as it was elaborate. I had yet to meet the man who owned the house. He'd hired me through the bank manager, Philip.

Apparently, Mr. Esposito was a very important client in need of a new house-cleaning service. Philip had said he was a private guy and didn't want a team of cleaners in his house. I owed Philip for getting me this job. I was aware that Philip liked me, but he was much older than me. Maybe forty, but I wasn't sure exactly. He had claimed he was separated from his wife when he asked me out once last month. Thankfully, he had accepted that I wasn't ready to date. I was still grieving my fiancé's death. I wasn't sure how long that excuse was going to hold though. He was an attractive man, but I had watched him flirt with other women at the bank. I had a feeling he was separated because he'd done something wrong. Not the other way around.

I would deal with that if and when the time came.

I had been working on my anxiety. The first few panic attacks I'd suffered through after Hayes's death were difficult. It wasn't like they were new to me. I'd dealt with them all my life, but Hayes had helped me work through them. When I went to my dark place, where I escaped from memories, that was a different story. Thankfully, that had to be triggered by something. It didn't happen often. I wasn't going to rely on another person again. If I let myself, I'd lose them. That was a lesson I'd learned. I had to be strong for myself.

Feeling more confident, I gave the last room on the main floor one more glance and felt good about how it looked, then headed for the stairs. I had been informed that Mr. Esposito was at home but that he was in his private quarters that I wouldn't be cleaning, ever. This was a sprawling residence and I was curious where those private quarters were located. Not that I'd go looking for them. I wasn't stupid, just intrigued.

As I made my way toward the second floor, I heard what sounded like a muffled scream. Was someone watching a television? I hadn't come across another human since Ms. Hottel had taken me through the house, going over what was expected. I paused and thought about going to investigate, then decided against it. Being nosy was a bad idea if I was going to keep this job. My foot hit the first step just before a cloth was shoved in my mouth from behind, muffling the scream that tore from my throat.

My heart slammed into my chest as the reality of what was happening hit me. Whoever was behind me grabbed my wrists and tied them so tightly that I cried out in pain.

"Where is the fucker?" a deep voice demanded near my ear.

What fucker?

I shook my head, panicking. I had to do something. I glanced around and tried to turn to see who it was that had me when my body was slammed against the wall. The side of my face pressed against the stucco, and I closed my eyes for a moment, wondering if I would cry now.

Was this enough to provoke my tears? My own death?

"Take me to the fucker." The threat in his voice was clear.

If I didn't do what he wanted, I wasn't going to live. Problem with this was, I had no idea who the fucker was or where the fucker was.

"Motherfucker," another male voice growled.

Suddenly, I wasn't being pressed against a wall. I didn't move though. I stayed still, afraid to breathe.

"What the hell?" the first man snarled.

"Not that one." The other man's deep voice made me shiver.

I closed my eyes, amazed that they were still dry. I was possibly in my last few moments of my life, and I still couldn't cry.

"Jesus, Huck," he said.

Then, I watched as a man climbed the stairs without looking back. The gun in his hand made me whimper. He was going to kill someone. Possibly me.

A large hand wrapped around my arm, and I winced as I was pulled away from the wall.

"Easy, Trinity," he said, close to my ear.

He knew my name. How did he know my name? I turned my head slowly until my eyes locked with the most unique color I'd ever seen. Was that what people referred to as cornflower blue? Why was I even thinking about this man's eye color at a time like this?

"Do you remember me?" his deep voice asked.

I blinked, then let my gaze take in the rest of his features. The strong jawline, defined angles, the ... oh my God. Huck. The other guy had called him Huck. It had been six months since the day in the church when Hayes's brother had walked into the prayer room and stood up to Tabitha.

I swallowed nervously and nodded my head.

"Don't fight me," he warned. "You've got to get out of this house. I'm going to get you to safety, but I need you to trust me."

Trust him? I was gagged, and my hands were tied behind my back.

Hayes had never spoken of a brother. That had bothered me. I was now beginning to understand why he hadn't mentioned Huck.

Huck was a criminal.

I nodded, not because I trusted him, but because I knew I had no other choice. The other man with him had no reason to help me. However, the determined look in Huck's eyes gave me a shred of security. I'd been his brother's fiancée. Was that enough for him to keep me alive?

He took my arm with one of his hands, and in his other hand was a gun. I followed him as we walked back through the house. There was no sign of life.

Where was Ms. Hottel? Had they killed her? My stomach twisted in a sick knot.

I had to almost run to keep up with Huck as he maneuvered through the hallways until he came to a door I hadn't been through. We stopped, and he listened before opening it and stepping out into the sunlight. I saw movement in my peripheral vision. Turning my head, I watched as a bullet went into a man's head, and he dropped to the ground.

I screamed into the cloth muffling me. Huck began moving again and followed, but my gaze was on the gun in his hand. The one he'd just killed a man with.

Why the hell was I not crying? Was I truly this broken? I had just watched a man get shot in the head.

A black SUV came around the corner, and I started to duck. In the movies, this always appeared right before the gunfire erupted. It came to a screeching halt in front of us, and Huck jerked the door open and threw me inside. I scrambled to sit up, but Huck shoved me back down.

"Stay," he barked.

"Where's Gage?" the driver shouted.

"There!" Huck replied, his hand still on my back, keeping me pressed to the leather seat.

A car door opened, then slammed before I was jerked back as the driver shot off. A gunshot caused me to flinch, and then sick, maniacal laughter followed.

"Find him?" Huck asked.

"Am I in the car?" the guy from the stairs asked.

I was looking at him as he turned to reply, and his eyes dropped to me. Without barely any movement or warning, the man had the barrel of his gun pressed to my forehead, but Huck moved almost as quickly and pressed his gun to the other man's temple.

I was frozen in shock. I didn't dare breathe.

"What the fuck?" The man sounded shocked at Huck holding a gun to his head.

"Drop the gun," Huck replied.

The other man took his gun back as he glared at Huck. "I didn't know we were taking souvenirs."

Huck removed his gun from the other man's head.

"If the two of you could refrain from killing each other while I try to get our asses out of this fucking compound, that would be fantastic," the driver drawled.

The other man looked at me one more time, then shook his head in disgust before turning back around. "This is your ass," the man said. "Blaise is not gonna be happy."

No one said anything for several minutes, and it wasn't lost on me that Huck continued to hold his gun as if he would need it at any moment. I was definitely not out of danger. His hand remained on my back, keeping me low, and I didn't try to move. My arms cramped, and I was sure my wrists were raw, but I didn't care. This was better than a bullet in my head.

Huck's hand wrapped around my arm, and he pulled me up. I cried out as the rope dug deeper into my tender flesh.

"Dammit," he muttered, and his hands moved to my wrists.

I remained still while he untied me.

"Did you just fucking untie the bitch?" Gage asked.

"Call her a bitch one more time, and I'll make you mine," Huck snarled.

"What the hell is wrong with you? I know you got a thing for big tits and fat asses, but, Jesus Christ, did you have to take that one? You could have gone to the damn club tonight and gotten one of the girls there."

I winced as my arms dropped to my sides.

"The two of you need to calm the fuck down," the driver said in an annoyed tone.

"He's the one taking a damn witness alive so he can fuck her," the other guy said.

I turned, my eyes going wide as I looked at Huck. His eyes met mine, and he sighed, rubbing his temples with his thumb and forefinger.

"God, Gage, what does it take to shut you the hell up?" he asked.

The guy who he had called Gage pointed at me. "Kill the damn witness and drop her on the side of the fucking road."

I inhaled sharply through my nose.

Gage shrugged when he saw my reaction. As if he was apologizing for something that was inevitable.

"She's Hayes's fiancée," Huck said. "Or was."

Gage looked as if he'd been slapped. His face paled as he looked at me. It was odd to see a killer with clearly no remorse or mercy turn from hard and ruthless to showing actual emotion. Pain flashed in his amber eyes, and he winced as he closed them a moment.

"Fuck," he muttered.

"I'll shoot him for you," the driver said to Huck, then glared at Gage.

They'd all known Hayes. These men, who had just gone into a house and murdered people in cold blood, had all known Hayes. How was this real life?

Huck reached up and untied my gag. When it fell, I sat there silently. Wondering if this meant I was going to get to live or if the man they'd called Blaise was going to kill me. I was afraid to ask.

"Why were you at that house?" Huck asked me.

I lifted my eyes to meet his. "To clean it. To-to-today was my first d-day," I stammered out.

Huck ran a hand over his face and groaned. "This is an awfully long way from home for you to be cleaning his house."

I frowned at him, then realized he thought I lived in Alabama. Hayes must not have told him much about me. Perhaps they had been estranged. Seeing as how Hayes was going to be a minister and this man was a murderer, that would make sense.

"My apartment is in Lake City," I whispered, afraid to incite anger in one of them.

Huck's frown deepened, but he said nothing.

"How the hell did Hayes get hooked up with someone from there?" Gage asked, looking at me with clear mistrust in his eyes.

Huck's gaze was back on me. I glanced up at him, knowing he was wondering the same thing. These men had guns and were killers. Probably in a gang. I would tell them anything they wanted to know if I could live.

"My father lived in Alabama, and his wife went to the Baptist church Hayes's grandfather is the minister at. When my dad had a heart attack, I, uh, left college to go help take care of him. My father wanted me to go to church because I think he believed I'd bond with my stepmother. I went, and Hayes was there. He followed me to my car after a service and asked me out. Then, the rest ..." I shrugged. Sure, I'd left out a lot of details, but I didn't think they wanted my entire life history.

"You moved out of your parents' house after Hayes died?" Huck asked me.

I realized I hadn't explained why I was now in Lake City, Florida.

"My stepmother's house. My father had another heart attack four months after my return, and it killed him. He left the house and all his belongings to my stepmother. She, uh, doesn't like me. Never has. So, yeah, I packed my things and drove south. Lake City was the first place I came to where I could afford an apartment and get a job immediately."

Huck's neck flexed, and I could see the muscles in it shift. The hard line of his mouth made him appear deadly, but then he was. I shivered at the thought.

"She's the redheaded bitch from the funeral," Huck said.

I nodded my head.

Nothing else was said for several minutes, and I rubbed my sore wrists as I looked out the window. We weren't in Lake City, but my new employer, who was also dead now, had lived in a much better area.

"Are you going to take me home?" I finally asked when I realized we were driving farther away from Lake City and not toward it.

"No," Huck replied without looking at me.

"Why not? I thought—I thought you weren't going to kill me. I swear I won't tell anyone anything," I told him. My heart was racing again, but then it hadn't ever slowed down completely.

Gage turned around and gave me an annoyed glare. "We don't know if you're telling the truth. Fuck, we don't know that you didn't get into Hayes's life on purpose. Who you might be working for and if you were really there to clean that house."

I shook my head. "But I told you, Hayes asked me out. I didn't go after him."

Gage laughed then, and although there were crinkles at the corners of his eyes, the gleam in them wasn't amusement. It was calculating and terrifying. "He was a fucking man. Anyone could have hired you and sent you to wiggle your juicy ass in front of him to get his attention."

My jaw dropped.

"Shut up," Huck barked at him.

"We can't take her to the house. We don't know if she's lying or not. What about the shop?" Gage asked.

"The house," Huck replied.

"Gage is right. That's not a good idea. Shop is neutral. Everyone knows its location and that you own it," the driver said.

"We are taking her to the fucking house," Huck said through clenched teeth.

I closed my mouth and turned my head to look out the window again. What in the world had I gotten myself into? These people were crazy. Who would hire me to go get Hayes's attention?

"Hayes was going to be a minister," I said just above a whisper. "I don't understand why you think someone would have sent me to get close to him."

I was afraid to look at Gage or Huck. The other guy remained silent as he drove.

"He was a fucking Kingston. Loving Jesus and shit don't change that. Not in our world," Gage said as if that made sense.

Chapter FOUR

HUCK

"Where are we?" Trinity asked as she looked around.

"My room," I replied.

"Are … are you going to let me go?" she asked, then bit her bottom lip.

I didn't have an answer for that. I wasn't sure what the fuck I was going to do with her. She'd been in the house of one of the biggest drug dealers in the southeast. He'd taken down one of our men last week. I wanted to believe she was what she had claimed to be. His house cleaner. But first, I had to pull her background. Do some checking of facts. As pissed off as Gage had made me in the damn car, he was right. We didn't know she hadn't been some plant. Hayes would have been a weak link, and anyone who did some looking into the family could have found him.

"I need you to stay down here. I've got to go to a meeting, and it's not safe for you to leave this room. I'm going to lock you in. Don't unlock that door for anyone," I told her.

They were my friends, but they were also loyal to the family. That came first for all of us. I just hoped she wasn't fucking lying.

Her gaze swung back to the stairs we had used to get down here. "You're locking me in a basement?" she whispered.

I looked around. This didn't look like a basement. It was an elaborate master bedroom with a living area and bathroom. This had been Blaise's room until he moved out with his woman to their own place. There was no reason for her to act as if I were locking her in a fucking cell.

"You've got a television," I said, pointing at the flat screen on the wall.

She glanced at it, then nodded, but said nothing.

She could have been fucking killed. If I hadn't found Gage with her, he'd have put a damn bullet in her if she hadn't answered his question. There was no reason for her to act as if I were the bad guy here.

"Listen, you need to stay down here. You're not safe without me," I pressed. I needed her to understand and obey me.

She nodded again.

My phone rang, and I saw Blaise's name light up the screen. He was here.

"I have to go," I told her, then started for the stairs.

Why did I feel so damn guilty about leaving her down here alone? Hayes would have been thankful I'd saved her. I had done what my brother would have wanted me to do. Except now, I had her in a world he had never wanted to be a part of.

"I had no other choice," I muttered under my breath as if he could hear me.

When I reached the top of the stairs, I used my key to lock Trinity safely downstairs before heading to the office to meet with the others.

I could hear Gage ranting about my taking Trinity when I walked into the room.

Blaise's eyes swung to me, but there was only concern in his gaze. "Where is she?" he asked.

"Downstairs," I replied.

Gage threw his hands up. "Fucking great. I get that she was Hayes's woman, and that makes her a priority, but did we have to bring her in here before knowing if she's as innocent as she claims?"

I glared at him, although I knew he was right. I'd taken a chance in trusting her at her word. "I took her phone. She had nothing else."

"We need her checked out," Blaise told me.

I nodded.

He sighed and leaned back in his chair. "I get why you did it. But Gage is right about bringing her into the house. Are we sure she's not got a tracking device on her? What all did she see of the house? The shop would have been a better choice."

I tensed. "I'll check her for a tracking device and keep her downstairs until we know she's clear. If they'd wanted her dead, they would have checked the shop. It's common knowledge I own it."

"Just because she was your brother's fiancée, don't skip anywhere. She has to be stripped and checked thoroughly. You know the drill. Until we know for sure, she is not to be trusted," Blaise said, watching me for any sign of weakness.

"Have you seen her?" Gage asked Blaise.

Blaise nodded, and his eyes stayed locked on me. "Can you keep your hands off her?"

"Are you fucking kidding me?" I asked him. "She was my brother's fiancée!"

Blaise inhaled and rubbed his chin. "And he's gone."

Dammit! I wanted to put my fist through a wall. "She's got big tits and an ass. That doesn't fucking mean I can't keep my dick in my pants."

Blaise shrugged and stood up. "Good. Do that."

I wanted to get away from them. I needed a fucking drink.

Blaise walked around the desk and headed for the door. "Get her checked out now. We need to know what we are dealing with," he said, then left the room.

Gage was looking at me, and I swung my gaze to glare at him.

"What?" I growled.

"Go check her for a tracker. I'll get us some pussy over here," he said.

I stalked for the door and headed back to the stairs. I hoped the pussy got here fast. I was going to need it after this. My only other option was letting Levi or Gage check her, and there was no way in hell that was going to happen.

Chapter FIVE

TRINITY

This was okay. It wasn't a closet. I fought the urge to curl into a ball and rock. If I let myself react that way, I wasn't sure how long I'd be checked out on reality. I could focus and stay calm. I looked around the room. It was massive. Almost bigger than the house I had grown up in. Definitely bigger than the closet in the basement.

Not the same, Trinity. It is not the same.

"You're fine," I whispered. "You got this. You survived a gun to your head. You can sit in this nice, large room and wait."

I felt the tension in my chest tightening, and I took deep breaths. I could not go there in my head. I was in a house with killers or gangsters or whatever the hell they were. I had to stay alert. Even if Huck was Hayes's brother. That man was nothing like Hayes.

They would check out my background or whatever they could do and see I was not in some drug gang thingy. I winced, thinking of the things they would also find. I wasn't sure if the bogus stuff Tabitha and Roy had tried to pin on me would show up. There was no proof because I hadn't done anything wrong. That'd all started when I threatened to tell my dad about Roy. The next thing I knew, I was getting arrested for crimes I hadn't committed. Since I had never been charged, then that shouldn't be on my record. The only item that might show up was the scholarship I had lost. My stomach twisted as I thought about that. No, I wouldn't go there. I was away from that. It was over. Professor Jonathon Kilgore couldn't do anything else to me.

I had to focus on the here and now. This situation was my current problem.

Philip had gotten me this job for Mr. Esposito. I didn't think Philip knew the man was a drug lord. Surely, he hadn't. Pushing that thought aside, I tried to think about the lovely decorations. It was a nice basement. I was sure the other doors led to more rooms. Glancing at my watch, I realized I had been sitting quietly on the sofa for almost an hour.

Before I had a chance to get more worried than I already was, I heard footsteps on the stairs. Huck was coming back, and I hoped he was ready to send me home. I needed a hot bath, a good book, and possibly three shots of tequila.

I watched him as he walked into the room, and his gaze found me. His neck was strained, like he was clenching his teeth. Had he been ordered to kill me?

I swallowed hard, afraid to ask. I didn't want to die down here. Alone. Having not one person come looking for me. Dying alone and unloved was a sad way to go. There was May at the bank, who I'd gone out to drinks with twice but she ended up leaving with men she'd met at the bar so I'd stopped going with her. I doubted she'd miss my absence. Rochelle was the head librarian, and we always discussed our latest reads when I came in to clean at night. She might be considered a friend.

"Stand up," he ordered me.

I did because I was afraid not to but I wanted to curl up in a ball and hide instead.

He stalked toward me and stopped a few feet from me. "I've got to check you for a tracker, Trinity."

Okay … what did that mean? I waited for an explanation, but he continued to stare at me as his neck muscles flexed and his jaw clenched.

"Take your clothes off," he grunted.

My eyes went wide. "What?" My voice cracked.

"You can fucking let me do this, or one of the others can do it. Trust me, you want me to do this. Gage would probably hold a gun on you most of the time."

My hands trembled, and I had to fist them at my sides to make them stop. "Are you serious?"

He nodded his head.

"Why?" I asked, trying to think of another way to do this.

He closed the distance between us, and I had to tilt my head back to look up at him. "I can only protect you as long as you do as you're told. This isn't an option. I brought you into our home without knowing if you're a liar or telling the fucking truth. If you are wired, then it's my fault. If someone can track you here, it is my fault. You were Hayes's, which puts you under the family's protection. Unless you are working with one of our enemies."

Okay. So, I had to strip in front of this man or possibly die. I could do this. It wouldn't be the first time I'd taken my clothes off for an audience, although that had been another mess I hadn't meant to happen. This was just the first time I'd be doing it for a man I'd watched kill someone. I took a deep breath and focused on a dark spot on the floor. This was a technique I'd learned as a kid. It helped me handle things I didn't want to do. Things I shouldn't have been forced to do.

However, this was a little different than the horror that I'd lived as a kid. Huck wasn't Tabitha or Roy. The idea of this man seeing my naked body was a completely different situation, but it was still uncomfortable. The main reason being, he was a massive wall of muscle without an ounce of fat, and Gage was right. My ass was fat. It had always been too big. No matter how much weight I lost, my waist just got smaller. My rear end did not.

My hands were shaking as I pulled the T-shirt I was wearing up and over my head. I refused to look at him when I reached for the button on my shorts and unfastened them, then slid them down my legs before stepping out of them.

Huck picked up the shorts and inspected them, then laid them on the sofa before doing the same with my shirt. When he laid it on the sofa, I reached for it to cover myself back up when his fingers wrapped around my arm. My eyes shot up to meet his.

"The rest of it," he said tightly.

"You … you want me to take off my bra?" I asked.

"And panties." It sounded like a command.

Oh crap, crap, crap. I took a few moments to try and calm myself before reaching for the clasp behind my back. Slipping it off my arms, I stared at the floor and held the bra out to him so he could inspect it. I couldn't watch him as he looked it over.

The panties. I had to take off the panties. Oh good Lord, this was not happening to me.

You want to live, Trinity. You need them to trust you.

I decided to do it quickly and get it over with. I stepped out of them and handed them over, keeping my eyes down. I shivered as I stood there, hoping he hurried.

"Lift your breasts. I need to see under them."

I knew my nipples were hard, and I was sure he could see them, but the fact that I had to touch them and draw attention to them made my body flush. I didn't meet his gaze as I held my breasts in my hands and lifted them up for him to see underneath.

"Turn around. Hold your arms out beside you," he said in a husky tone.

"Why?" I asked in a whisper. I didn't want him to see my butt. It had dimples in it. The humiliation was just getting worse.

"I have to check you for a tracker," he bit out.

"On my body?"

"Trinity." His tone was a warning.

Okay, fine. I could survive this. Maybe they'd let me go after this, and I would never see him again.

I turned slowly, biting down on my lower lip so hard that I tasted blood.

I felt his body come up behind me, and I stiffened. What was he doing? My heart was racing in my chest, and I began to tremble.

"Spread your legs and bend over," he said.

I looked back over my shoulder at him, but he didn't meet my gaze. His eyes were on my ass, and the heat I saw in them made me feel things other than humiliation. I was apparently a bad person. I should feel nothing but embarrassment right now. Jerking my head back around, I opened my legs and leaned forward. I held my breath, wondering if he could see the wetness between my legs.

"Fuck," he swore under his breath, and I closed my eyes, feeling a tingle as if he'd touched me with more than his gaze. "Get dressed!" he demanded, and I straightened, turning to see his back as he walked away.

I wrapped my arms around my waist and stood there until I heard the door at the top of the stairs slam shut. Moving, I went to get my panties and dressed myself. There had been no trackers on my clothes or body. I knew that. I had proven myself. Surely, he'd come back soon and let me go. I could lock myself in my apartment and try and forget this day had ever happened.

Once I was finished, I sat down on the sofa and waited. I would not check out on this. I would not.

"You stay alert," I told myself. "This is not a place to have an attack. You will be leaving soon."

Time ticked by, and he didn't return. What was taking so long? Why was I still here? I kept looking around to remind myself how large this area was. Not a closet. I wasn't locked in a closet. I was fine. I was going to be fine. The cold sweat started to creep over me, and I stood up to walk around.

"Get control of yourself."

I had to stop this. I began pacing back and forth, telling myself that, tomorrow, I would be cleaning the library at this time, and all would be well with the world. Rochelle would want to hear about the fairy romance I'd just read, and although the first book had been hard to get through, this second one was awesome.

My mouth was dry, and my stomach grumbled. I looked back at the stairs. Was he going to come back? I needed some water. Anything. I walked over to the bottom of the stairs and listened. It was quiet, but that could be that it was soundproof down here. My stomach rumbled some more. I needed something to drink and eat. I'd been told to stay down here, but he had checked me for a tracker since then. Maybe I was expected to come up when I was ready. He hadn't told me to stay down here after he checked me and left.

I headed up the stairs, unlocked the door, and stepped into the hallway. The windows up ahead told me it was almost dusk. Why hadn't they sent me home already? Had they forgotten I was down there? I began to walk, not sure which direction I should go when I heard something or someone. Following the sound, I listened for more, but it sounded like muttering.

The light was on ahead, and I could tell the noise was definitely coming from that direction. I walked toward it, and just as I stepped into the open room, I realized it wasn't a mutter but a groan. My gaze went to the sofa. Huck was leaning back. I could only see the profile of his face, and his mouth was slightly open. I took another step in and started to say his name when his arm moved up and down. Pausing, I waited, unsure what he was doing.

"Harder," he demanded, and I heard the gagging sound.

Before I covered my mouth, a sound escaped me. Huck's head turned, and his eyes locked on me. I stood there, knowing I needed to leave the room, but unable to make my legs work.

The look of pleasure on his face made my stomach feel funny. I saw the brown hair clasped in his fist as he jerked up the head of the woman who was between his legs before shoving it back down. He kept his gaze on me. I watched as he lifted his hips to thrust into her mouth.

"Take it. Suck it like a good little whore," he growled. "That's it. Just like that."

He wasn't talking to me, but it felt like it. His eyes were locked on me as he talked to her. I should go, but I didn't. I wasn't sure I could. Huck's face tensed up as a groan tore from him. He jerked, looking satisfied.

"Swallow it all," he said as a smile curled his lips.

Forgetting about food or water, I spun around and rushed back to the door leading downstairs. I had just watched Huck get a blow job. What was wrong with me? Why was I so messed up? As if it wasn't bad enough that he'd had to see every imperfection of my body today, now, he'd seen me be a full-blown voyeur. Surely, I'd be going home now.

Chapter SIX

HUCK

Gage was sitting on the edge of the desk in the office, holding papers in his hand with a grin on his face. He lifted his eyes when he heard me enter and shook his head. "Damn, I didn't know Hayes had it in him. Seems like he was a fucking Kingston after all."

I scowled at him. What the fuck was he talking about? "Stop grinning like a moron and explain."

Gage held the papers up. "Got that background check on his girl. She's not Baptist at all. Not even fucking close."

I reached out and snatched the papers from his hand.

"I just want to know if we can keep her." Gage's amusement annoyed me, and I hadn't even read the report yet.

I reviewed the first page. Trinity Camille Bennett, age twenty. Birth date: November 5, 2002. Known addresses, Social Security number, phone numbers, employment. I scanned through all that, and then I tensed. Affair with a married fifty-year-old professor at Howell University, where she'd had a full ride and lost it. Worked at Diamond Heels, a strip club thirty minutes from where she'd attended college. In the photo attached she had been wearing a wig and colored contacts but that body had been hers. No fucking doubt in my mind. Tabitha Bennett had claimed she had used her identity for several credit cards, but that was never proven, and case dropped. Roy Hayley had filed a police report, claiming she had stolen five thousand dollars' worth of rare first-edition books from him. Again, never proven, but that would be hard to prove. Arrested for grand theft auto but later released.

Had my brother known any of this? I knew he'd believed the Lord forgave, but I couldn't imagine the folks who had raised my mother would accept this. Fuck, Hayes wouldn't have been able to accept any of this. There was no way he had known. Hayes had never broken a law. The kid had never even gotten a speeding ticket.

"I mean, the fraud is impressive," Gage said. "And the grand theft auto? Levi and she can bond over their similar felonies. I bet she uses that hot little body to her advantage."

"Why the fuck was she cleaning houses and businesses? For someone who had done all this, why wasn't she hitting a pole somewhere else? And this address is a shit area to live. At least with stripping, she could afford to live in a decent area."

"About that. Levi and Kye called. Her place had been trashed. Torn to fucking shreds. Everything had been destroyed. Looked like they were after something," Gage informed me. I should have gone but I hadn't wanted to leave with Trinity here. Kye, who had recently stepped up to begin family after graduating high school, wasn't my first choice in something like this. He wouldn't have known what all to look for but Levi would had been thorough.

My grip tightened on the papers. What the fuck had she gotten herself into? There was nothing incriminating after she'd hooked up with Hayes. For the six months, they had been together, her record was clear. If someone was after her, then they had to be after her because she'd been the only one not left dead in that house. She'd escaped. We'd put her on their radar.

"Fuck," I grunted, trying to figure out what the hell I was going to do with her.

"Want me to get a room ready for her?" Gage asked, still grinning.

I glared at him. I knew what the fucker was thinking. He wanted her at his disposal. That shit wasn't happening. She might be a liar and a slut, but at least Hayes hadn't died without having had a hot piece of ass. Slamming the papers down on the desk, I turned to see Levi walking into the office.

"You look thrilled about the sis-in-law," he drawled with a smirk. "Her place is torn the fuck up. Barely found her anything worth salvaging. She can't go back there, so I vote she stays here. We need a cook. Gina's gone, and I'm tired of not getting a hot meal."

"I'm behind that idea," Gage piped up. "She can take Gina's spot. In the kitchen and on my cock."

Like hell. He'd been ready to kill her. Held a gun to her head twice. Fucker wasn't getting his damn cock anywhere near her.

"No," I said, stalking toward the door.

"To the cooking or the fucking?" Levi asked.

"Only cock she's riding is mine," I growled before walking out. "And only once or twice," I muttered. Just to fuck her out of my system.

I'd had to rub one out after getting sucked off and fucking the bitch I'd had over earlier. Seeing those big brown eyes watching Destiny between my legs messed with me. That juicy, bare ass was the reason I'd needed an outlet to begin with. Then, she'd appeared, and I'd gagged Destiny with my load.

Hayes would hate me for this. Even if he'd known about her past. But I wasn't Hayes. I didn't have damn morals. I fucked when and how I wanted to. No remorse, no attachments. And Hayes was dead.

Slamming my fist into the brick wall, I took out my frustration.

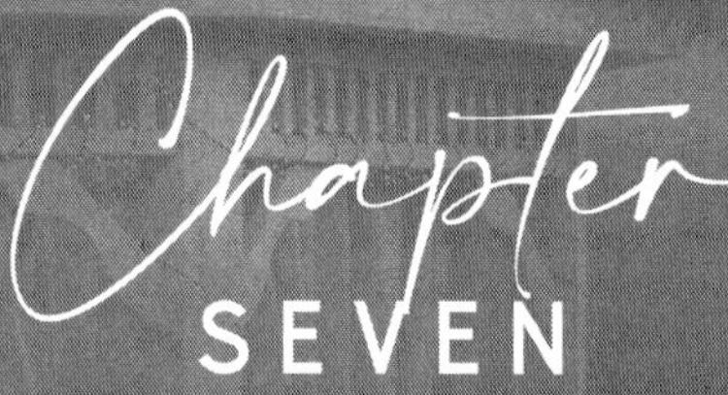

Chapter SEVEN

TRINITY

It was two hours before I heard footsteps on the stairs. I'd sat silently on the sofa, staring at the wall, trying not to think about what I'd seen.

How was I going to look at this man after all this? *Please let me be going home now.*

I didn't turn to see him walk into the room. I stayed where I was, studying my hands that I twisted in my lap. A tray of food was put down on the coffee table in front of me, and my stomach growled at the sight of the pizza. Old habits died hard, and my first thought was to grab a piece of pizza and cram it in my mouth while I had a chance. Thankfully, years of teaching myself control kept me from embarrassing myself further.

Lifting my gaze to meet his, I started to say *thank you*, but he spoke first.

"Take a bath or shower when you want. Here is a shirt you can sleep in. There are extra toothbrushes under the sink," he said, then turned and headed to leave me.

I stood up quickly. "Wait. You're leaving me down here? All night?"

He stopped and turned back around to look at me. "Yes."

"Why? You checked me for a tracker. Can't I go home now?" *Please let me go home.*

I couldn't stay down here. No matter how nice it was, I was exhausted from battling my inner demons to keep myself alert.

He shook his head. "No," he replied, then turned and went back to the stairs.

I opened my mouth to plead with him, but he was gone. I stood there, feeling hopeless. When the door upstairs closed, I sank back down and looked at the pizza. Grabbing a slice, I began to eat it like the starved kid I had once been. He wasn't going to make me go without food. Perhaps he was just waiting on the background check to come back. How long did those take?

Swallowing the slice, I grabbed another, but didn't eat it as quickly. My stomach would rebel if I ate too much. I picked up the bottle of water he'd brought and took a long drink.

This was going to be fine. I'd faced worse. I could survive this.

Finishing the pizza, I drank down the rest of the bottle of water, then stood up to go get a shower. I felt dirty and wanted to wash this day from my body. The threat of anxiety tried to creep in, and I fought it. This would not get to me. I could live through this. They would see I was harmless soon and let me go.

The warm water washed over me, and I imagined it was cleaning me of all I'd been through. I soaped my body twice and washed my hair three times before finally stepping out of the shower and drying off. The T-shirt that Huck had left for me was huge. It had to be his. I took the fabric and held it to my nose to inhale. It smelled like him. I slipped it on over my head, and it hung off one shoulder and hit me just above my knees.

Sighing at myself in the mirror, I turned out the lights to the bathroom and went to the king-size bed. Taking a pillow from it and the blanket folded up on the end, I went to the sofa and lay down. I didn't know if Huck intended to sleep in that bed or not tonight, but I wasn't going to be in it if he did return.

Opening my eyes, I blinked, confused as I looked around the room. Where was I? Sitting up, I realized I was on a sofa, and with that, it all came back to me. I was in a basement, being held prisoner by my dead fiancé's criminal older brother. I stretched out my legs and dropped my head back on the sofa. Would today be the day I could go home? Unsure of the time, I walked over to a lamp and turned it on, then looked at my watch. It was seven thirty-three.

I glanced back at Huck's bed, and it looked exactly how it had last night. He hadn't slept down here. Hopefully, he'd return soon, and I could go.

I looked around for the television remote and found it on the table beside the recliner. Picking it up, I managed to figure out how to turn it on and change the channels. It was complicated, so I stayed with the basics. I stood there, flipping through the channels until I found the local news. Once I had some other voices to fill the silence, I put the remote down and went to use the bathroom and get myself ready to go home.

Twenty minutes later, when I stepped out of the bathroom, my eyes locked on Huck, and I stopped. He stood, scowling at the sofa as if it offended him. I waited until he noticed me, afraid to say anything. I still didn't know what to think of this man. Should I be afraid of him, feel safe with him, stop noticing how attractive he was?

His gaze lifted to find me standing across the room, watching him.

"You slept on the sofa." He sounded angry.

I nodded, unsure if that was an insult of sorts.

"Why?"

I tucked some hair behind my ear. "I, uh, well, that's your bed. I didn't think you'd want a stranger in it."

His scowl deepened.

"Sit down," he demanded.

I wondered if anyone had ever told this man no. The way he ordered me around made me want to stand my ground, but then there was the other part of me that knew better than to push the person in charge. I walked over to the sofa and sat down, telling myself that I'd get to leave soon and I'd never have to lay eyes on him again. Which was a good thing because the dirty, twisted part of me, which I had worked so hard to hide from the world, was attracted to this brutal killer. No amount of ipecac would get that demon out of me. But then it had never worked when Tabitha shoved it down my throat. Whatever demons she thought were inside of me hadn't left. My boobs had only gotten bigger. If she had known about my sexual thoughts and the books I read, she'd never have let me sleep under her roof while I dated Hayes.

Huck didn't sit down, but remained towering over me while he looked down at me. "For six months, you had to put on a fucking good act for my brother."

The disgust was clear in his tone and expression. I was used to disgust. I'd grown up with it in my face daily. But seeing it on his face bothered me.

What all had he found out about me? How much could he have learned in such a short time? Did those things I had been wrongfully accused of show up? And why the heck did I care if Huck Kingston was disgusted with me?

Fine! Be disgusted with me. But get in line, buddy. You aren't the first one.

"Hayes would never have put a ring on your finger had he known the truth, but then you know that. How did you think you were going to pull off being a minister's wife?" He let out a hard laugh then. "You were good at it. I was even fucking fooled at the funeral."

I fisted my hands in my lap. I would not let this man get to me. He wasn't a saint. His judgment was laughable. At least I'd never killed anyone. I should be disgusted with him.

"Not gonna defend yourself?" he asked, raising one eyebrow as he looked down at me. "Not gonna tell me that you can explain things? You had to have made up some crock-of-shit story to tell my brother in case he ever heard the truth about how you'd lost your scholarship and when. Because it sure as fuck wasn't a year ago, when you'd finally gone back home."

He bent down until his eyes were level with mine. The disgust was still there, but I saw something else. Something that should send me running from this room and this house. It wasn't the first time a man had looked at me like that. I knew what it meant. I'd learned from Roy that a man could be disgusted with you and feel lust at the same time.

"And to think, I had felt like a fucking asshole for making you take off your clothes for me," he said, tilting his head as a slow, sadistic smile spread across his face. "Then, you spread those legs and bent over, and that pink pussy was glistening with your arousal. I should have known it then."

His hand shot out, and he grabbed my face with his massive hand. Squeezing my chin so hard that I wanted to cry out from the pain, but I didn't. I was afraid to move or make a sound.

"You played that part so well. Embarrassed to strip for me when you had done it for money. And my baby brother never knew, did he?" He let go of my face, shoving it away from him as he stood up.

He had found out I'd worked at a strip club for almost six months. No one knew that. I'd worn a wig, colored contacts, and gone by a different name. I hadn't applied to be a dancer. I didn't think anyone would want to see my body naked. I started as a server. I was just required to wear a short skirt and pasties over my nipples. After one week, they convinced me to get onstage. Customers had wanted me up there, and the money was the reason I gave in, but I would have done anything to keep from having to go back to my father's house. Tabitha had made my life a living hell. She was the reason I'd studied so hard in school, determined to get a scholarship to a college as far away from her and the home I'd been forced to live in.

This man didn't deserve that explanation though. I didn't know him. One day, I would have told Hayes. He'd have understood. At least, that was what I had told myself when the guilt of my lies taunted me.

"Your disguise was a good one, but that ass?" He released a dark chuckle that made me shiver. "Any man who's seen it bare would recognize it."

The dark part of my soul that I feared would always make me bad, no matter how hard I tried, flickered inside me. My body wanted him to like it. That was sick, and I knew it, but it didn't matter to the demons I tried so hard to fight.

"Don't get me wrong; your stepmother is a horrible bitch. I get why you didn't want to go home, but then if you hadn't been fucking your married professor, then you wouldn't have lost your scholarship," Huck drawled.

He was wrong there, but then telling him that was pointless. No one had believed me then, and this man sure wasn't going to believe me now. I dropped my gaze to my lap and held my hands together, hoping this would end soon and I could go.

"The cleaning business can't pay as much as that fucking body of yours did. What was it, the guilt over lying to Hayes? He's dead. You could have gone right back to the pole. More money. Less work."

No. I had hated every moment on that stage. I'd hated myself for doing it. When my dad had had his first heart attack, I'd gone home and sworn to myself I'd never do something like that again. If I had to work myself to death, doing shitty jobs, I would.

Huck sat down on the table in front of me. His knees pressed against mine. When he leaned forward, resting his elbows on his thighs, and looked at me, I had to remember to breathe. Up close, it was hard to remember how dangerous he was. Those eyes of his were consuming.

"The man you were working for is dead, but there are those who aren't happy about it. You escaped that day while everyone else in that house was found with a bullet in them. They know by now that you were the fiancée of my brother. You're a walking target. Your apartment has already been broken into and ransacked. There is little left of your things, but what is left is being brought here." He paused and leaned closer to me. "The only way to keep you from being killed is for you to stay here. But you're not getting a fucking vacation. You'll cook for us and keep things clean. When we have people over, you'll cook the food. You'll fill drinks. You'll do whatever we ask of you. So, what's it gonna be?" He tilted his head and narrowed his eyes. "Leave here and get yourself killed within the hour or stay?"

Was this really a choice? I wanted to think he was lying about my apartment and being a target for some crazed drug gang or whatever they were. But I had seen him shoot a man in the head. These people didn't joke about this kind of thing.

It was clear he didn't want me here, but he was doing this for Hayes. Maybe he was right, and Hayes wouldn't have had anything to do with me if he'd known about my past. I didn't mind cleaning, and I loved to cook. I was good at that.

Huck cupped the side of my face roughly. "What's it gonna be?"

"I'll—I will, uh … I'll stay. I can clean and cook," I stammered, feeling slightly off-balance with his face so close that I could smell the scent of spice and cigarette smoke. I didn't care for cigarettes, but on Huck, it was different.

"Can you cook?" he asked me.

I nodded, then licked my lips. My mouth felt dry, and I had to squeeze my legs together to relieve the ache between them. Huck was a bad man, and I was turned on by him. Was it the evil in his gaze that I was drawn to? Tabitha would say it was.

Huck slid a hand between my legs until they brushed the cotton fabric of my panties, and I gasped. That, I hadn't expected. My eyes went wide, and my breathing quickened. He ran a finger over the fabric in a circular motion. Only my fingers had touched there. Having someone else do it was different. Having Huck Kingston do it was sinful, but I didn't care.

"That's all it took, and your panties are wet," he said in a husky whisper, then slipped a finger under the fabric and pushed it inside of me.

I cried out from the shock and pleasure of it. That was very new. When I touched myself, I only rubbed my clit until I orgasmed. I had never stuck anything inside of me. I realized my mistake now. I should have tried this years ago.

There was no longer disgust in his eyes, I realized. They were like two blue flames as he watched me. He looked on edge, as if he might bolt at any moment. He began to press his thick finger further into me.

"Fucking hell, that's a tight pussy," he growled.

I whimpered as he began to pump his finger in and out of me. My mouth fell open as I took short, fast breaths. I dropped my gaze to his hand between my legs.

"Oh God," I moaned.

That was too much. Seeing his big hand inside my panties was something that fantasies were made of. I didn't want this to ever stop.

"Too fucking easy," he said, jerking his hand away from me as if I had bitten him, and he stood up.

His fingers wrapped around my arm tightly before hauling me up. When I was flush against him, he grabbed my waist and spun me around to face the sofa. His hand pressed against my back, forcing me forward. I placed my hands on the back of the sofa before I face-planted on it. I opened my mouth to ask him what he was doing, but he shoved the T-shirt I was wearing halfway up my back, then grabbed my panties and ripped them off my body.

There were so many things going on at once, and I was battling to figure out which one I should be feeling. Excitement, arousal, fear, or were all of them at once acceptable too?

His hand landed on my left butt cheek with a loud smack, causing me to cry out from the pain. "Spread 'em," he barked at me.

He grabbed my butt cheeks with his hands. "Fucking hell," he said in a hoarse whisper that I felt all the way to my clit.

The arousal was definitely winning in my swarm of emotions. No man had ever touched me like this. I was having a morning of firsts, and so far, they were all something I wanted to do again. Many times.

The heat from Huck's breath caressed my throbbing clit. His face was between my thighs. I should probably be embarrassed, but his tongue ran along the sensitive folds, and my knees buckled. I cried out as I gripped the back of the sofa harder. The room was spinning.

"Damn, you taste sweet," he growled.

His hands continued to squeeze my butt cheeks as he buried his tongue inside of me. This was bad. I shouldn't just be letting this happen, yet I wasn't sure I could stop it even if I wanted to. Nothing had ever felt this incredible.

Another slap to my bottom, and I cried out in shock, pain, or was it pleasure? I didn't know the difference anymore. A long, thick finger slid inside of me, and I began to pant.

"That's a tight pussy for a slut," he said, plunging it into me. "No man's had this cunt in a while."

Unable to control my body, I moaned and rocked against his hand. No man had ever had my cunt. His fingers were the first ones to be inside of it. I should tell him this in case he planned on putting his penis in me. But I was afraid he'd stop, and I wanted more. The build inside of me as I drew closer to my release was stronger than anything I'd ever managed to do to myself. I wanted to know what that felt like. I was having to bite my bottom lip to keep from pleading with him to get me there. The throb between my legs was verging on painful as I began to pant.

Before I could spiral out of control, his hand was gone. There was nothing there but cold air.

"No!" My voice sounded as desperate as I felt.

I held myself like that, with my body trembling from the lack of fulfillment as Huck walked away. I watched as he turned the corner. He didn't look back once.

When I heard the door slam at the top of the stairs, I sank down onto the floor and curled my body up into a tight ball. Slowly, I began to rock, but no tears came. They never did. Not anymore. I banged my forehead on my knees, wishing I could be anyone else.

Hating myself was a plague that I was finding out didn't go away. The truth was, Hayes wouldn't have married me. Even if he had lived. Because eventually, he'd have seen the evil in me too. The girl that was impossible to love. How could I expect someone to truly care for me when I hated myself?

Chapter EIGHT

TRINITY
ONE YEAR AGO

No one wanted me here. Not even my father. Even after he'd almost died of a heart attack, he hadn't cared that I'd come home. For him. To help Tabitha, who hated me, take care of him. This stupid church that Tabitha loved so much had been brutal to sit through. Hearing the minister preach about how hidden sins would find you out.

Well, I sure as hell hoped not because my father would have another heart attack.

Rolling my eyes, I jerked the door handle on my car harder than necessary, wishing I'd just stayed in Georgia. Perhaps I should just go somewhere else. Find a new place to move to. Start a new life. Tabitha had said Roy and his wife, Anita, were coming for a visit next week. I hadn't seen him in four years. I'd not gone to his wedding. I refused to be anywhere he was going to be. If he was coming, then I was leaving.

"Excuse me. Trinity, right?"

A male voice startled me, and I spun around to see the man who had spoken before the minister this morning. He looked to be about my age. I wasn't blind. This man was nice to look at, but he was also a minister of sorts. He was probably coming to save my black soul. I forced a smile and hoped that Tabitha was not out in the parking lot yet, seeing this. I'd come to this church because my father had asked me to. When I was growing up, Tabitha wouldn't bring me to church with her. She would tell me that those with demons in them weren't allowed inside the doors. Why my father had thought I should attend church now, I had no idea.

"Yes," I replied.

His grin spread, making a dimple appear in his left cheek. Okay, so he was handsome and had a dimple. He still loved the Lord and all. Not for me.

"I was, uh, well, I noticed you this morning, and I asked around."

He looked unsure of himself. That wasn't expected. I said nothing, curious as to what this was about. He cleared his throat and looked down, then back up at me through his ridiculously long lashes.

"Sorry. I'm not normally so bad at this. You make me nervous," he explained. "Would you like to go have coffee? Or lunch maybe?"

That was not what I had guessed this was about. I opened my mouth and closed it.

Was this him asking me out? Or had Tabitha told him I was a sinner, bound for eternal damnation, and he was going to try to save my soul?

He ran a hand through his hair and lightly chuckled. "I'm Hayes Kingston. My grandfather is the minister here. I swear I'm not as crazy as it currently seems."

Wow. The minister's grandson. I wondered if the man knew his grandson was asking me to coffee. I glanced around the parking lot and immediately saw Tabitha glaring at me. I was speaking to her beloved minister's grandson. She wasn't happy about it. I was sure to shame her by simply breathing.

Snapping my gaze back to the man standing in front of me, I smiled brightly. "I'd like that," I told him.

When he smiled this time, his eyes twinkled with excitement, and I felt a little flutter in my chest. Hayes Kingston was very good-looking, I realized. This would probably be a one-time thing. Tabitha would be sure to bash my name the moment she could. He'd never want to see me again. For now, I'd enjoy a meal with a handsome man who I made nervous. While also making Tabitha furious.

PRESENT DAY

Eventually, I was able to get myself together, get up from my pathetic breakdown on the floor, and go to the bathroom. A long, hot shower, cleansing myself from the ugliness that I had accepted and even embraced, helped me clear my head even if it didn't do anything for the pain that was a part of me. When I exited the bathroom, I saw food had been delivered, but I had no appetite. Forcing myself to eat would only make me sick. I'd tried that in the past.

I curled up on the sofa to watch mindless television shows. Sitcoms where family life was entertaining and all was well at the end of the thirty minutes it took to air. I didn't know how long I'd sat there, nor did I care what time it was when I heard the footsteps on the stairs once again. The sound caused a sick knot in my stomach, and my eyes shifted to the food I hadn't touched.

Would I be forced to eat? It wouldn't be the first time.

Tabitha had caught me sneaking a handful of chips from the pantry once. She then forced me to eat the entire bag and then another until I threw up. Then, she'd given me a spoon and stood over me with a long, thin hickory switch, snapping it across my back until I ate my vomit. To this day, I couldn't eat plain potato chips.

I fisted my hands in my lap. I wasn't a child anymore, and physical and emotional pain were things I had learned to survive. Huck was a large man, and as much as I disgusted him, I didn't believe he would hurt me physically. But then I had been wrong about so many things in life.

My eyes stayed trained on the television show I had been watching. I had no idea what the name of it was, but that didn't matter. It kept my thoughts preoccupied.

"You didn't eat."

His deep voice made me tense.

I would not let this man do any more damage. He had no idea the level of suffering I could endure.

I shrugged. "I didn't have an appetite." My eyes never left the television.

Silence. I fought against counting the seconds that ticked by. If the man lunged at me and strangled me to death or began hitting me, then perhaps death was something I could embrace. End this life I'd been given.

"Get up. Get your things."

He liked to order me around. Perhaps if I were a stronger woman who had a backbone, I would stand up to him. See how he liked being told no. But I'd been beaten down long before I met Huck Kingston.

Standing, I walked over and picked up the few things that I could call mine, then turned to look at him. He was scowling, as if being down here this close to me was his own form of punishment. I wished I didn't care. Perhaps it was the way he frowned or the way his eyes were set in his head. It reminded me of Hayes. The only person in my life to not see my faults. The only male to ever make me feel special.

"Is that it?" he asked.

I nodded.

"Follow me."

He turned and started toward the steps. Was I being moved to a room now so I could cook and clean, or was I being sent home to possibly be murdered? At least I wasn't being left locked up in his basement. If he sent me away, I might possibly survive long enough to leave the state, change my appearance, but then all of that took money. I wasn't sure my car could get me that far at the moment.

Panic slowly began to trickle in, and I focused on my breathing as I followed Huck up the stairs. Either option was terrifying.

No … no … stop! I wasn't going to fall apart in front of this man. If I didn't live to see another sunrise, then so be it. But I would not let this man see me crack. He wouldn't get the satisfaction.

At the top of the stairs, he turned left, and I followed him. We turned to go up another flight of stairs. That was my answer. I was to stay and be the housekeeper and cook. The panic clawing at my chest eased some.

The new set of stairs was impressive, wide and curved. A chandelier hung overhead, and I realized I'd never seen this part of the house. It was open with windows and light pouring in everywhere. This wouldn't be bad. I could do this.

Huck stopped at the top of the stairs, then barely glanced back at me before pointing toward the wide hallway. "The third door on your right. You'll stay there. We will expect breakfast at seven thirty every morning, we aren't here for lunch, and you'll be notified if we will require dinner. Keep a list of items you need from the grocery store, and that will be handled. Every room needs to be thoroughly cleaned each week. The rooms that are occupied, you will straighten and clean daily. Don't leave the house without permission. You can't be without protection." Huck spoke as if this were something we'd already discussed.

When I said nothing and only nodded, he glared at me.

"If you don't want to die, you'll refrain from stealing shit," he snapped. "Do your job and stay out of the way otherwise."

I wasn't a thief, but explaining what he'd seen on my background check wasn't something he wanted. He believed what he wanted to about me. Most people did. I wasn't going to lose sleep over that.

I managed a nod, took my things, and walked past him toward the third door on the right. For now, I was safe, out of the dungeon, and no one was going to starve me or force me to vomit. This wasn't living free, but it was living. I would just be thankful for that.

Chapter NINE

TEN MONTHS AGO

Hayes's hand held mine tightly as we left my father's gravesite. Everyone else had already gone. Including Tabitha. I hadn't been able to move from that spot, looking down where they had lowered his casket into the ground. It was so strange that my heart ached like it did.

Not once in my life had I felt like my father loved me. He was never my safe place. I'd never had a safe place. Yet, now, we would never get that chance to have a relationship. There would be no apologies. We wouldn't hug each other and say *I love you*. Knowing that left a hole in my heart. He was the only parent I had ever known, and he hadn't loved me.

Growing up with that knowledge had twisted and shaped me into the person I was today. If your own parent couldn't love you, then could anyone?

I hadn't had boyfriends when I was in high school. Tabitha didn't allow me to go anywhere but to school and home. When a boy showed interest and dared to call our house, I was punished. Eventually, I did everything I could to be invisible wherever I went. The baggy, unattractive clothing Tabitha had supplied for me helped me fade into the background. There was no young love, first love, nothing of the sort. By the time I was out of the house, I'd grown accustomed to being alone. I never managed to form any relationships.

Truly being loved was a foreign thing to me. Hayes hadn't said he loved me, but he showed me more compassion and understanding than anyone in my life. He was the only person to put in the energy to get down my walls. He was patient and kind, yet I knew I wasn't in love with him. I'd read books and heard other girls talk. Hayes didn't cause butterflies in my stomach or make my heart race. Don't get me wrong; I did love him. I would do anything for him. He gave and thought about others, never once worrying about what he wanted. I loved him in a way I had never loved anyone. I could trust him. He'd become my best friend—my only real friend.

"Where would you like to go?" he asked me as we reached his car.

I shrugged. I had no idea. Tabitha hadn't kicked me out yet, but my father had only been dead for five days. There was a good chance I would find my bags waiting on the front porch when I got home. Sure, she had been nicer since Hayes had begun taking me out and giving me attention. However, I doubted she would want to keep me in the house that my father had left solely to her.

"Okay, let me ask this another way. Do you want to go watch back-to-back movies at the theater until we are so full of popcorn that we are sick, or do you want to head to the beach and watch the waves in silence until it's too dark to see them?"

How could you not love someone like that? Hayes was the perfect human, and although I had tried to tell him I wasn't good, he'd refused to listen to me. We did not belong together, and deep down, I was sure he knew it too. If he didn't, he would figure it out. My chest ached at the thought of not having him. With Hayes, I didn't feel alone anymore.

"Beach," I said.

"We'll stop and buy unhealthy snacks and eat those," he replied.

My lips curled into a smile as he opened the car door for me. Turning to him, I placed a hand on his cheek and kissed him. I'd never kissed anyone. Not even a relative on the cheek. But I was too emotionally wrung out to find the right words. I owed him so much. I wasn't sure I could have survived this had he not stood by my side the entire time.

Hayes's left hand touched my waist, and he returned the kiss. It wasn't passionate, and no new feelings emerged within me as I slipped my tongue inside his mouth. This was safe. It was comfortable. I enjoyed the connection with another person. Perhaps I should have tried this sooner with other guys. It was pleasant, and although it wasn't true affection, it stood in for the emptiness. I could pretend it was more.

PRESENT DAY

I was pulling the biscuits from the oven when Gage walked into the kitchen. Glancing at the clock, afraid I was running past the time Huck had said I was to have breakfast ready, I realized Gage was early. With a sigh of relief, I placed the biscuits on the island.

"Can I get you a cup of coffee?" I asked him.

Gage looked at the food I had already prepared before grinning. "Damn, girl. You even made French toast," he drawled, then walked over to study the other items. "What's that? It smells fucking amazing."

"It's sausage and gravy breakfast lasagna," I replied feeling anxious.

He then pointed to another item. "And that?"

"Breakfast fried potatoes. I just added some onions, peppers, and seasoning."

He shook his head, still grinning. "Where're the fucking plates? I'm gonna want to come back for seconds and thirds. I need to start now."

Relieved that I had made someone in this house happy, I hurried over to grab the plates and set them on the end of the island.

He picked up a plate and then groaned. "Please tell me that's homemade cinnamon rolls."

"It is," I replied.

He looked up at me seriously now. "Listen, if Huck pisses you off and you want to leave, then come see me. I love the man, but I have priorities. He's not gonna mess this up for us. And if Levi proposes, say no. He'd make a terrible husband."

I laughed, surprising myself. I hadn't wanted to laugh in a very long time. I turned to get the sausage from the stove and bring it over, then headed to the fridge for butter and jelly. Remembering I still hadn't gotten Gage's coffee, I turned to see him walking to the table with a plate piled high with food.

"How do you like your coffee?" I asked him.

"Black," he replied. "Could I have a glass of milk too?"

"Of course," I replied and hurried to start making his drinks.

I tried to relax since he was pleased but he still needed to taste it first. Although I was pretty confident in my cooking skills. There wasn't much I felt good at. Cooking was something I had taught myself to do to fill the time. It was good therapy. I rarely had anyone to cook for, which was why my butt was larger than it needed to be.

"What the fuck is this?" Huck's deep voice filled the kitchen.

I turned around so quickly that the hot coffee sloshed over the cup and burned my hand. I winced, but said nothing. My attention was locked on Huck. He was scowling at the food like it offended him.

"Br-br-breakfast," I managed to reply.

He waved a hand at it and looked at me like I was insane. "I said to cook breakfast, not a fucking buffet. There is just the three of us. Who the hell is gonna eat all this?"

I opened my mouth and closed it again.

"Shut the fuck up!" Gage called out from the table. "I'll eat it. No one asked your ornery ass. If you're gonna bitch over this, then go eat at the big house."

What was the big house? I didn't ask that though.

Levi walked into the room then, and his eyes went from me to Huck to the food. When they widened and a smile spread across his face, I felt somewhat better. Two against one. That was good odds.

"Holy shit, I've died and woken up in heaven when I was sure hell had a room ready for me," Levi said, then walked past Huck to grab a plate. He looked back at me. "You did all this?"

I nodded, afraid to look back up at Huck, who was still standing there.

"I think I fucking love you," he said and began filling his plate.

I picked up a plate and held it out to Huck. "Try it at least. You need to eat."

He looked down at the plate as if it were disgusting. "I don't like wasting food," he said to me.

I swallowed. "I wasn't sure how much y'all would eat," I replied honestly.

Huck pointed at the food. "No one eats that much."

"Excuse me! I do. Stop bitching," Gage barked. "Ignore him, sugar. I'll worship at your feet if you feed us like this every morning."

Huck muttered a curse and snatched the plate from my hand.

Levi put a cinnamon roll on his plate. "Sweet mother of God. I'm gonna propose. I swear it. Just let me get the ring."

"Told you. Ignore him," Gage told me with a mouth full of food.

Huck put food on his plate with more force than necessary. I tried not to worry about it and asked Levi what he'd like in his coffee. When I took Levi's cup to him, he grabbed my hand and kissed it.

Huck said nothing, and I noticed he had his own cup of coffee when he sat down. He also had a lot less food than the other two men. I tried not to let that bother me.

"Fuuuuck," Levi groaned loudly. "This is better than getting sucked off."

Gage laughed out loud, and I found myself smiling again.

"Must be putting your cock in the wrong mouths," Huck said in a tone that made it clear he was not impressed with my cooking.

Why did this man hate me? Because I'd let him touch me? I hadn't asked him to. He had started it. I'd just not stopped him. My mistake. It wouldn't happen again.

"You going into the shop?" Gage asked Huck.

"If I want to keep it open."

Levi chuckled, and I glanced over to see if Huck was at least enjoying his breakfast.

"Ray-Ray coming in today?" Gage asked over a mouthful of food.

"Keep your dick out of Ray-Ray." Huck's response sounded annoyed. "She's my fucking secretary."

Gage leaned back and smirked. "So, she gets to suck your cock when you want it sucked, but the rest of us don't get the goods when we come in to work?"

My face heated as I turned away from them and went to cleaning up the things I'd used to make breakfast.

"She begs to suck his cock," Levi said. "Bitch has a thing for Prince Albert."

What did that mean? Had he named his penis?

I wished I could unhear all of this.

Chapter TEN

HUCK

The living room was crowded with those of us not at the Kentucky Derby. Typically, I'd be there. This year, I had planned on going, but Trinity had screwed that up. Gage didn't go to most of the races, and he'd stay here, taking care of things and running my bike repair shop, but that shit wasn't happening. I didn't trust him or her. Last thing I needed was for Trinity to start fucking Gage or Levi. She'd get attached, they'd get bored with her, and then I would be stuck trying to relocate her somewhere safe.

Glaring at the television as everyone was ready for the turf race to begin, I tried not to be bitter that I was missing the real thing. So far today, Pyros had won Churchill Downs, and Galahad had won La Troienne for Hughes Farm. Moses Mile had gotten their first win with Firefoot in the Distaff Turf Mile. The fucking energy in this room was nothing compared to being there.

"We're celebrating. Or did you miss that?" Gage asked as he walked up beside me.

I didn't look at him when I grunted my response.

"You could have gone," he said. "I would have kept her safe."

Like hell he would have. Moving Trinity from my room up to the second floor three days ago had been hard enough. She was already walking around and in my fucking way all the damn time. Cooking elaborate meals that had the guys praising her and offering marriage. She would blush all the way down to those big, natural tits when they gave her attention. Her pussy was probably soaked, thinking one—or both—of them was going to bend her over and finish what I had started. The more they did it, the more pleased she looked, the fucking angrier I got. She was driving me mad. I'd had Ray-Ray suck me off twice today because I kept thinking about Trinity's tight pussy. I shouldn't have touched it.

"I'd have gone, and she'd have been tag-teamed by the two of you," I snarled, shoving off from the wall I'd been leaning on and stalking toward the bar.

"Hey," he called out. "You said that was off-limits. What? You don't trust us?" Gage called out as I walked away from him.

Yeah, I fucking trusted them with my life. They were my brothers. The ones I had killed beside, the most loyal sons of bitches I'd ever known. But I didn't trust her. She liked men, and she liked sex. It had been clear when she'd let me eat her like a damn buffet, not caring that I was her dead fiancé's brother.

"Okay, who the hell made this crab dip? It's the best shit I've ever put in my mouth," Red's loud mouth bellowed as he walked out of the kitchen.

"We replaced Gina," Gage replied. "You should see what we get for breakfast these days."

Mattia grinned as he walked over toward the bar with an empty glass. "The brunette, right? I got me a look at that. I approve. Got a fucking boner over that ass. Now, I know she can cook too. Shiiit."

I stiffened and took a step toward him. Gage stepped in front of me.

"Easy," he said, and I wasn't sure if he was talking to me or Mattia. "Trinity was Hayes's fiancée."

Mattia's olive skin went pale as his eyes widened. He looked past Gage to me. "Fuck, man. I didn't mean disrespect. He said y'all replaced Gina, so I thought ..." He stopped before going any further.

"No one is fucking her," I ground out between clenched teeth. Not even me. If I couldn't fuck the slutty, lying cunt, then no one was getting a piece.

Mattia nodded and turned to go back to the sofa instead of filling his glass.

"If I go in the kitchen to get some of the dip, do you promise not to kill someone if they mention Trinity and her world-class ass?" Gage asked me.

I gave him a warning glance, then went back to watch the next race.

Destiny walked up beside me and wrapped her arm around mine. "Can I get you anything?" she asked, pressing her tits against my arm.

"Later," I replied.

Ray-Ray's blow jobs hadn't helped. Maybe fucking Destiny would.

She pressed a kiss to my bicep because she wasn't tall enough to reach any further and winked at me. "I'm available whenever you want me."

No shit. I was relieved when she walked away. I wasn't currently in the mood for her to lick all over me.

"Not everyone knows about Hayes," Gage said as he came to stand beside me with his plate of food. "You need to be prepared for some of them to hit on Trinity. Technically, she's a widow in the family. Even if Hayes chose another path, he was a Kingston. There are those who will see that as Trinity needing another man in the family to take care of her. Sure, you're the first choice, but if you don't want that, then …" He stopped talking and put a chip with dip in his mouth.

I shifted my gaze to Gage. "Who the fuck is hitting on her?" I asked, already knowing he was right.

Having her here in front of the others was eating at me. I hated that I cared. Hayes had been so damn good. He'd deserved more than what he'd ended up with. Sure, he'd died before she could crush him, but that didn't change the fact that I knew it would have happened. She had used him. Poor little brother had been blinded by big brown eyes and a body made for sin.

Gage cut his eyes at me. "Every man here with a dick."

Fuck.

"Where is she?" I bit out.

Gage finished chewing the food he'd shoved in his mouth. "Kitchen. Making shit that tastes fucking delicious. Wearing shorts that don't cover her ass. And—" Gage didn't get to finish that sentence.

I didn't have time to listen to this. As I stalked toward the kitchen, a ball of rage coiled tight in my chest. Was she trying to get fucked? Or was she looking to replace Hayes? Wanting a man to take care of her? That wasn't what she was going to get here. They'd take care of her all right, but not the way she had planned with my brother. No fucking white picket fences and Sunday church picnics.

When I walked into the kitchen, my eyes zeroed in on one of the younger men, Bart. He stood too damn close to her as she cut up something in a baking dish. She was smiling at whatever he was saying. She couldn't stop flashing that damn smile around. I swore to fucking God if Levi got up from the table one more time with a boner, I was going to cut it off.

Did those damn shorts even cover her ass? Why hadn't she just shown up naked?

"Out!" I roared before I could stop myself.

Bart's head snapped up, and he tensed, then made his way out of the kitchen without another word. I didn't have a problem with the kid other than the fact that he was sniffing around pussy that was off-limits to him.

Once he was gone, I moved my gaze to Trinity. She was watching me with those big brown eyes. Confusion, uncertainty, and a little touch of rebellion danced in their depths.

Was it those eyes that had caught Hayes's attention? Or had that juicy ass been his weakness?

"You looking to get fucked?" I asked her.

She stiffened, and the hurt that flashed across her face made me feel shit I didn't want to acknowledge. I knew she wasn't going to respond. She'd barely spoken to me since I'd eaten her pussy, finger-fucked it, then walked off.

I placed my hands on the counter, leaning closer to her. "In this world, you are now free fucking game. Hayes wasn't one of us, but he was born into this. You're protected by the family. Which also means one of us can decide he wants you and then you're his. You become his piece of ass. You have no say," I explained in a low voice, not wanting anyone to walk in and hear me. Mostly because I was making some of this shit up. She had a say. It might not be enough of a say, but she had one.

"Bart's young. He's got little power. Harmless. But he's not what you need to be worried about," I warned her. "Do you want to open those legs for anyone who wants it? Keep smiling pretty, blushing, and wearing fucking shorts that don't cover your ass. You'll get what you're begging for."

Trinity stiffened and blinked several times. "I don't," she replied and then took a deep breath. "I don't mean to do that or those things. The shorts are some that were left for me in my room. Most of my clothes"—she paused—"didn't make it here. The clothes I have aren't my size, but I didn't pick them."

Fuck. Fine. She must be wearing shit Gina had left behind, and Gina didn't have an ass like that.

"You've got two options," I reply. "Let one of them claim you. Or ..." I paused, knowing that I was going to fucking regret this but the shit was coming out of my goddamn mouth whether I wanted it to or not. "Or pretend you're mine."

Trinity stood there, looking up at me as if she wasn't sure she'd heard me correctly. Shit, I wasn't even sure if I had heard me correctly. Why had I even offered this? She was a burden I didn't want.

"What does pretending mean exactly?" she asked softly.

The fact that my cock got hard wasn't a good sign.

"You act like we are together when others are around. Not Gage or Levi. They will know this is bullshit. But anyone else."

I wasn't sure I believed what had just come out of my mouth. Did I really want to do this just to save a lying stripper from a man who might truly want her? Most of these guys wouldn't give a fuck she'd lied, stripped, stolen, committed fraud, committed adultery, and whatever else she'd done. Hell, they'd think it was a great résumé.

Even if I didn't want her, I wasn't willing to let someone else have her. That was my fucked up shit. I couldn't stop thinking about how her pussy had tasted like honey and smelled even sweeter. Maybe she'd refuse and save me from my stupidity.

"I'll pretend," she whispered.

Fuck me. My hands fisted on the bar, and I managed a nod. "Starts now. They're already out there, talking about you. Asking questions. Go upstairs and get those goddamn shorts off. Find something else. Anything else. Then, come back down."

She nodded and turned away without argument. I waited until she was gone before rubbing my face with my hand, then adjusting my damn cock. Destiny was gonna get her ass pounded tonight.

Chapter ELEVEN

TRINITY

Three sundresses, one hoodie, and a pair of jeans were all the clothing I'd been brought from my apartment. Everything else had been destroyed. Gage had brought me a box full of clothes and said I could have whatever I wanted out of it. Problem with those clothes was, they fit in my waist and most in my chest, but the butt and hips were an issue.

Standing in front of the mirror, I chewed on my bottom lip, wondering if Huck was going to be okay with this. The shorts I had were all going to fit me the same. They weren't mine. Two of my three sundresses were too dressy for things downstairs. That left me with the one hot-pink sundress that was low-cut and short, but it did cover my butt. After all, that had been his complaint. It was ninety-three degrees today. Wearing a hoodie and jeans was not happening.

I was a ball of nerves. I had agreed to what Huck had said because I was worried about what would happen if I didn't. Every man downstairs was scary and intimidating.

Huck might not like me, but I knew he was hell-bent on protecting me for Hayes's sake. He had seemed like the safe choice because he had already made it clear he didn't want me sexually. I wasn't in danger of being raped by him—not that it would be rape. Sadly, I had used the memory of what he'd done to me in the basement to pleasure myself more times than I could count. Although sticking my fingers inside myself had done nothing for me.

Not to mention, the more I was around him and watched his large, muscular, tattooed body move, the more fascinated I became. He was so hard not to look at and want. What female wouldn't want a man like that taking control of her body? He made me think about naughty things without even speaking.

Squeezing my eyes closed tightly, I took several deep breaths, then headed back downstairs. Huck hadn't said where to go or if he would meet me. I wasn't even sure he planned on doing more than just telling people we were together. He'd just wanted me to change my clothing. Deciding to walk to the living room so he could see me before ducking back into the kitchen to hide, I hoped I was doing the right thing.

The living room was full of people. It seemed like more had appeared since I had gone upstairs. I scanned the room to see Huck in the large leather chair that sat to the right side of the room. A blonde with boobs falling out of her … bra—was she just wearing a bra?—sat on the armrest beside him. Her hand was on the back of his neck, rubbing it.

Okay, well, I wasn't wanted in here, it would seem. Instead of waiting on him to notice me, I decided to walk behind the crowd and go to the kitchen entrance. In this strange world I was now in, did it mean he could claim me as his, but still let half-naked women hang all over him? I wasn't sure us being together was believable if he had other women pawing at him. But what did I know?

I was almost past the bar when a deep voice carried over the crowd. "Trinity."

Huck had seen me. I stopped and turned to look at him. He was leaning back with his left ankle resting on his right knee. A cigar was between his lips, and I hated smoking, but why did that look so sexy? His gaze traveled down my body, and then he held out a hand toward me. Obediently, I went to him, careful not to make eye contact with the blonde beside him. That was just awkward.

When I reached him, I stared down at his hand, then back at him. He raised his eyebrows at me, and I lifted my hand slowly before placing it in his. I sure hoped that was what he was wanting. His large fingers wrapped around my hand, and he tugged me toward him. He took the cigar out of his mouth with his free hand.

"You can go, Destiny," Huck said, not taking his eyes from me.

The blonde stood, but I didn't dare look at her. Huck tugged me closer before reaching up and grabbing my hips with the one hand to pull me down to his lap.

Oh. Okay.

"Relax," he said near my ear, and I leaned back against his chest in hopes that it was what he considered relaxed.

My body was tense, and I knew it. But he smelled like cigar, whiskey, and spice. I was torn between snuggling closer and inhaling or jumping up and running.

Huck brushed his lips against my ear. The heat from his breath made me tremble. I felt like he could swallow me whole, and unfortunately, I would go willingly.

"I don't bite unless you ask me to." His voice was low and husky.

I managed a nod and tried to loosen up. Act like this was normal. Huck's hand moved to my leg, then slid up and under my sundress before moving it between my thighs. I stopped breathing.

"You're too tense. No one here will think I'm taking that cunt if you look ready to bolt," he told me.

"I'm trying," I whispered, looking down at his hand between my thighs.

"Open them up just a little," he urged me.

My breathing was so erratic that even I could see my chest rising and falling too fast and hard. "My legs?" I asked in a whisper.

"Mmhmm," he murmured in my ear.

This man ran hot and cold. Mostly cold, but Lord help me when he ran hot. I felt like I was already burned, and he'd not even done anything yet. I eased my legs open enough so that his hand could slide further up. I didn't breathe, waiting for him to touch the silky crotch of my panties, but he didn't go that far.

Great. I was going to be panting like a dog in heat. This was a bad idea. Maybe Gage … no, Levi—he was less threatening-looking. Levi could pretend we were together. I didn't get all wet and bothered by Levi or even Gage. Huck seemed to hold that power exclusively.

"You come down here in a fucking short dress with those big tits about to fall out, and I'm gonna play. Everyone in here would expect it. I've been sucked off in front of these men. I've fucked in front of them. Destiny and others have bounced on my dick on days like this. So, if we are going to be believable, then you're gonna have to let me touch you."

I inhaled sharply. I was not having sex in front of people. Or sucking him off. This was a bad idea. "I won't do those things," I said, moving to get up. His one hand held me firmly in place.

"What won't you do? Bounce on my cock or do it in public? Because we both know you'd have bounced real fucking easy when I had my face in your cunt."

My entire body felt like a live wire. I should be mad at him. I should get up and walk away. I should not be getting wet because of the way he had been talking to me. But the memory of his tongue pleasuring me wasn't one I would forget anytime soon.

"In public," I replied. No point in saying I wouldn't let him screw me. It had been clear downstairs that I was willing to do whatever he wanted.

"What, a stripper who won't fuck in public? I thought you'd get off on it." His voice was cruel. I could hear the disgust in it.

"This was a bad idea. Maybe Levi would be a better choice to pretend with."

I had barely gotten the words out of my mouth when Huck's hand gripped the inside of my thigh so tightly that I let out a whimper.

"No. Not Levi. Me," he growled, then took a nip at my ear with his teeth. "I won't let anyone see your cunt, but I'm going to fucking touch it."

His hand moved up then, jerking the fabric covering me away before sliding two fingers along the wet folds. My hand went to his arm, and I squeezed, which only got a low, deep chuckle from him.

"You sure are fucking wet," he said as he kissed my neck. "Makes me think you liked the idea of fucking with an audience."

I shook my head, but I couldn't form words. Huck's fingers continued to slide back and forth inside my panties.

"The crab dip is incredible." Gage's voice broke into my lust haze, and I lifted my eyes to see him standing beside us, eating from a plate in his hand.

Huck didn't stop. In fact, he pressed the tip of his finger inside me just barely. I made a noise and tried very hard not to show on my face what was happening. Although if Gage looked down, he'd see Huck's hand between my legs.

"Th-th-thanks," I replied, trying to smile.

"Easy, just relax," Huck said against my ear.

"Levi's gonna have competition after tonight," Gage said with a laugh. "He might need to put a ring on it fast."

Huck shoved his finger inside me fully then, and I turned my head away from Gage to bury my cry in Huck's chest.

"She's not available," Huck said.

"Oh?" Gage's tone was amused.

"Mine. Make sure they all know," Huck replied.

Gage laughed then. "Oh, brother. There's not a fucker in here that doesn't know now."

I squeezed my eyes closed, and the pleasure was mixed with humiliation. Huck lifted his hand holding the cigar toward his mouth, and I tried to calm my heartbeat. The man wasn't even affected by this. He was casually smoking his cigar while he played with my vagina.

Just when I was sure I couldn't take much more teasing, he stopped and moved his hand down and rested his large palm on top of my thigh. "Legs together," he told me.

I quickly did as I had been told because I needed to ease the ache he'd created. I glanced at him to see his eyes were on the television. Scanning the room, I realized everyone's eyes were on the horse racing up on the big screen. Finally, I was about to relax. When I shifted so that I could see the television better, Huck's hand tightened its grip on my leg.

"I'm just trying to see the race," I explained.

"Be careful where you wiggle that ass," he warned.

I was no longer relaxed.

The people around me cheered, yelled, and talked about what was happening on the screen. I tried to focus on it, but Huck made it hard, just by breathing. Some man he'd called Red was sitting on the sofa with a woman in his lap. When the room erupted in cheers, she pulled her top off and swung it around in circles over her head before tossing it. The man laughed and pressed his face in between her now-naked breasts.

I dropped my gaze to my hands, wondering how much longer I had to sit here. It was clear the horse they'd wanted to win had won. The celebrating was beginning. Destiny, the blonde who had been beside Huck earlier, stood and took off her bra, then flashed a smile at Huck before straddling Levi.

It was clear she wanted Huck, and this was her way of getting his attention. I glanced back at him, and he was watching her with the cigar between his lips. A knot of something I did not want to admit curled in my stomach. He liked her body. She had a perfect one. I didn't want to look her way again though. It stung, and that was just sad. I shouldn't care. So what? Huck didn't want me like he did her. He didn't like that I hadn't been good enough for Hayes. Well, Hayes had loved me.

Hayes had been a good man. He'd just wanted me. Granted, we had never done more than kiss, and even I had kissed him first. The few times I'd tried to get him to do more, he would stop me, reminding me we had to wait until marriage.

Gage walked over toward where Destiny was straddling Levi's lap. I could tell he was watching them. The interest in his gaze was clear. He stopped behind Levi and reached forward to squeeze Destiny's breasts. She threw her head back and moaned.

When was I going to get to escape upstairs? I didn't want to watch this. Huck placed his hand on my stomach and moved me back further against him. The hard ridge of his erection pressed between my butt cheeks. A tingle ran through me before it hit me that his erection had nothing to do with me. He was turned on from a topless Destiny.

I was done here. He couldn't make me watch this. I tried to get up, but he was surprisingly strong with one arm.

"Let me up," I hissed.

"No," was his response.

Destiny cried out Levi's name, and I was almost positive they were having sex now. I must have missed when he had unzipped his pants. I struggled to get up again.

"Be still." It was yet another command from Huck.

I fisted my hands in my lap. "I don't want to watch live-action porn," I told him angrily.

He let out a low chuckle. "You forget I know you worked at a strip club. Stop with your virtuous bullshit."

I glared at him. "I didn't claim to be virtuous. I just don't want to sit on your lap with your hard-on pressed against my bottom while you watch some girl screw your friends."

He pulled the cigar from his mouth and laid it in an ashtray on the table beside him. "My hard dick has nothing to do with Destiny's performance. I've seen it many times. She's bounced on my dick just like that."

I was the one who laughed this time. "Yeah, okay. Whatever." I rolled my eyes. I now had an image of that in my head, and I was mad that he had put it there.

He grabbed my face with his hand and held me still. I stared at him, afraid he was going to bruise my face if I moved. My breathing became quick, short breaths. It was times like this he scared me and excited me at the same time.

"Don't roll your eyes at me," he warned.

I started to be obedient when I heard Destiny yell the word *fuck*, then squeal loudly.

"Don't tell me what to do," I shot back at him.

His grip on my face tightened, and two things happened. It hurt—bad. And I felt a small jolt of pleasure between my legs. What was wrong with me? I needed to be slapped.

"Are you trying to see how far you can push me, Trinity?" His voice sounded deadly.

I was an idiot. "No," I whispered, hoping he'd let me go before he broke my jaw.

He studied me for a moment, then let go of my face and grabbed my waist to stand me up. I stumbled by the sudden movement, but Huck was standing up in front of me, and his hands steadied me before he wrapped his fingers around my wrist and pulled me through the people. I had no option but to follow him. As we passed behind Gage, going toward the door I'd entered the room from, his hooded eyes turned to meet mine, then flickered to Huck's.

The grip Huck had on my arm tightened, and I hurried to keep up before he pulled my arm out of the socket. I doubted I'd get to see a doctor if it happened. I would have to make my own arm sling and hope for the best. Good news was, I knew how. Tabitha had twisted my arm once until something cracked. I was twelve. For three months, I had to wear a sling I'd made for myself with an old T-shirt when I was at home. In public, I hadn't been allowed to wear it and had to pretend as if I wasn't in pain.

Huck hauled me up the stairs, and I realized he was taking me to my room to get rid of me. Perhaps he was next in line with Destiny. Why I was sour about that, I didn't want to examine. If he wouldn't touch me like he had downstairs, then maybe I could stop thinking about him sexually.

We walked down the hallway to the room he'd assigned to me. I didn't call it mine because nothing was mine. Remembering that was the best way to protect myself. There was no use in pretending.

Huck shoved the door open and then pushed me inside. I almost fell from the force of it but caught myself on the bedframe. Crossing my arms over my chest, I waited until the door closed behind me. I didn't want to look back at him. There was a moment's pause, and I began to think he was either going to say something or join me.

Before my body could get too excited, the door slammed, and I listened as his footsteps retreated down the hallway. Turning then, I sank onto the edge of the bed and stared at the closed door. I was tempted to take my sandal off and throw it at the wall, door, something.

Instead, I stood back up to go get a bath and try not to masturbate to Huck Kingston.

Chapter TWELVE

TRINITY

It took me most of the day to clean up the mess from the party. When that was done, I worked on the rest of the house, then started dinner. This was going to be a full-time job. How long was it going to last? I wasn't getting paid for this. Just room and board. I guessed my life was safe too.

Gage came inside the back door about the time I finished making dinner. He inhaled deeply and grinned. "That smells fucking amazing. Now, let's pack it all up and head to the shop."

I'd heard them talk about the shop, but I wasn't sure what it was. "What is that?" I asked.

"Huck's bike repair shop. We got some shit to finish up, and we'll be there late. Huck sent me to get you and the food. Well, just the food, but you've been here all damn day, and I getting out will feel good."

He was taking me without Huck telling him to. I wasn't sure that was a good idea.

He raised his eyebrows when I didn't move. "What?"

"I, uh … is that smart if Huck didn't say I could?"

Gage grinned and put both his hands on the island between us, then leaned toward me. "He might be big and fucking bossy, but make no mistake—Huck isn't in charge of me. I'm a crazier son of a bitch than he is. He knows it too. Now, pack the shit up, and let's get you out of the damn house for a while."

He was right. It would be nice to get out of this house. I nodded and started packing up the lasagna, Caesar salad, and garlic bread. There was an apple pie on the counter and vanilla ice cream in the freezer.

"Need a cooler for the ice cream?" Gage asked.

I nodded.

He left the kitchen, then came back in with a navy cooler that I added ice to before putting the vanilla ice cream in.

"Should I pack an ice cream scoop, plates, forks?"

He shook his head. "Nope. There is a mini kitchen at the shop. It has all we need."

I was still a tiny bit nervous about going without Huck's permission, but Gage did seem sure of his decision. He was the one who had put a gun to my head—twice. Obeying him would be a solid decision.

Gage took most of the food with him out to the truck he was driving. I followed with the pie and garlic bread. He took over arranging everything in the backseat, so I let him handle it and went to get into the passenger seat. It felt good to be getting out. Last night had been difficult. Huck seemed to be a problem for me, and as much as I wished I could hate him, I couldn't.

"What exactly does Huck do at the bike repair shop?" I asked when Gage was pulling out of the garage.

"Mostly works on Harleys. That's his Harley in the last parking spot in the garage. It's his specialty. But he works on all kinds of bikes."

"Motorcycles then. Not actual bikes." I realized I had misunderstood.

Gage laughed. "Yeah, motorcycles."

I could see Huck on a motorcycle. He looked like the type. I remembered the Harley I'd noticed outside the church when we left to go to the gravesite for Hayes's funeral. I'd wondered then who it belonged to, but with all the other going on at the moment, I'd forgotten about it.

"Do you and Levi work there too?" I assumed he had to have help other than Ray-Ray, who apparently liked to give blow jobs.

He smirked. "I can't fix shit. Levi knows a little. Huck has a few guys who work for him."

I watched out the window as we drove away from the house.

"How did you like last night's get-together?"

I turned to look at him to see if he was being serious. He was grinning. Figured. For a man who would hold a gun to your head with no issue whatsoever, he sure liked to make jokes.

"Memorable," I replied.

He threw his head back and laughed. Gage wasn't as tall, wide, attractive as Huck, but he wasn't hard on the eyes. Neither was Levi. They all had their own appeal. If you overlooked the fact that they were criminals.

"Can I ask you something?"

He glanced over at me. "Shoot."

"Are y'all in a gang?" I asked.

He let out another laugh and flashed me a grin. "No, Trinity. We are not a gang."

I continued to look at him, waiting on some kind of explanation.

He shrugged. "There is some shit that I can't share. You're new. You checked out, but that doesn't mean we just trust you. Think of it as a family. We might not be related, but we are thicker than blood."

That answered nothing. I wanted to point out his attempt at killing me, but I let it go. They didn't want me to know. I was stuck with them until it was safe for me to be on my own again. I could live with that. How long could that take?

Gage pulled into a parking lot. The sign out front said *Huck's*, nothing more. However, the motorcycles lined up outside and the ones that could be seen through the windows made it clear what this was.

"Good luck," Gage said, opening the door and getting out.

"With what?" I asked.

He opened the back door and started taking out the food. "With Huck."

I froze. "But you said—"

Gage started laughing again, cutting me off. "Kidding, Trinity. Get your cute ass out of the truck and come on."

All I could do now was hope that Huck was in a good mood. I had apple pie and ice cream. He couldn't be mad at me if I had that, right?

Gage led the way as we went to the side door of the shop, and he opened it, then held the door for me to go inside.

"Turn right, head to the back," he told me.

I turned right but waited for him. I was not about to walk into a room with Huck without Gage being in there first. He walked past me and smirked. I sighed and followed behind him. Right now, he was my only champion, and I didn't need to make him mad. No need to say anything sarcastic.

Gage opened a door, then stepped inside, keeping his foot on the door so I could enter.

"Before she has a fucking panic attack, I made her come. She's been in the damn house for days. And she made us apple pie. I had to break her out," Gage announced as I walked slowly into the room following him.

There was a long table, where I noticed Levi sitting to the far side, a guy I didn't know across from him, and at the far end was Huck. I met his gaze. A redhead with a tube top on stood behind him. I forced a smile as she looked me over.

"Thanks for consulting me about it," Huck replied.

Gage shrugged. "I made the call. I don't answer to you."

Huck's jaw clenched, and I set down the garlic bread and pie. I would remain quiet and stay out of the way. He would have no reason to be angry about my being here.

"This looks incredible," Levi said as Gage set the food down in front of them.

"Fuck, I'm moving in with y'all," the other guy chimed in.

"Ray-Ray, go fetch the plates and flatware," Gage said while taking the lids off the lasagna and salad.

The redhead ran her hand over Huck's shoulder, and I wished I hadn't watched that. She walked as if she knew everyone was watching her every move. The tiny skirt she had on covered her butt but little else. Her flat, tanned stomach was completely bare. I tore my gaze off her and tried to focus on something else.

"Follow Ray-Ray and take the ice cream to the freezer," Gage told me.

I silently pleaded with him not to make me go with her, but he cocked an eyebrow, as if to challenge me. Damn him. Why was this so amusing to him? I turned and took the ice cream from the cooler and hurried to catch up with Ray-Ray. What kind of name was that anyway?

She was turning left up ahead, and I walked faster so I wouldn't lose her. Thankfully, when I turned the corner, I saw her walk into a brightly lit room with a refrigerator in clear view. I slowed down, hoping to give her time to get what she needed so we weren't in there together long before I made it to the door.

I turned the knob and stepped inside as she put flatware on top of the plates. Her bright green eyes locked on me. There was no way those eyes were real. They were too bright. Almost alien-like. Or I was being critical because she was sexy and worked for Huck.

"Can I help you?" she asked.

I held up the ice cream. "Gage told me to put this in the freezer," I replied.

She said nothing as I walked over to open the freezer and place the ice cream inside. When I turned around, she was standing there, looking at me. I forced another smile.

"You must be the chubby former fiancée of Huck's little brother," she drawled with a smile on her face.

That hurt. She had no idea the old wounds that brought up. I wasn't fat. I knew that. But I wasn't her kind of skinny either. I doubted my body would ever be that slim. I tried to exercise. Body image and being called fat were parts of my past that still haunted me. It was clear that the big boobs on her had been bought. But acting like I didn't want a body like hers would be a lie. She was tall, thin, and had a great boob job.

I managed a nod and headed for the door.

"You might be in his house, but it's just because of his brother. Huck isn't into"—she paused and waved her long red nails at me—"all the extra baggage. I keep his dick sucked and taken care of."

My cheeks heated. There was a part of me that wanted to tell her to fuck off. I didn't care what she did with Huck. But I also wasn't so sure making Huck's female angry was smart.

I needed to stay alive. Not piss off the one keeping me alive. Although last night, he'd tried to make the people at his house think I was his. If they knew he liked the Ray-Rays of this world, would that even work?

Smiling at her, I held the door for her since she was carrying all the plates and flatware.

Ray-Ray walked past me with the same sway to her hips, as if I were interested in her body. Perhaps that was how she always walked. I'd worked at a strip club, and there were girls there much like her. However, they hadn't been so territorial. Neither had they taken shots at my body.

I followed her back to the room the men were in, and the moment I stepped inside, Huck's eyes locked on me. I dropped my gaze to the floor and walked over to the corner and waited until someone needed me. It was clear Ray-Ray was in charge of feeding the men here. Stepping in her way wasn't something I wanted to do.

The heat of Huck's focus on me made me nervous and uncomfortable. I turned my head so that I was looking out the one small window in this room. I should have stayed at the house.

"Trinity, come eat. You worked your ass off on the house today," Gage called out from the table.

As if I could eat with Ray-Ray watching me. I almost laughed at the idea. I started to tell him I wasn't hungry.

"I don't think she's missing any meals," Ray-Ray said with a syrupy-sweet accent.

My face flushed, and the heat went from my temples to down my neck. I could deal with the mean girl. Wasn't the first time.

"I'm good, thanks," I told Gage, unable to hold a real smile very long and turning back to the window. Why, oh why had I let Gage talk me into coming here?

"What's that supposed to mean, Ray-Ray?" Gage challenged her, and I closed my eyes, praying this would end.

She let out a soft, throaty laugh, and if I could turn any redder than I already was, then it was happening.

"Leave." Huck's command was harsh.

I swung my eyes back to him, only to see he was glaring at Ray-Ray.

"What? I thought you needed me … later," she said, leaning into him so that her cleavage was on display.

"I don't," he snapped.

She frowned and glanced around at the other men, as if they were going to defend her but no one spoke up. Unable *not* to watch this play out, I noticed as she stiffened, tossed her shoulders back, and ran her hand along Huck's neck with her nails.

"Call me if you change your mind."

He didn't look at her or respond.

When she turned to walk away, I was pinned with her hateful glare, as if this were my fault. I dropped my eyes to the floor and waited until the door closed behind her. Letting out a breath of relief, I closed my eyes and relaxed.

"The jealous bitch is gone. Come eat," Gage said.

I lifted my gaze to meet his, and he waved a hand toward the table. I shifted my focus to Huck, not wanting to be anywhere I wasn't wanted, and he took another bite of the lasagna on his plate, but his eyes didn't meet mine.

"It's fucking delicious. Come on and eat with us," Levi called out.

"Ray-Ray has no ass, Trinity. That was straight-up jealousy talking," Gage said.

Their attempt at trying to make me feel better was the only reason I walked over to the table and pulled out a chair.

Huck wasn't talking, but with two against one, I figured sitting down was safe. Besides, I really liked my lasagna.

Gage slid a plate over to me. "Get you some."

I glanced at Huck as he picked up a glass and took a drink. His eyes locked on me. I wanted to apologize for being here.

Why did I want his approval so much? He had done nothing but turn me on, then humiliate me since he'd saved me from death.

"Eat." Huck's one-worded command surprised me. I glanced at the lasagna, then back at him. "Get some fucking food."

Gage slid the lasagna toward me, and I put some on my plate. Next time though, I wasn't coming to the shop. I would stay locked up in that house before I did this again.

Gage placed a slice of garlic bread on top of my lasagna. "That'll keep your ass juicy."

"Gage." The warning in Huck's tone wasn't lost on me.

I picked it up and took a bite. Gage nodded his approval, and for a moment, I relaxed enough to eat.

Chapter THIRTEEN

TRINITY

Another week passed with my feeding the guys breakfast, them leaving for work during the day, and then them returning for dinner most nights. At least up until last night.

There had been a fight on pay-per-view, and the house had filled up. After making the appetizers Gage had requested, I escaped to the room I'd been given and locked myself in for the evening. However, on my escape, I noticed Ray-Ray sitting on Huck's lap the way I had at last week's party. Seeing her was enough to keep me hidden away.

I fell asleep around ten last night, and the party was still going downstairs. It had been loud and only gotten louder.

There was a knock, and then a note slid under my door this morning. After opening my eyes and squinting against the morning sun pouring through the blinds, I noticed it on the floor.

Business to handle. We're gone. Not sure how long. Most likely until tomorrow.

—Gage

I was thankful I wouldn't have to look at Huck this morning or today. Simply because I was jealous. Admitting it didn't help, but at least I was honest with myself. Gage had said Huck liked fat asses, but apparently, not my kind of fat ass. Mine had dimples, and it probably wouldn't hurt if I did squats daily. Not that I was going to start that crap.

There was no reason to cook breakfast today, and I had no idea what I was going to do after I cleaned. There was probably more of a mess than usual after the party that had gone on so late last night. If I finished in time and had nothing to do, I could make use of the pool. There were five bikinis in that box that Gage had brought me. None fit me properly, but since I was here alone, I could wear one.

Deciding that was my plan, I did my morning routine upstairs, then headed downstairs to find a complete mess. Plates with half-eaten food, empty beer bottles, a broken glass, several used condoms, some dip smeared into the rug. I was only in the living room. If the other rooms down here were this bad, then I was going to be busy for hours. The pool might be an evening event.

Getting to work, I filled five big trash bags before I could even start anything else. Someone had thrown up in the bathroom beside the living room, and it was on the walls and floor. Three used condoms were on the bathroom floor, and I sincerely hoped those had been used before someone spewed vomit in here.

Seven hours and thirty-eight minutes later, I wiped the sweat from my forehead and sighed. The house was back in order and smelled like the citrus cleaning solution I'd used, and even the rug cleaner I had found made the rug look new. I deserved pool time after that. Maybe even a cocktail.

After putting on a red bikini that went straight up my ass with no coverage at all, I went back down to the kitchen to make myself something to eat. I took my time making avocado toast before taking it and a bottle of water outside. I'd make myself a cocktail later.

The late afternoon sun was bright, so I sat down in a lounge chair that had a table beside it with an umbrella for some shade. I couldn't remember the last time I'd lain by a pool or gotten in a pool. The temperature had to be in the nineties. I couldn't wait to sink into the pretty blue water. It was calling to me.

After finishing my meal, I closed my eyes and enjoyed the warmth of the sun until I couldn't take the heat any longer. I swam a few laps, then lay back out again, wishing I had a good book to read. Closing my eyes, I must have drifted to sleep because the next thing I heard was the slamming of a door.

I sat up, startled by the sound, and swung my gaze toward the house. Huck was stalking toward me. Although he had on sunglasses, I could tell by the set of his mouth and the veins in his neck that he was angry. Maybe I wasn't allowed to relax or swim. Gage could have mentioned that in his note. Also that they COULD be home today. He'd made it sound like they wouldn't be.

"Where the fuck is your towel?" he growled as he approached me.

"I don't have one," I replied. "Am I not supposed to be out here? It took most of the day to clean the house. You weren't here, so I was just going to enjoy the sun a little after I finished cleaning."

Huck inhaled sharply through his nose. "Do you at least have a cover-up? Clothes? Something other than the tiny pieces of fabric on your body?"

I shook my head. "I thought I'd be alone all day," I said, getting angry.

"Fuck," he said, reaching down to grab my arm and pulling me up.

I glared up at him. "Stop jerking me around by my arm! You're going to pull it out of the socket with the way you manhandle me. Just ask me to get up, and I will." I was almost shouting. That wasn't my smartest move, but I was mad at him for more than just this.

Seeing him with his wide chest and thick, corded arms on display just made it worse. I hated that I was attracted to him. He was an asshole. Not to mention, I'd had to pick up more than two dozen used condoms and wonder how many had been his.

"Stop bitching," he replied.

I shoved his chest, which did nothing. I might as well have shoved a brick wall. "Leave me alone. I'll go get dressed and start cooking dinner. No need to act like an ass," I told him.

He didn't release my arm. Instead, he hauled me up against his body. The warmth radiating off him made every square inch of me feel as if it had been zapped by an electric current. My body was a traitor. I tried to pull away, and his other hand pressed against my back, keeping me against him.

"What are you doing?" I scowled, wishing he'd let me go.

He smelled too good. It was unfair.

"Blocking their view." His reply was a deep rumble in his chest.

"Of what?" I asked, annoyed.

"You."

"Why is that?"

His hand pressed me harder against him, and it was then that I felt his erection. My eyes widened in shock, and I tilted my head back to look at him.

Why was he hard? It couldn't be because of me. We both knew I did nothing for him but piss him off.

"Because they're men and you're basically naked."

His deep voice made me shiver. Or maybe it was the size of his erection that was causing that reaction.

"I'm in a bikini," I tried to argue, but my voice sounded breathless. "Ray-Ray runs around the shop dressed in less than this." That was an exaggeration, but seeing her in his lap last night had stung. I knew what he did when I sat in his lap, and thinking about him doing that to her had made me feel things I didn't need to be feeling.

"I don't give a fuck what Ray-Ray wears," he whispered.

Huck's hand slid down to my butt, and he grabbed a handful of my bare bottom. The bikini had a small strip of fabric that might have covered the crack if I had a smaller rear end. He made a low sound in his chest as he began to knead my fat with his hand. I closed my eyes, I hated that this was turning me on because it was embarrassing.

I didn't want him reminded of my dimply bottom, and that was the only way I could find the will to try and move away from him. His hold, however, didn't budge.

"Stop," I begged.

"Touching your ass?"

I nodded.

"You of all people should know if you go around showing your bare ass, a man is gonna touch it." His tone was condescending. It was like ice water being dumped over my head.

I pushed harder against his chest. He chuckled at my attempts, as if they were amusing.

Breathing hard, I glared up at him. "I thought I was alone. If you'll let me go, I can go get dressed," I hissed at him.

He took that moment to move his other hand to my butt and then slipped a finger under the strip of fabric that was currently between my butt cheeks and pulled it out. I closed my eyes, wanting this humiliation to end. Both his hands were now squeezing my bottom, and he groaned.

My eyes snapped back up to look at him. Why was he groaning? That sounded an awful lot like he was enjoying himself. My nipples were suddenly so hard that they ached. He lifted me off the ground as if I weighed nothing. Which was so not the case.

"Legs around my waist," he told me, and I didn't argue.

The pulsing between my legs wanted that very much. Something about him being able to pick me up so easily while he palmed my bottom was incredibly sexy.

He started walking then, and the movement made my sensitive clit rub against the hardness beneath his jeans. I had to bite my bottom lip to keep from making a noise that would embarrass me. I would ask where we were going since it wasn't toward the house, but I was afraid I'd moan instead.

"Fuck," he muttered as he looked down, and his hands gripped me tighter.

I glanced down to see what he was looking at and realized my nipples had popped free of the bikini top. My entire body felt like a live wire.

"Pull them free," he ordered me.

I swallowed, unsure of what we were talking about. "What?" I asked.

"Your fucking tits, Trinity. I want them both bare."

Oh. I looked back down at them and slowly lifted my hands up to do as I had been told. When they were no longer covered by any fabric, I glanced back up at him. He opened a door behind me then, and we walked into a dark room. This wasn't the house, and I had no idea where we were, but at the moment, I couldn't care less.

Huck lowered me to my feet, then turned and pressed me against the wall before his mouth went to my neck. His tongue flicked out and licked at my flesh before he made his way down past my collarbone, then onto the tops of my breasts. Both of his large hands cupped my boobs, and he brought my left nipple to his lips. He made a sound that reminded me of a snarl before he bit down on it.

I cried out at the sharp pain, although my vagina clenched with pleasure. Huck continued to suck and bite on my breasts, moving from one to the other. I could see marks left from his teeth on my pale skin, and it only made the ache between my legs worse. I was getting so desperate for attention in that area that I was close to touching myself so I could orgasm. I needed relief. I didn't trust him not to leave me without finishing what he had started.

When he began licking at my nipple as if it were a lollipop, I gave in and slipped a hand inside my bottoms. The moment my finger found my wet clit, I moaned, arching my back and pressing my nipple further into his mouth. Huck stopped. I wanted to scream.

My eyes snapped open, and I realized it was about to happen again. He was going to leave me wanting. Walk away with no backward glance. I might kill him this time.

His hands grabbed my bottoms and yanked them down my legs as his gaze locked on my hand buried between my thighs. He reached up and took his sunglasses off, tossing them aside.

"Don't let me stop you." His voice was steady.

He was going to watch me and not touch me. The image of that only turned me on more. Fine, if he wanted to watch, it was better than him walking away. I began to move my finger again, sliding it in and out, enjoying the pressure on my aroused clit. I could hear my own juices as I brought myself closer to a climax. I might be a virgin, but I'd been masturbating for years. This was something I could do.

My body began to shake as I drew closer. With my eyes closed and my head thrown back against the wall, I prepared to feel the sweet pleasure rush over me. My hand was suddenly pulled away, and my eyes opened as I cried out. I had been so close.

Huck took my hand and began to suck on my fingers. Oh God, that was something I never wanted to forget.

"Fucking honey," he said in a hoarse whisper.

He held my hand in his mouth and sucked some more while moving his other hand between my legs. I held my breath, watching him, until his fingers slid over my needy spot before he shoved one of his thick fingers inside me. I screamed his name, and he let my fingers pop out of his mouth.

I began to ride his hand. The last time this had happened, he'd left me wanting and humiliated.

This time, I was so desperate for release that I would finish myself off if I had to and deal with his rejection later. The build was more intense than it had ever been, and I grabbed his shoulders as I felt a tremor run through me. He was hitting something inside me that I'd never touched before. I knew I was close, and suddenly, the power of it began to scare me just before I felt an explosion that made my entire body convulse. The wetness that gushed from between my thighs should have been a concern, but the nirvana my body was currently in as it shook uncontrollably made everything else fade away.

I heard myself crying out Huck's name, but it sounded like it was far off. I held on to his shoulders, and my knees buckled beneath me. One of his arms wrapped around my waist and held me up as more tremors racked through me, bringing even more pleasure as I moaned.

When I finally came back down from the world's best orgasm, I remembered the gush between my legs, and I tensed.

Oh dear God, had I peed on him? My eyes widened in horror, and I stared at him, expecting to see a similar expression.

He didn't look disgusted or horrified. Instead, he was watching me with a feral-looking expression. I was still gasping for air. Dropping my eyes to between my legs, I saw the wetness running down my legs and some on the floor. That wasn't normal.

I covered my mouth. "Oh God! What did I do?" I asked, although my words were muffled by my hand.

"You've never done that before?" Huck's deep voice sounded surprised.

I couldn't look at him. I shook my head.

"Not even during sex?" he asked.

I'd never had sex, but, no, that would have been traumatizing if I had. I doubted I'd ever let a man touch me again, for fear of doing it.

"God, no!" I said, panicked.

Huck ran his hand up my leg, and I winced as he touched the wetness. How was he not grossed out right now? This had gone from the best moment in my life to the worst. Okay, not the worst, but still humiliating.

"I'm sorry," I told him.

"Trinity"—he said my name in a way that made my eyes snap up to meet his—"you're a fucking squirter."

If I could cry, I would. "What does that mean?" I asked, almost afraid of the answer. If it meant you peed during sex, then I was going to die a virgin.

He ran his hand up my thigh with that same savage look in his eyes. "It means, if I ever stick my dick in you, I might never be able to stop," he said slowly. Then, he jerked his hand away from me like I was diseased before standing up. "Jesus Christ," he growled, then stalked away from me.

"I didn't mean to. I don't know what that means, but I swear it's never happened before. I'm sorry," I told him. But then no man had ever made me orgasm before.

He spun around and looked at me. "You're sorry?" he asked me. "Because you can fucking ejaculate? That I'm gonna think about you squirting on my dick all the damn time? Yeah, well, me too, baby. Me too," he said, then headed for the door.

"Wait, I don't know where you brought me. Don't leave me here," I begged, bending down to get my bottoms.

"Walk straight once you exit. The house is up ahead. We didn't go far," he replied, then swung the door open and stormed out as if he couldn't get away from me fast enough.

Did he mean ejaculate, like a man? Ewww.

I covered my face and sank down to the floor. Wrapping my arms around my legs, I began to rock. I couldn't stop it. I wasn't strong enough to fight it off.

Chapter FOURTEEN

TRINITY
THIRTEEN YEARS OLD

I waited until I was sure the house was empty before leaving my room. Roy was here for his winter break, but Tabitha had taken him to church with her. Dad always went when Roy was here too. I had to be careful what I got from the kitchen to eat though because Tabitha kept track of everything. I had to get things she couldn't be sure of exact amounts on, like peanut butter, shredded cheese, dry cereal, that kind of thing. Also small amounts. I usually got a little of everything I could.

She'd told Dad that I wasn't feeling well and didn't want to join them for breakfast. I was standing at the door, listening for him to enter the kitchen so I would be safe to go eat. But she'd stopped that. It smelled so good, and I almost went out there anyway just so I could have some. My fear of punishment later was all that kept me from it. I'd wanted some bacon, but not bad enough to be forced to eat it until I vomited, then forced to eat my vomit.

I took a spoon and filled it with peanut butter, then stuck it in my mouth. Turning to get a bowl for the cereal, I almost screamed when my eyes landed on Roy standing in the doorway, watching me. Why was he here?

I swallowed the peanut butter, but it went down like cement. "You aren't at church," I said as the dread coiled in my stomach.

He smirked. "Nope. Seems I wasn't feeling well. Needed more sleep."

Did my dad stay home then? Hope sprang in my chest. If Roy hadn't gone, then Dad wouldn't go. I wasn't going to be locked in the closet in the basement for hours, sitting in my urine.

"Tabitha and Benjamin went on without us," he said menacingly, as if he knew what I was thinking.

I decided to get back to my room, and luckily, Roy didn't stop me. However, he was behind me. Following me. I tried not to show panic or concern.

Keep it cool. This is okay. I am fine.

When I reached my door, I turned to close it quickly, but his hand shot out and stopped it.

"Not so fast," he said, shoving it open and making me stumble backward.

"What are you doing?" I asked, glancing around for some kind of weapon.

Sure, Tabitha would punish me if I hurt him, but sitting in a dark basement closet with bugs and peeing on myself because she wouldn't let me out to use the bathroom was better than Roy being in my room.

"Mom is going to be pissed when I tell her about the peanut butter," he said with a smile curling on his cruel face.

I would not beg him not to tell her. I refused to ask him for anything. I lifted my chin in defiance.

"Act like you don't care. I know you do. I was already planning on offering you something to eat before I found you in there, helping yourself."

Sure he was. I rolled my eyes.

He snarled at me then. "Do you like sitting in the basement?"

I said nothing. I wasn't going to give him the satisfaction.

"Take off your shirt and unwrap your tits for me. Let me see what my mom is so determined to keep hidden."

I shook my head and backed up to put more space between us. He closed that space and more as he continued toward me.

"What? You enjoy eating your vomit? Starving? Pissing on yourself in a dark closet?"

He knew I didn't, but I wasn't showing him my boobs either. They had started growing two years ago, and now, I was glad for the wrap that Tabitha wanted me to put around them. I didn't want anyone seeing how big they were. She had said it was because I ate too much, but she didn't let me eat most of the time.

Roy reached for my shirt and grabbed it, then ripped it open, making the buttons pop off and fly around the room. "You want me to see them. Touch them. I'll even suck on them. You'll love it," he said, grinning like a crazy person.

I slapped at his hands and pushed him back, but he was stronger than me. The slap that landed across my face was so hard that my vision blurred and I lost my breath for a moment. Those few seconds was all it took for him to unhook the fabric wrapped around me and let it unravel and loosen enough for him to jerk it down.

My boobs sprang free, and I screamed, kicking and hitting him. He didn't seem to care. His awful, horrid gaze was locked on my chest as he licked his lips, then grabbed handfuls of them and squeezed hard.

"They're so big," he groaned.

Tears were streaming down my face as I pushed at his chest, begging him to stop. He didn't look at my face or even act like he had heard me. His hands moved to my shoulders, and he shoved me down hard until my knees buckled and I fell to the floor.

I watched in horror as he pulled his penis out of his pants. I shook my head and scrambled, trying to get away from him and up onto my feet. He made a sick sound in his throat and kicked me so hard in my ribs that I couldn't breathe. Grabbing my side, I gasped for air.

Roy straddled me and began rubbing his penis over my boobs. I was in so much pain that all I could do was cry and beg him to stop. I tried to get up, but it was impossible. He began moving his hand up and down his erection as he pressed it to my breasts. I felt like I was going to be sick. The peanut butter was coming back up my throat.

"Stop! PLEASE! STOP!" I cried out, holding my side and trying once again to get up from the floor.

Roy began grunting and calling me names. Talking about my demons, my being dirty, and how I loved this. I cried harder, wishing I were locked in the basement closet. At least there, I was safe from him.

He let out an awful grunt, and a stream of white shot all over my bare breasts. When he stood up, he was smiling again. I heard the front door close, and Roy jerked his sweatpants up and gave me one last evil grin before turning to see his mother standing in the doorway of my room.

She looked at me on the floor, holding my side with my breasts bare, and I thought she might throw up. I was about to, so that would make two of us.

"What have you done?" she asked me.

I shook my head. I was hurt, lying on the floor, my shirt had been ripped open, and there was semen on my boobs. What had *I* done?

"She called me in here," Roy said to his mother. "Jerked open her shirt and showed me her bare breasts. I'm sorry. I'm a guy, and I couldn't help myself."

She looked at her son with a look that was normally directed at me. "Men are so weak," she spit. "Go to your room and pray for forgiveness."

Roy hurried out of the room as Tabitha leveled her hate-filled eyes at me.

"You fucking whore. Tempt my son with your disgusting obesity. You knew how he'd react to your bare breasts. You want to show them off. It's disgusting. You are filthy!"

I held my side and hoped she didn't touch me. If she jerked me up right now, I was going to black out or vomit. I wasn't sure which one.

"Go wash my son's sin from your body. I don't want to see the proof of his earthly desires. God will punish you for what you've done to him. That is meant for his future wife and to produce children. Not to be wasted on you and your horrible body!"

I was going to have to stand up. How was I going to do that? I leaned forward until the pressure wasn't completely on my side. Then, I used one hand to balance myself and put my feet under me carefully.

"GET UP! GET IT OFF OF YOU!" she yelled at me. "Benjamin will be back any minute with lunch. He doesn't need to see the filthy whore his daughter is. You've always been possessed by a demon, but it is getting worse. None of us are safe in this house with you here."

Closing my eyes and holding my breath, I forced myself to my feet. A cry tore from my chest as the pain seared through my side. My eyes met hers, and I swore then that I'd never waste one more tear. I wouldn't be weak. I would find a way out of this hell. This was going to end.

Chapter FIFTEEN

HUCK

Throwing the back door to the house open, I stalked inside, needing to get the hell away from Trinity before I slammed my dick into her and fucked her like an animal.

"You look ready to kill someone," Blaise drawled, and my eyes locked on him, then swung to his wife, Maddy, and their one-year-old son in her arms, Cree Elias Hughes.

"Would you take a towel outside to Trinity?" I asked Maddy.

She smiled and handed Cree to his father. "Of course. I came to meet her. I'm starved for female companionship," she said.

"I need a fucking drink," I said to no one in particular as I went to the bar, not looking at Blaise again. He was watching me too damn closely. "Where are the others?" I asked while pouring myself a drink.

"Here. Somewhere," Blaise replied. "They mentioned you stalked off, carrying Trinity in your arms. I find that interesting. Care to explain?"

I slung back my glass and then looked at Blaise. "What? You want me to admit I want to fuck her?" I asked, scowling. He was my boss, but he was also my best friend. But right now, I had shit I didn't want to talk about.

"You don't have to admit anything," he replied. "You're a walking billboard."

I poured another glass. "You saw her rap sheet, and she was going to marry my clueless brother. She was using him. And, *boss*, you told me not to stick my dick in her," I said, disgusted with myself for wanting her so bad.

"I don't think what we saw is considered a rap sheet," Blaise replied. "That's a little harsh."

He knew what the fuck I meant. "I let Hayes down in life. I wasn't around. Fuck, he died, and I hadn't seen him in over a year. I can't bring him back and fix that. What does it make me if I fuck the woman who was using him? Huh? I can't do that. Not to his memory. He deserved a good girl. One worthy of him. A woman who was his equal. Who belonged by his side. Not that … that lying slut." I realized I had been shouting.

Two things happened at once. Cree shouted the word *slut*, and a door slammed behind me. I turned to see Maddy glaring at me, and then beside her, Trinity was wrapped in a towel with those big brown eyes looking hurt. I stared at her, not sure what to say. She'd heard me. Fine. She'd needed to. If I had really hurt her, she'd have tears in her eyes. Women cried over that shit. She was acting the part.

"I'm sorry I talked like that in front of Cree," I told Maddy.

Her eyes narrowed. "Are you serious right now?" Maddy snapped.

That sounded like a trick question, and my fucking stomach was in a damn knot because of the look on Trinity's face. I tore my gaze from her and wished like hell things were different.

She ran then. I watched her go through the door. Fucking running. Good. I wanted her out of my sight. My damn dick was still throbbing after she'd squirted all over my hand.

"Huck, I could slap your face right now," Maddy said angrily. "You might believe what all you just said, but no woman deserves to walk in and hear that about herself. You should have apologized, groveled at her feet, anything!"

Maddy walked toward me with her finger pointed at me. "Not only are you an asshole, but you are also cruel."

"Mommy!" Cree called out. "Hut asshole!"

Maddy shook her head at me as if she was disappointed. "While y'all are gone, she's coming back to the house with me. I am not leaving her here alone. She ..." Maddy paused, and I could tell she wanted to say more and stopped herself. "She could use new scenery."

"Mommy! Hut asshole!" Cree shouted and clapped his hands.

I turned to look at Blaise, who was grinning. He shrugged and pressed a kiss to his son's head, then sat him down. When he stood back up, he looked at Maddy. "Have her go pack her things," he told her. "I've got Cree."

Maddy nodded and turned to follow Trinity.

Once she was gone, he looked at me. "You pissed off the queen. I'm not sure anyone can save you now."

I scowled and poured another drink. Maddy was soft-hearted. She was the reason Gina was alive and living God knew where with a new identity. Blaise would have put a bullet in her head had Maddy not stopped him. She was the savior of all women, apparently.

"You know what I don't get?" Blaise asked me.

I didn't care at the moment, but he was going to tell me anyway.

"Why you think she's so damn bad. Sure, she fucked a married man. We don't know he and his wife weren't separated. Who the fuck cares that he was fifty? She was a stripper. So? We've known a lot of strippers. You have a couple who visit this place frequently. As for the other shit, it was never proven. She wasn't officially charged. They were accusations. There is no reason for you to be so hard on her. You put bullets in men. We all do."

I downed the drink in my hand and slammed the glass on the table.

"Hayes was a good kid. He deserved a woman who was equally good. Someone who loved him. Not someone who was lying to him."

Blaise chuckled. "Hayes was a man, not a kid. He might have been in the ministry, but he was a man with a fucking dick. She walked into his church, looking like a damn smoke bomb, and he moved in on it. He was smart. If he was going to settle down and do the church shit, at least he would have a wife with a body that knew how to dance on a pole for him. You are putting him on a pedestal that he never asked you to put him on. If he'd lived and married one of those good girls you think he deserved, do you think she'd have been fun in bed? Highly doubtful."

I glared outside, hating that Blaise might have a point. "How likely is it that she was accused of so many things and not guilty of at least one of them? I could see it if that was a one-time thing. Maybe revenge or some shit from her stepmother. But why the hell would that other person who'd accused her of stealing make that up? She's got enemies for a reason."

"Roy Hayley probably did it for the same reason his mother did," Blaise replied, sounding smug.

I turned to look back at him. "Who's his mother?"

"Tabitha Bennett."

Fuck. That, I hadn't expected. "What about the grand theft auto?" I reminded him.

Maddy had made him weak. Too soft. At least with women.

"Oh, the car she supposedly stole, which belonged to Benjamin Bennett, her father? She was eighteen. It was the night of her high school graduation, and her father was out of town on business. She used his car, and when Tabitha found out she'd taken it, she called the police and claimed she'd stolen it. Benjamin had the charges dropped."

I was going to need another fucking drink.

Chapter SIXTEEN

TRINITY

This house was even more impressive than Mr. Esposito's house. It was bigger and brighter, and it felt less like a museum and more like a home. The photos of Madeline, Blaise, and their son, Cree, filled the walls. Random toys were scattered around. From where I stood in the room with floor-to-ceiling windows overlooking rolling hills and green pastures with horses off in the distance, I could hear laughter.

Maddy had taken Cree upstairs to bathe him and get him ready for bed. Blaise had driven us here, then left to go meet Huck, Levi, and Gage. They had some business that would be taking them out of town for a few days. Although I'd told Maddy I would be fine back at the house, alone, she'd insisted, saying she could use the female company.

Deep down, I'd known she was worried about my mental health and leaving me alone. She had found me in the garden shed behind the house. I was checked out, having one of my episodes, rocking back and forth on the floor. When I came back from the dark corner of my brain I'd escaped to, her blue eyes were the first thing I saw. For a moment, I had stared at her silently, unsure of where I was. At first glance, she looked like an angel. As in an otherworldly being. Her platinum hair, perfect heart-shaped face, blue eyes, and genuine smile were shocking. Then, she spoke. Introduced herself and held out her hand for me. She stood up, pulling me with her. Then wrapped her arms around me and hugged me.

I was stunned. I wasn't sure anyone other than Hayes had ever hugged me and meant it. Sure, the church people at his funeral had hugged me, but that had been required. This woman had done it because she wanted to.

She wrapped me in a large white towel and talked about everything from the weather, to her son, to how nice and clean the house was and asking me if I'd done that, to telling me that she was happy to have another female around. Somehow, she'd managed to get my thoughts off of what had happened with Huck in the shed until she opened the door to him saying how I wasn't worthy of Hayes and calling me a lying slut.

Why did I want the man to touch me when he always ended up hurting me? Was it because of my past? Was I so broken that his cruelty was a turn-on for me? Or was it that, deep down, I thought that was what I deserved?

"Mommy!" I heard Cree calling out as little feet hit the ground running. "Hut asshoooole!" Then, he giggled.

"Cree, I told you to stop saying that. It's not a nice word. Mommy is sorry she said it," Maddy told him.

They were downstairs now and coming this way. I could hear their footsteps getting closer.

Cree wasn't running full blast just yet. It was more of a wobbly run, where he looked like he might tumble over at any moment. Maddy had told me he turned one last month.

He was doing really well for his age. When he entered the room, he saw me and grinned, then clapped his hands before noticing a red toy car on the floor and making his way over to pick it up.

Maddy followed him into the great room, as she had called it earlier. She sighed and pushed her hair back out of her face. "Bathing him should be an Olympic sport," she said with a smile. "How about you help me drink a bottle of wine once I get him in bed?"

I nodded. "That sounds good."

She turned her gaze to Cree and smiled lovingly at him. My chest squeezed. That was what it was like to have a mom. Lucky little boy. He was loved. He was wanted. Maddy squatted down and opened her arms up wide. Cree turned to see her and dropped his toy, then ran over to her, wrapping his arms around her neck.

"La lu, Mommy," he said, nuzzling his little face close to hers.

"I love you most," she replied, then stood up with him in her arms. Her gaze came back to mine. "I'll be back in a bit. Go to the kitchen and fix yourself a snack. Make yourself at home. Whatever we have, you're welcome to it."

I stood there and watched her walk away, holding her son, and my chest ached so bad that if I could still cry, I would be a mess right now. She wanted me to make myself at home. That was laughable. I hadn't truly ever had one of those. My apartments hadn't been home. They had just been a place to live. There was never a place with family who loved me to call home.

What must that feel like?

I had watched how her husband looked at her. It was as if the sun rose and set at her feet. She was beautiful and kind. It was easy to see why he loved her.

I had often wondered why Hayes loved me. He never gave me reasons. He never said the words but he'd wanted to marry me. I had thought that meant he loved me.

Even if he had lived, we would never have had this. A home where laughter and love filled it. We hadn't looked at each other the way Blaise and Maddy did.

Knowing that I had said yes to him because he loved me made me feel as if Huck's words had some truth to them. I had just never wanted to admit it. I had lied to Hayes. I let him think I loved him the way a wife should love a husband. I agreed to marry him because I wanted a family. I wanted to belong.

That hadn't been fair to him.

Guilt wasn't something new to me, but each time it dug its claws in, it was hard to face.

EIGHT MONTHS AGO

Most nights that Hayes took me out on a date, it was centered around some church function. But occasionally, there was a weekend that the church didn't have something planned, and we were free to see a movie, go to dinner, drive to the beach. Tonight, was one of those nights.

We had driven to the beach, had dinner at his favorite seafood restaurant, then walked over the bridge onto the sand. Hayes had brought a blanket with him for us to sit on as we watched the waves crashing against the shoreline as the sun set. I leaned back against his chest, and he wrapped his arms around me.

He was careful to keep from touching my boobs. I had thought it was sweet at first. He was taking it slow. Not wanting me to feel like he just wanted sex. But we had been seeing each other exclusively for four months, and we had only kissed. He never tried anything more.

I hated to admit that my insecurities were starting to raise their ugly head. My body was something I had never been comfortable with. I saw more flaws in it than other people did. That had been clear when the manager at Diamond Heels insisted I get onstage. Men had requested me. Hearing their approval of my naked body should have given me more confidence than it had.

Now, here I was, with my first boyfriend at the age of twenty, and he didn't seem interested in touching me. I kept telling myself it was because he was going to be a minister. He was waiting until marriage for sex. I got that, but did he have to wait for everything?

I hadn't wanted to be touched intimately since the day my stepbrother had violated me. It had terrified me when guys looked at me with interest in their eyes all throughout high school and even in college.

Then, Professor Kilgore had taken some sick fascination with me, and when he was caught trying to rape me, he accused me of coming on to him and said he had fallen for my Lolita ways. The university took away my scholarship, and he lost his job. He was now working at a community college in Texas the last I'd checked. His wife hadn't left him, and she'd believed whatever lies he'd told.

I wanted to wipe those memories away. Hayes could do that for me. I wasn't scared of his touch or attention. I doubted he'd ever lose himself to any lustful desires. He was so careful and in control. But if we could do more than the small amount of kissing and cuddling we'd done, it would be nice.

Like right now, he could move his hand up just a few inches and touch my breasts. I was ready to see how that felt when it wasn't being forced upon me. He could move his hand down to the hem of my sundress and pull it up and touch me between my legs. I could see if an orgasm that I didn't give to myself was better.

Shifting so that his hand was closer to the bottom of my breast, I held my breath, waiting until it would brush against his hand. Before I could get in the right position, Hayes moved his arms down lower on my stomach. Well, crap.

"Are you uncomfortable?" he asked me.

I was thankful it was getting dark and my back was to him. My face was flushed. "No, I'm good," I told him, then decided to try something else.

Scooting my bottom back until it was pressed against his crotch area, I waited until I felt the hard ridge of an erection, but he shifted back enough so we were no longer touching.

That had been obvious. He didn't want that kind of connection. Did he find me unattractive? He'd told me I looked beautiful many times, but maybe my body as a whole didn't do anything for him.

"Hayes?" I asked, keeping my eyes straight ahead.

"Yeah?"

"Are we ever going to do anything more than kiss? Or are you not attracted to me like that?"

He was silent for a moment, and I prepared myself for a letdown. I'd asked him, and if he told me the truth and it hurt, I would have to accept it.

"I want to wait until marriage," he said finally. "You know that."

I nodded. "Yes, I know, but I'm not talking about sex," I said, then took his hand and placed it on my left breast. "This isn't sex."

He went very still. I held my breath and waited for him to do something. My heart sank when he pulled his hand free and moved back from me. I curled my legs up behind me and stared down at my hands. This was the end. I'd asked for more than he wanted with me.

"That leads to other things, Trinity. If we touch each other in ways that feel good, we will want more. That's what happens. You touch and get carried away, and then you're having sex."

I didn't see how touching my boobs or me pressing my butt against his crotch was going to have us ripping each other's clothes off. But I said nothing. I continued to look at my hands.

Hayes reached over and slipped a finger under my chin and lifted my head up so that my eyes met his. "You're beautiful. Inside and out. There isn't a heterosexual man on this planet who wouldn't be attracted to you. Don't get in your head like that. This isn't about you or your body. I promise you."

I nodded, and he leaned forward, then pressed a kiss to my forehead.

"I want to marry you," he whispered.

Chapter SEVENTEEN

TRINITY

The wine bottle was almost empty. I'd taught Maddy how to make my favorite chocolate chip cookies, and we each had three of them. We hadn't talked about anything very deep or personal. She entertained me with Cree stories and Blaise being a dad. I laughed so hard that I choked on my wine when she told me about Blaise's first experience in changing a diaper.

I hadn't laughed like this in … well, ever. It felt good to laugh and talk to someone. Maddy made it easy to relax around her.

"We need to do this more," she said, still smiling.

"I would like that," I told her.

She took another drink from her glass, then looked at me. "About today," she began, and I inwardly winced.

I had expected this to come up, and when it hadn't, I had been relieved. I didn't want to mess up a great night with that.

"Listen, if you don't want to talk about it, I get it. But just know, I've got a past too. I've dealt with some bad things. My emotional baggage is something I still struggle with."

I frowned, and my gaze shifted to the picture on the wall of her, Blaise, and Cree. They looked happy. Perfect. As if they belonged on a television ad. I doubted she would understand the kind of emotional crap that haunted me.

"Yes, I'm very lucky," she said, and I turned to see her looking up at the picture I'd been staring at. "Blaise Hughes loves me. That's the only reason I'm even alive. I shouldn't be. My mother died of breast cancer before I was three. I barely remember her. The man who I thought was my father wasn't. The brother I had all my life wasn't my brother.

"Long story short, my mom had run away, pregnant, and married a widower with a kid. Not planning on dying and leaving her child with him." She sighed and shook her head. "I won't bore you with all the details, but if Blaise hadn't been watching over me, I'd have been a victim of sex trafficking, only it would have been the man I thought was my father handing me over to the men who planned on selling me."

My mouth fell open as I stared at her. "Oh my God," I whispered.

She nodded. "Yep."

"Where is your dad now? I mean, the man you thought was your dad," I asked.

"Dead. Both him and his son."

Holy crap. "How? I'm sorry, you don't have to answer that."

"Blaise said Huck saved you when Gage had you tied up with a gun to your head. You had been cleaning the house of a man who had wronged the family. Everyone in that house was to be taken down. You're lucky. You knew from the first day what they were. I hadn't. I was clueless and fell in love with Blaise before I knew he was the next boss. Anyway, they killed the men I thought were my family. Because they were going to sell me."

I had no words. I sat there for a moment, letting that sink in, then asked, "Boss of what exactly?"

She laughed then. A soft one that sounded as perfect as she looked. "Maybe you don't know what they are. I'm not surprised Huck hasn't explained. They keep their secrets close. But you're living in their home. Hayes was your fiancé, so you're family now." She shrugged, as if that made sense. "The boss is exactly what it sounds like. He's the leader, calls the shots. The guys don't just go around, killing people. It only happens when business goes bad. They beat all around the bush, explaining it to me, to make it sound better. I am going to just be blunt with you. They're the Mafia."

I started to smile. "You're kidding, right?"

She shook her head. "Not even a little."

Holy shit. Okay. Whew. I needed a minute.

"Horse racing is their main thing. They're good at it, but the Hugheses come from a long line of crime bosses. They have those around them who work for them. Families pass it down from generation to generation. They're wealthy and smart with money, but they're powerful and connected. Those connections are how they control things."

So many questions were swirling in my head, and I wasn't sure what to ask first or if she'd even answer. Finally, I asked, "And Huck is one of them? Since he works for your husband?"

Her husband was a Hughes. That had to be it.

"Huck and his father and his father and his father. The Kingston men have been loyal to the Hugheses for generations," she replied. "And, yes, Blaise is who Huck answers to because they've also been best friends their entire lives. When my father-in-law steps down, Blaise will take his position. But until then, Garrett is the boss."

Huck was in the Mafia. I shook my head. Hayes hadn't been.

"But Hayes was a Kingston."

Maddy gave me a sad smile. "Yes, but their parents died when he was young. I'm sure you know that. He chose to stay with his grandparents and eventually the ministry. Huck only ever wanted this life. This world."

I stared at this sweet, delicate blonde in front of me. The adorable little blond boy, full of laughter, and this house, which was so clearly a happy place. How was this family not only in the Mafia, but also the head of the Mafia? I'd never imagined it this way. But then all I knew about organized crime was what I'd seen on television.

"What Huck said today, that wasn't like him. I was shocked and disappointed. I don't know what is going on in his head, but he's a good guy. He's saved me more than once from people trying to kill me and from myself. He is someone I consider a friend. Although the words he said were horrible, the passion he said them with, I've never seen it from that man. He never shows his emotions like that. It was different. Don't ... don't write him off just yet."

There was nothing to write off. She didn't know that though. I was a burden he hadn't asked for, and as mad as I wanted to be at him, his words had held truth.

A chime went off, and Maddy stood up. "Uh, someone is here."

We were two women, alone with a kid.

We had passed a mansion on our drive back here that she had referred to as the big house. But we were about a mile away from that house.

I stood up to go with her. She went over to one of the paintings of Cree on the wall and opened it like a door. My eyes widened as she pressed in a code, and another metal door opened. She reached in and pulled out a gun.

Oh shit.

She glanced back at me and smiled. "It's probably nothing. Whoever it is got through the guards at the main gate, mansion, and our gate. I'm just being careful since the guys are gone."

I managed a nod, but no words were coming out. She walked casually back through the house and held the gun at her side. I stayed back, unsure of what I should do. When she got to the door, she opened another secret compartment on the wall behind what looked like artwork, and a screen appeared. On it was an attractive, well-dressed guy with dark hair standing outside the front door.

She laughed and shook her head. "Nosy," she muttered, closing the artwork and going to answer the door.

"What are you doing? Why didn't you call first?" Maddy asked as she held the door open for him to come inside.

The guy walked inside and looked down at the gun in her hand. "Nice. You've gone all badass. Have a baby with the future boss and start answering the door with a Glock in your hand," the guy drawled, then winked at her.

Maddy closed the door and rolled her eyes. "Trinity, meet Trev Hughes. My brother-in-law and oftentimes a smart-ass."

Trev was dark, where his older brother was light. He also didn't look intimidating, or maybe it was that he didn't have an air of power radiating off him.

"Trev, this is Trinity. My house guest," she informed him. "I'd offer you wine, but it's almost gone."

Trev gave me a crooked smile. "It's nice to meet you, Trinity," he said. "Like she said, I'm the better-looking brother."

I laughed, and his grin spread.

"Come on in and join us. You knew she was here, and you're being nosy. Admit it," Maddy said as she walked past us and back toward the great room.

"Maybe I came to see my little buddy," Trev said, then winked at me this time.

Major flirt. But I liked him.

"Cree has been in bed for two hours. You know that," she said as she put the gun back in its hiding place.

Trev walked over to the nearest leather chair and dropped down into it, then turned his smile on Maddy. "You might almost be finished with the wine, but what about Blaise's whiskey stash?"

"You know where the bar is," she replied and sat back down on the sofa.

I walked over and returned to the spot I'd been in before Trev arrived. He was watching me.

"Tell me, Trinity, how is life with the guys?"

I shrugged. "Fine," I lied.

"You need to work on your lying skills. That sucked," he told me.

That was a touchy subject I wasn't about to venture into.

"Trev, don't stir the pot, please," Maddy said. "Huck isn't Blaise."

He didn't seem concerned, and truthfully, he didn't need to be.

"How old are you?" he asked.

"Twenty-one."

"Just one year older. I like older women."

Maddy grabbed a pillow and chucked it at him. "I am serious. Stop."

Trev held up his hands. "I was just making small talk," he said. "Trinity, how do you feel about Grand Theft Auto?"

Did everyone know what was on the background check? My face heated, and I dropped my gaze to stare at my hands in my lap. Apparently, the family had passed around the details of my past.

"Did I say something wrong? If you don't like video games, it's cool." Trev's voice sounded concerned.

Video games? Oh. He wasn't asking me about the real thing.

I laughed then and lifted my eyes up to meet his. He had an unsure look on his face as he stared at me.

"I like video games. I used to play with Hayes sometimes," I told him.

He nodded and kept looking at me. "Did you think I meant real grand theft auto?" he asked.

I pressed my lips together, unsure of how to explain this. I didn't want them to know that I'd been arrested for it, although I hadn't been charged.

Trev leaned forward, putting his elbows on his knees as he held my gaze. "Holy fuck. You've stolen a car." Then, he threw his head back and laughed.

I glanced at Maddy, worried she'd think I was a bad person to have in her home, but she was smiling at me. Did she know about my history? Had Blaise let her read my background information?

"Blaise knows the truth," she said softly. "The real truth." Her smile was reassuring.

"We're going to the game room. It's time to see how good your skills are. Maddy sucks at it. Don't let me down," Trev said, standing up and holding out his hand for me.

I glanced at Maddy, and she nodded. Standing up, I put my hand in his, and he held it up in the air.

"Come on, you naughty little felon. Let's go play."

Chapter EIGHTEEN

HUCK

The past forty-eight hours had been all work. Pulling through the arched entrance of Hughes Farm was a fucking relief. I'd get some sleep. After eating and taking a shower, I might not get up until tomorrow.

Blaise was out of the passenger side of the Escalade the moment I put it in park outside the stables. He'd been texting with Maddy, and she was working in her office inside the stables today. Maddy had wanted a job, and working on the ranch was the only thing Blaise had been willing to let her do. I would have gladly let her work at the shop, but she was his, and that made her a weakness to the entire family. Having her out there, available for any attack, wasn't smart. Here, she could work and be safe. When it came to the woman, Blaise Hughes was owned.

In the past forty-eight hours, Blaise had scared the literal shit out of a man twice his size. That was a first, having a grown-ass man shit his pants, but then when Blaise turned on the crazed look, it was impressive. He'd also tortured another man for information and put a bullet in a few others. Yet he was so damn pussy-whipped that he couldn't get to his woman fast enough. I wondered if she'd mention the blood splatters on his shirt. He hadn't even taken the time to change.

Stepping out of the vehicle, I headed into the stables. Maddy had only said that Trinity was with her. I had to pick Trinity up and take her back to the house. Gage and Levi had been talking about her cooking since we had headed home this morning. If I didn't bring back their cook, they'd lose their damn minds. The stables were busy, but that was typical this time of year. I nodded at one of the jockeys, stopped to talk to Kye about a follow-up we needed done with one of our high-end dealers, then headed toward Maddy's office. I didn't get far when laughter stopped me.

It wasn't just the pleasing sound of the laughter, but also the feminine huskiness in the voice. I recognized it even if I'd never heard that laugh myself. My body suddenly felt on edge as my teeth clenched, grinding together as I walked toward the sound. Trinity had never laughed for me. I hadn't given her a reason to, but it still didn't sit well.

"I will not!" She let out a squeal.

She was fucking squealing too. What the hell?

My hands fisted at my sides as I turned the corner. Whoever the fucker was making Trinity laugh like that had messed with the wrong man. I wasn't in the mood for this. I needed goddamn sleep. Not another damn dick trying to get in her pants.

Then, I saw them.

Trev motherfucking Hughes was smiling from ear to ear as he pointed a water gun at Trinity. Shit. It would have to be a damn Hughes. Did the kid have to flirt with every woman he met? Yes. He was a playboy. Why hadn't Maddy warned Trinity about him?

"Fair is fair," Trev called out, making Trinity laugh more.

Why was he so damn funny? I wasn't fucking laughing. Nothing about a water gun was that damn hilarious.

"I'm sorry. Truce!" she cried, holding her hands in front of her face as she turned to run. Her eyes collided with mine then, and the smile that had lit up her face vanished, and she stopped.

Just the sight of me could turn her mood. I hated the way that sat in my chest like a damn ton of bricks.

"And the rodeo squad is back," Trev said.

The kid had no fear. Stupid fucker knew he was untouchable.

Trinity frowned, glancing back at him.

Trev dropped the water gun and walked up to stand beside her. He nodded his head toward me. "When Maddy met them all the first time, she called them the rodeo squad. It stuck."

"No, it didn't," I snarled. "You're the only fucker who uses it."

Trev shrugged, grinning at me.

"Time to go," I said, turning my gaze back to Trinity.

"Okay," she replied. "My things are in Maddy's office."

"Go on out to the Escalade. I'll get them," I told her, then shot little Hughes one last warning glare that only made the fucker grin bigger.

Trinity glanced back at Trev. "Bye. I had fun."

What kind of fun had she had with Trev? He was a damn kid. Had they done more than this stupid water gun shit? Where the hell had Maddy been when this was going on? Trinity was too old for him … fuck. Trev was twenty. It was hard to remember that. In my head, he was still a teenager. She was only a year older than him. Yeah, no more of her coming to stay with Maddy.

I waited until she headed toward the exit, and then I turned to go into Maddy's office to get her things. The door was open, but Blaise had Maddy up on the desk, and he was standing between her legs, kissing her like he was about to eat her alive. I cleared my throat, and Maddy pulled back, breaking the kiss. Blaise kept her face cupped in his hands and his eyes on her.

She blushed as her eyes met mine. "Hey, Huck. Did you find Trinity?" she asked.

I nodded. "Need her things."

She started to move, and Blaise put his hands on her thighs to stop her.

"He can get them. You're not moving."

Maddy shifted her gaze to Blaise and scowled at him, but it was only a second before she softened again. "They're behind my desk," she said to me.

I didn't say anything or look at them again. Blaise wanted me out of here. I grabbed the bag that Trinity had brought with her and headed for the door.

"Remember the cameras," I said before locking, then closing the door behind me.

When I reached the Escalade, I opened the door to the back and tossed her bag in, then climbed into the driver's side. Trinity looked tense. Nothing like the girl I'd walked up on a few minutes ago with Trev.

I'd had two days to think about what Blaise had said to me back at the house. When we hadn't been torturing traitors, I'd let my thoughts go to Trinity. There was a lot I had assumed about her because I didn't trust easily.

Especially someone who looked like her but had been engaged to my religious younger brother. That pairing made no fucking sense. The way she had reacted to her squirting on me wasn't an act. She'd been as shocked as I was. One minute, I got the feeling she was naive, and then the next, she was a willing piece of hot ass. I couldn't figure her out.

Once we were on the road back to the house, I glanced over at her. She wasn't going to talk—that was clear. I'd said some hard shit, and I knew it had hurt her. Blaise had had a point. I needed to find out some things about her.

"Tell me about the fraud," I said, keeping my eyes on the road.

"Is that what it was described as?" she asked softly.

"It said you stole your stepmother's identity to get credit cards that you maxed out."

I heard a deep sigh. "She claimed that, but I wasn't charged with anything because once it was investigated, they found most of the charged items were in her possession or there was evidence she'd been the one on the trips where the cards were used. Tabitha had gotten herself into a financial bind and decided to blame me so she wouldn't have to pay her debt."

Motherfucker. I knew I hated that bitch. She'd been fucking evil at the funeral. However, that was the one thing on the background check that I'd overlooked. If Trinity had committed fraud with that woman's identity, I would have commended her. Not judged her. I'd met the woman.

"You don't believe me," Trinity said with a trace of annoyance in her tone.

I wanted to smile, but didn't. I had more questions.

"Tell me about the book theft."

She shifted in her seat, and I was tempted to look down at her legs and see if those shorts had ridden up any further. At least these covered her ass. I wasn't sure where she had gotten them, but I was damn thankful there had been no asscheek showing when I showed up to get her.

"Roy is Tabitha's son," she said, then paused. There was something in the way she had said his name that bothered me. As if saying it was difficult for her. "He needed money and sold all the rare books from Tabitha's library on eBay. They were to go to him at her death one day, but they weren't necessarily his yet. Anyway, when Tabitha found them missing, she accused me, but when I had no idea what she was talking about, she dropped it. Then, the next thing I knew, Roy had filed a police report, claiming I had sold his rare first-edition books. Since Tabitha had already tried to charge me with something I hadn't done, my guess was, they thought it might work better if Roy did it. But again, no proof that it was me. Charges dropped."

She was telling the truth. It was in the way she'd spoken and the defeated tone in her voice. There was no pausing to think about what she would say or how to explain it. She'd just repeated it as she knew it. I had forced the truth out of many men, and I knew the tells of a lie. Trinity wasn't lying.

My grip on the steering wheel tightened. I wasn't sure if I even needed to hear about the car. Blaise had already found out the truth. But I needed to hear her tell me. I wanted to see what her story was.

"And the car," I finally said.

She let out a laugh that held no humor in it. More than anything, it was laced with pain. What the fuck had she grown up with? Where had her father been when that bitch of a stepmother was doing this shit to her? Why hadn't he protected her?

"My dad missed my high school graduation. No one came. I would never have expected or wanted Tabitha there, but I had thought my dad would at least come. Someone to watch me." She paused then, and I looked at her. She was staring straight ahead, but the look on her face killed me.

"Anyway, I didn't have many friends—or any friends. I never went out. I always studied and focused on getting out of that house after graduation. It paid off at first. I got the scholarship. That night, one of the girls in my class was having a graduation party for the entire class. This was my last time to do something in high school. I didn't want to stay home in a house with a woman who hated me. I wanted to celebrate that it was over. I'd be free soon. I called my dad and asked if I could use the car and go to the party. He said yes, probably because he felt guilty for missing my graduation. Tabitha was at a church event when I left. My dad didn't tell her I was taking the car, so she thought I'd done something she could punish me for. She called the cops and reported it as stolen and accused me. The cops showed up at the party—I had been there maybe fifteen minutes—and I was arrested. They took me in. I told them to call my dad since it was his name on the title of the car. They did, and my dad confirmed he'd let me use the car. Then, I was released."

I couldn't ask any more questions simply because I couldn't fucking handle the answers. The damn ache in my chest was new for me. I was struggling to take deep breaths. Motherfucker, I needed to kill someone. Or at least break them. My body was strung so tight that I could hear my heartbeat pounding in my ears. It didn't help that every shitty thing I'd said to her and accused her of since I'd brought her to the house was just more cruelty that she had to endure.

Apologizing to her now would sound fucking weak. There weren't words to make that go away. Dammit, why hadn't Blaise cleared that shit up with me on day one? She had been through enough bullshit. Had Hayes known this? If so, why hadn't he dealt with that fucking redheaded bitch? He had been religious, but even the God he believed in had dealt out consequences. Hayes had been a Kingston. He'd turned from that, but it had still been in his blood. I wanted to ask her if she'd told him these things, but I couldn't because if she had and he'd not done shit about it, I didn't want to be angry with my dead little brother.

"Since you aren't going to ask me, I'll tell you. I never did anything with Professor Kilgore. Not willingly. He flirted, and I ignored it. Then, he gave me an F on a paper I had turned in and told me he needed to meet with me in his office. I couldn't fail that class, or I'd lose my scholarship. I'd never made anything lower than a C in my life. I was devastated. I went to his office, and he pushed me against his desk and told me all I had to do was fuck him for an A." She stopped and took a deep breath. "I tried to get away from him. He grabbed my boobs and said things about my body. His hands were up my skirt, grabbing my butt, when another professor entered the room. Except she was also currently having an affair with him and was furious. She told the board that she caught us having sex. They believed her."

I hadn't asked. Because this was what I had been afraid I'd hear. My chest burned. Fucking son of a bitch. I was going to find Jonathon Kilgore, and he was going to fucking wish he'd never laid eyes on Trinity.

I pulled through the security gate that surrounded the house. The more I thought about all the shit I didn't know, the life she'd lived, the more the fury inside me began to get dangerous. These things couldn't have been the only problems Trinity had dealt with in that house. When I could gain control of the rage licking at my pulse, I'd ask. That wasn't now. Not when my need to put a bullet in Kilgore was clawing at me.

I parked inside the garage and turned off the ignition before looking at her again. She had her hands gripped tightly in her lap, and her shoulders were slumped, as if she was defeated. That shit only made the monster inside me roar to life.

"Trinity ..." I said her name as calmly as I could, considering the shit stirring inside me.

She turned her head to look at me.

"I would apologize to you, but the words *I'm sorry* don't feel adequate."

Those big brown eyes blinked twice as she studied me.

"The family is my family. It always will be. But Hayes was my blood. Even if he didn't want to be a part of this world, he was my brother. I protected him from the moment he was born. He was never like me. He was softer, kinder, understanding—things that make a man an easy target."

A sad smile touched her face, and then she licked her lips, and my fucking dick got hard.

"And you thought I had used him," she said. "You were right. There is no reason for you to apologize. The things you've said to me and about me, most are true."

What the fuck was she talking about?

"I wasn't good enough for him. I've been broken a very long time. If it helps, I don't think I could have walked down that aisle. He wanted a girl that I tried very hard to be, but I knew I could never be her. I'm not good. I don't think there is a god we can pray to who answers us. I tried that many, many times, and there was no answer. But more than that, I did love Hayes. Who wouldn't love him? He was impossible not to love. I just … I wasn't in love with him. That wasn't his fault. It was mine. I'm not sure I can love that way. He deserved that love. I knew it even when I said I'd marry him." She stopped and dropped her gaze from mine. "You were right about me."

Jesus Christ, I couldn't take any more of this shit. I reached for the handle and swung the car door open with more force than necessary. I needed air. The kind that didn't smell like honeysuckle and jasmine.

What the hell perfume did that woman wear? Was it not enough that her damn pussy tasted like honey?

I slammed the door behind me and stood there, taking several deep breaths as I tried to separate my rage from my arousal. The two did not go together.

I heard her get out of the vehicle, and I closed my eyes tightly, forcing myself to get control. I was tired. I needed rest. I'd be better after sleep. This had all come out at a bad time, but then I was the one who had asked her for answers.

"If you want me to leave …" Her voice sounded so damn nervous and unsure.

She was used to people abusing her. I hadn't even asked about the stripping because I no longer gave a shit. I'd learned enough so far, and already, I was planning on a road trip to kill a man.

"No," I bit out, opening my eyes to turn and look at her.

She was biting her bottom lip, and the defeat in her eyes as she stood there, ready for someone else to let her down, broke me. I stalked toward her, and she backed up, her eyes going wide until she hit the Escalade and couldn't go any farther. She let that bottom lip go as she gasped.

It was then my mouth claimed hers.

II

"She's mad, but she's magic. There's no lie in her fire."
—Charles Bukowski

Chapter NINETEEN

TRINITY

Spice, cigar, and mint infiltrated my senses. I'd never understood kissing. It had never made me want to cling to Hayes or press against him. Most of the time, kissing had been quick, comforting, nothing more.

This was not that.

My grip on Huck's arms was so tight that my nails were biting into his massive biceps. I was squeezing my thighs together because with each thrust of his tongue inside my mouth, I felt my clit pulse and ache. His grip on my hips was almost painful, which only heightened the desire pounding inside my body. This wasn't comforting. It was demanding, and I was desperate for more of it. Reminding myself that, at any moment, Huck would release me, step back, and leave me standing here alone was hard to accept. I wasn't so sure I wouldn't chase after him, pleading for more.

His hands moved down to grab my butt, and he groaned against my mouth. I was beginning to think the man did like my butt. I pressed against him and felt his erection. Even beneath his jeans, it was intimidating. The size of it. There was a part of me that didn't think it would fit inside of me, and then another part of me knew that was never going to happen anyway.

Hayes hadn't been my first kiss, but I'd only kissed one other guy before him. Jeffrey had been in one of my classes at Howard. We went on two dates, and then he realized how inexperienced I was. We became acquaintances that barely spoke when we passed each other on campus. That was the end of my dating. I'd figured I was too broken to do it correctly.

Kissing Huck was nothing like the others. He made me frantic for more. I wanted to climb up his body and never let go of him.

Then, he broke the kiss. I had known he would, but it was soul-shattering nonetheless. A pathetic whimper slipped out of me, but I couldn't help it. I was devastated that it had already ended. His hand wrapped around my wrist, and then he began walking, pulling me behind him. He wasn't leaving me here to stalk off. That was a good thing. Hope stirred in my chest as he led me through the house. His long strides made me have to jog to keep up. It was either that or have my arm pulled out of my socket.

Gage stepped out of the kitchen, and I saw him open his mouth, then close it as we passed by. Huck said nothing but continued. I began to worry that he was taking me to my room to slam the door in my face again. We had been down that path, and I didn't want to repeat it.

When we reached the door leading to his basement room, he unlocked it, then slung it open with more force than necessary before continuing to pull me behind him. I almost tripped twice on my way down the stairs, but I managed to keep up. He didn't stop until we were at his bed. His hand released my arm, and I looked up at him.

My breath caught in my chest when I saw the wild gleam in his eyes. He was watching me, and although it was slightly terrifying, it was also exciting. When he yanked his shirt up and over his head, I realized I might have an orgasm from the simple sight of him.

Tattoos decorated his chest. I'd seen them on his arms and assumed he had more, but actually getting a look at the ripped chest, covered in art, was another thing. Holy crap, he was hot. I wanted to touch him. Feel the warm skin under my fingertips.

"Take it off," his deep voice commanded.

I blinked, looking up at him.

"Your clothes. All of 'em."

Okay. This was what I had wanted. When he had been kissing me, I had wanted it. Why was I nervous now? He had seen me naked already. I watched as his hands went to his jeans, and he began unbuttoning them. He was getting naked.

"If you don't fucking strip, I'm going to tear your clothes from your body, Trinity."

That was hot. I needed to focus. He was huge, and I was a virgin. Did I tell him? Would he stop if I did? I didn't want him to stop. I might die if he stopped.

I pulled my shirt up and over my head, then dropped it to the floor. His hungry gaze was on my chest. Reaching around to the back, I unsnapped my bra, then let it slide down my arms. My nipples were instantly hard under his intense gaze. I had never felt sexier in my life. I had rarely felt sexy, but in this moment, with Huck's complete attention on me, I was beautiful. I unbuttoned my shorts, then pushed them down before stepping out of them. A low growl came from his chest, and I shivered.

He shoved his jeans down, and there was no underwear beneath them. The thick, long erection was even bigger than I'd imagined. A silver glint caught my eyes, and I sucked in a breath.

"What …" I started to ask, but the words fell away.

There was a bar—a curved bar—in the head of his … oh-my-God.

"Panties off," he said as he took a step toward me.

I was trembling, unable to look away from the piercing I had been unaware a man could have, as I slid my panties down, then kicked them away.

"It's pierced," I whispered.

His hand wrapped around the hard length, and he began to stroke it. I watched him as I began to pant. That was the sexiest thing I'd ever seen.

"Get on the bed." His voice sounded hoarse.

I glanced up at him, and his eyes were on my breasts. To think I had once hated my chest size. The way Huck was looking at me now, I decided they might be my most favorite body part. I backed up until my butt hit the bed, then lifted myself up and sat on it, scooting back as he advanced on me.

"Open your legs."

When I did, Huck stopped stroking himself. I should tell him now that this was my first time and his size might not fit inside me. But he grabbed my legs and put them over his shoulders as his hands slid under my bottom. When his tongue slid between my folds, my hips bucked as a strangled cry tore from my chest. His hands squeezed my ass, and he pressed his face in closer, making a growling sound.

This was even better than I remembered. Maybe it was the position. Lying back and seeing his head buried between my thighs only added to the sensation of his tongue licking me as if he couldn't get enough. I was moaning, pleading, riding his mouth, and no longer caring what came next.

He looked up at me and took one of his hands from my bottom to run a finger from my clit to my entrance before slipping it inside of me.

"AH!" I grabbed handfuls of the sheets beneath me.

"This pussy is tight, Trinity," he murmured, then placed a kiss inside my thigh. "Real fucking tight, baby."

If he stopped, I was going to fall apart. I didn't say anything. Maybe he wouldn't notice. Unless, of course, he didn't fit. He'd notice that.

"My dick is big," he told me as he continued to kiss and lick my clit while fucking me with his middle finger.

Was he telling me it wasn't going to fit? I would cry.

"You want to tell me something?" he asked, shoving his finger deep inside me.

He could tell. Was that possible? Was his finger long enough for that?

I moved against his hand, desperate. Not wanting him to stop.

"Trinity?"

"Is it not going to fit?" I asked him.

He chuckled and kept his eyes on me as he ran his tongue where his finger had been. "Oh, it'll fit. But that's not my question."

He sat up on his knees, letting my legs fall back to the bed. The statues of Greek gods did not hold a candle to the image in front of me. Solid muscle, tanned, decorated in art, and that silver bar taunting me on the head of his penis.

"Bend your knees up and open wider for me," he told me as he watched.

I swallowed hard, then did as I had been instructed.

He came over me then, holding himself up. His hands on either side of my head. I stared up into his eyes and shivered. He wanted this too. I was a virgin, but I saw the lust in his gaze. The throb between my legs grew stronger.

"Tight pussies are one thing," he said to me. "But untouched pussies are another."

I said nothing, wishing he'd stop asking me to tell him. I didn't want to say anything that might put an end to this.

He leaned down and brushed his lips below my ear. "Am I about to thrust my dick into a virgin pussy?" His voice was soft in my ear.

"Yes," I replied.

He knew. He wouldn't be asking if he didn't already know.

"Jesus." He muttered it like a curse.

"Please don't stop," I pleaded.

I considered locking my legs around him and holding him there. Sure, he was strong enough to break free, but I might get a few more seconds of begging.

"This fucking house could catch on fire, and it wouldn't keep me from taking this tight cunt." His voice sounded angry. "My cock is big, baby. It hurts any pussy I shove it in."

I didn't want to hear about any other pussies he had shoved it in.

"Okay," I replied.

He groaned and kissed the corner of my mouth. "I don't have a condom on," he said.

Oh. What was I supposed to say? Did he not have any left? I could believe that after the amount of used ones I'd thrown away.

He ran the tip of his nose along the side of my neck and lowered his hips so that his erection touched my clit, and then he rocked his hips, letting it slide over the wet entrance, but he didn't do anything more.

"So wet," he murmured in my ear. "I want to feel your tight cunt as I slide inside you for the first time. I don't want a barrier. I've never fucked without a condom."

I was willing to let him do whatever he wanted if he stopped torturing me. Every time that metal bar ran over my swollen clit, I made a sound and jerked. I was going to combust like this.

"Okay," I agreed.

"There was no record of you taking birth control." His voice sounded aroused. "I might not be able to pull out in time. When was your last period?"

I shook my head. I couldn't answer questions like this right now.

"I don't know," I panted as his cockhead slid through my folds again. I whimpered, lifting my hips up for more.

"Fuuuuck," he groaned, aligning himself with my entrance. "Take a deep breath."

I did, my eyes never leaving his face.

"God, you're sweet," he said before he pressed inside me, stretching me as he slowly lowered his hips.

Then, he pulled back, and I thought he'd changed his mind. My hands gripped his sides harder, and then he thrust inside of me. A scream tore from my chest as the searing pain burned, as if I'd been ripped open.

"SHIIIT!" Huck groaned.

I held on to him as he remained still. Moments passed, and the pain slowly began to ebb away. He didn't move. The veins on his neck stood out, and his jaw was clenched tightly. I listened to him taking deep breaths through his nose. He exhaled heavily, and then his eyes locked on mine.

He began to slowly move so that he slid out. My nails bit into his skin, trying to hold him inside of me. Just when I thought he was going to pull out, he sank back inside me.

Deeper this time until the metal bar I'd forgotten about hit something that sent a jolt of pleasure through my body.

"AH!"

Huck pulled back, then did it again. I moaned, wanting more of that. The pain was forgotten now. It was there, but whatever he was doing was making it worth it. I'd go through that a million times over to feel this.

"Never," he growled. "Never had a pussy this good. So tight."

The words made my arousal intensify. I wanted more of that. Hearing how he felt inside me. I had no idea what to do to make it good for him, but his words sounded like he was enjoying this. His next thrust was harder. I made another needy sound and arched my back.

"You want more of my cock?" The threatening sound in his voice only excited me.

"Yes," I panted. I wanted to feel everything.

"Sweet little virgin pussy"—he sounded sinister—"taking my big cock like a good girl."

I cried out his name and clawed at him. The pleasure felt as if it was swelling inside me. Ready to burst and send me crashing into bliss. He had given me one orgasm with his hand, and that had been earth-shattering. The thought of feeling that with him buried inside me, stretching me, caused a frenzy. I wanted it more than I'd ever wanted anything.

"Is that what you want?" he asked as his thrusts came faster and harder. There was pain mixed with a madness that promised more.

"Yes, yes," I moaned, arching my back to meet him.

His eyes went to my breasts, and he growled, then lowered his head to pull a nipple into his mouth. When he began to suck, my eyes rolled back in my head. This was too much.

"OH-GOD!" I screamed when he bit down on the nipple in his mouth.

My body clenched as a euphoria engulfed me, taking me under. It was a form of delirium. Nothing mattered but this. The gush between my legs only enhanced it. I heard myself crying out Huck's name.

"FUUUUCK!" His shout filled the room as his hips jerked, and a warmth filled me.

When the second pump of his release shot inside of me, I was hit with another crest, and for a moment, the world went black.

Chapter TWENTY

HUCK

Trinity went limp beneath me, and I pulled out of her before cupping her face in my hands. Had she passed out? Holy fuck. Her lashes began to flutter, and I sighed in relief when they finally opened and she stared up at me. Jesus Christ, she was going to ruin me.

I lay down beside her and pulled her to me so that she was lying against my chest. Now that I knew I hadn't fucked her to death, I needed a minute to gather myself. The amount of women I had fucked, I didn't even know. I'd lost count when I was a teenager. What I did know was, nothing had compared to that. Not even remotely close. Hands down the best sex I had ever had, and she had been a virgin.

Damn animal inside me wanted to roar with satisfaction that I'd been the first dick inside her.

"Oh no," she whispered and started to move away from me.

My arm tightened around her. She wasn't going anywhere.

"I did that thing." Her voice wavered. "I got your bed wet."

Yeah, she'd fucking done that thing, and I'd never come that hard in my life.

"I don't care," I said. "If you do that thing every time I fuck you, then I might chain you to my bed."

She tilted her head back and looked up at me. I met her gaze.

"There's gonna be blood too. Don't get all upset when you see it. We made a fucking mess," I told her.

She winced. "I'm sorry."

"You're sorry?" I asked her, wanting to laugh. "About what exactly? Squeezing my dick with your hot little cunt so hard that I became a madman? Or for ejaculating on my dick, which is something I'd never experienced bare, and it made me come so damn hard that I might never recover?"

She didn't say anything. I watched her lay her head back down on my chest, and then I closed my eyes. I needed to get a handle on this. She'd been a fucking twenty-one-year-old virgin. I hadn't even thought that existed. I'd shot a load into her that I hadn't even been aware I could produce. Yes, I wanted more of that tight, magical pussy, but could I do that without her getting emotionally attached? I didn't do attachments, and she'd already been hurt enough.

Fuck me, this was not good. My dick wanted to stay buried in her, but my head knew that a girl like this one was not able to keep sex and emotions separate. She had said she didn't think she could fall in love. That was promising, but I wasn't sure if I could trust that. I fucked women who knew the score. They didn't expect monogamy. They didn't expect anything but a few orgasms. And they sure as fuck were not virgins.

What had I done? I knew her pussy was too tight. I could feel the damn hymen in there when I shoved my finger deep inside. And I'd been so overcome by lust that I'd done it anyway.

Dammit!

She was quiet for a female who'd just had sex. I looked back down at her and saw the slow, even breathing. My chest tightened. Why was it doing that? Shit, my dick was now controlling other parts of my body. I needed to get my head on straight. Trinity did not deserve to be hurt more. I eased out from under her, and thankfully, she didn't wake up.

I had to get her sweet smell, mixed with sex, out of my head. I pulled the covers up over her and headed for the bathroom. Turning on the shower, I glanced down at my still-semi-hard dick. There was a smear of blood there, but that warm gush of her release had washed most of it off. Thinking about it made my cock start to harden and lengthen again.

Cursing, I reached in and turned off the hot water, then put the cold on full blast. Taking a cold shower after the best sex of my life. This was going to be fucking hard to control. But I would. She might have claimed she couldn't fall in love, but she was a woman. They tended to do that shit anyway. I had to make sure it didn't happen.

When I was showered and dressed, I walked back into the room to see Trinity still sleeping. I didn't need to be down here when she woke up. That wouldn't be good for either of us. Cuddling after sex was a bad idea too. That would only confuse her.

I headed upstairs and went straight to the kitchen. Gage was standing in front of the fridge with a bag of chips in his hand. He looked at me as I walked in and narrowed his eyes.

"You couldn't wait until she cooked us something to eat? And how long does it take to fuck her? Jesus, you were down there forever. I'm starving. Is she coming up?"

I scowled at him and went over to the pantry. "She's asleep. Cook your own damn food."

"Asleep? Why the hell is she asleep?"

I wasn't talking about what I had done with Trinity with him or Levi. Or fucking anyone. Not their business.

"She's tired," I bit out.

Gage grabbed a container of dip and slammed the door. "Great. We've not had a good meal in days, and you fucked our cook to the point of exhaustion."

"Who fucked our cook? Huck?" Levi asked, walking into the kitchen.

"Who do you think? We were told we couldn't touch her," Gage replied, sounding annoyed.

Levi looked at me, but said nothing.

"I'm ordering pizza," Gage announced, pulling his phone out of his pocket.

"Get a large cheeseburger pizza," Levi told him. "Extra bacon."

"What do you want?" Gage asked, looking at me.

"Meat lovers," I said.

"I'll order it, but tomorrow night is fight night, and we need food. Don't fuck her all damn day."

I was going to plant my fist in his fucking face if he didn't shut the hell up.

"Can I ask how it was, or will that get me killed?" Levi backed up a few steps after he said it.

"No," I snarled and headed for the bar.

Levi turned on the Heat game and flopped down on the sofa. I finished one drink and poured another before going to my chair. Once Gage was done ordering, he sat down on the other side of the sofa.

Levi yelled at the television some. I never got into basketball, but Levi had always been a die-hard Miami Heat fan.

No one discussed anything important, and when the pizza arrived, Trinity was still downstairs. I considered going to check on her but decided that would send mixed signals.

This wasn't a relationship. We fucked. I wanted to do it more. A lot more. Possibly for many years. But no strings. No emotions.

Chapter TWENTY-ONE

TRINITY

After waking up and finding myself alone, I climbed out of bed, then took a look at the bedding. It was not good. I stripped the quilt, sheets, and mattress pad. These needed to be washed, but first, I had to take a shower. There was blood between my thighs, but I didn't think that was the reason I was sticky.

I took a quick shower, then put my clothes back on. Rolling up the dirty bedding in the quilt, I headed for the stairs. Thankfully, I didn't have to go through the kitchen or living room to get to the laundry room. If Gage or Levi saw me carrying this, I would likely die of embarrassment.

I started with the mattress pad, adding bleach to the machine before turning it on. Once that was going, I headed for the stairs to go up to my room, but the smell of pizza caught my attention. I debated on going upstairs to change or going to get something to eat first.

They had probably expected me to cook tonight and had to order pizza since I was sleeping. What would Huck have told them? Or had Gage already figured it out since he had seen Huck dragging me through the house?

Taking a deep breath, I decided to go face them and get this over with. I should apologize for not cooking dinner. I'd make it up to them tomorrow at breakfast. If only I wasn't nervous about this. I was a grown-up. I'd seen Levi have sex on the sofa while Gage participated. There was no reason for this to be a big deal.

I could hear the television, and it sounded like they were watching some sort of sports game. Making my way down the hall, I entered the room quietly and had a moment before they noticed me. My eyes instantly went to Huck, who was sitting in the leather chair he seemed to always sit in with a glass of whiskey in his hand and a cigar between his lips. My chest felt funny, and I wanted to smile just from the sight of him.

His head turned then, and he looked at me. I was happy, but it was very brief because he nodded his head once in acknowledgment of me and turned his attention back to the television. My chest no longer felt funny; it hurt. I had expected something different. Why? I didn't know. I should have known better. This was me we were talking about here. I didn't get to feel happy.

My feet wouldn't move. I was glued to the spot, looking at Huck, thinking maybe he would turn back to me. Downstairs, he'd seemed … different. He had held me and said things to me that made me feel special. Maybe that was what he did after he had sex.

"Trinity!" Gage called out my name, and I jerked my gaze off Huck to meet Gage's smile. I tried to return it with one of my own, but it was a struggle. "We got pizza. You hungry?"

Not anymore.

"Sorry you had to order pizza," I told him, feeling my face get hot. "I promise to make it up to you at breakfast."

Gage's grin grew. "Deal. My favorite meal of the day." He glanced back at Huck, who was watching the television and taking the cigar from his lips.

When he swung his gaze back to me, I could see the pity in his eyes.

"Come sit." He patted the spot beside him. "You've got a choice of meat lovers, cheeseburger, buffalo chicken, or pepperoni."

I looked from him to Huck again, who was still watching the television. I wasn't going to be able to eat, but if I walked out of here, all three of them would know why. Huck would know I had thought what we had done meant something. They would all know that I had misunderstood. My pride wasn't going to let me do that. I had to face these men every day.

I walked over to the sofa and sat down beside Gage. Not close enough to touch, but beside him. He had been the one to invite me to sit. No one else had asked. Levi was eating a piece of pizza, but I could feel him watching me. He hadn't said anything.

"What's it gonna be?" Gage asked me.

I was almost positive if I tried to eat something, I would throw up. I shook my head. "I'm not hungry."

He frowned at me. "You sure?"

I forced a smile. "Positive. I might have some later."

Gage seemed appeased by that, and he leaned back on the sofa with another piece he'd taken from a box in his hand. I started to look at the television, but Huck's eyes stopped me. They were locked on me, and there was a scowl between his eyes. Unsure of what I'd done to deserve it, I turned my attention to the television.

"You like basketball, Trinity?" Levi asked me.

I shrugged. "I honestly don't know. I don't think I've ever watched an entire game."

Levi took a bite of pizza, winked at me, then turned his attention back to the television.

Gage had invited me to sit by him, and Levi had winked at me. A sick feeling began to settle in my stomach. Did the fact that I'd had sex with Huck now mean they expected me to have sex with them? They shared women. Was that why they were being so friendly? They were normally nice, but they didn't bring me into their space like this. What was happening now was definitely new. I liked Gage and Levi, but I didn't want to have sex with them. I wasn't attracted to them in that way. Huck held that position. The thought made me flinch. I'd opened my legs for the man every time he asked. He always walked away. Why had I expected him to be different this time? Because we'd had sex? Because of the conversation in the car?

"I'm going to get some water," I said, standing up. "Can I get anyone something?"

Levi held up his beer bottle. "A new one? Please?"

"Same," Gage added.

I turned to look at Huck, and he shook his head, then put the cigar back between his lips.

Trying not to run out of the room, I focused on keeping myself calm. No one was going to force themselves on me. Gage and Levi wouldn't do that. I would handle this like an adult. Tell them no if it came up. This would be fine.

I walked over to the fridge and pulled out two beers like the one Levi had shown me. There were three different kinds in this fridge. I realized I needed to make a grocery list. We were low on several items. Closing the door, I turned and almost dropped the beers when Huck's chest was blocking me.

I looked up at him, and he reached for the beers in my hand and set them on the counter. I watched him, unsure of what this was about. Were we going to talk about it? Somehow, I doubted that.

"You come on my dick, then go sit beside Gage?"

Was he seriously upset about that?

"You barely acknowledged me. Gage invited me to come in and have pizza."

"I acknowledged you. What did you expect from me? We fucked."

That stung. I wasn't going to let him know it.

I placed a hand on my hip and straightened my shoulders. "I didn't say I expected anything from you. I said you didn't seem interested in my presence, and Gage was."

Huck took a step closer to me, and I took a step back. We did this until my back was pressed against the fridge. He placed a hand on either side of my head, caging me in.

"If I leave you sleeping in my bed after we fuck, then I care about your presence. But this is fucking. Not a relationship or shit with emotions. I don't do that."

That cleared things up. I wanted to roll my eyes, but I didn't.

"I didn't call it anything. I didn't assume we would ever do it again." That was a lie, but one that was required.

Huck smirked. "You expect me to believe that?"

God, this man was full of himself. Did he think because he had a big dick with a piercing in it that did really amazing things that women worshipped at his feet? Probably. I wanted to hit him, but it would do no good. I'd seen his chest naked. It was a chiseled sculpture.

"As you know, this fucking thing is new to me. I wasn't told the rules," I snapped at him angrily.

His eyelids lowered, and he leaned closer to me. "You say *fucking* with that pretty little mouth again, and I'm going to shove my dick back into your tight pussy before it's recovered."

I swallowed hard. There he went with his dirty talking again. I said nothing. I wasn't sure I trusted myself.

He ran a finger down the side of my face. "Good girl," he whispered.

When he praised me with that endearment, I wanted to climb up his body and lick him. I was insane. Sex with this man had flipped some switch in me. I needed to find it and flip it back.

"Now, you're gonna go back in that room, give them their beers, and bring your ass over and sit in my lap."

"Are we playing pretend for them now?" I asked, shocking myself with my sass.

He grabbed my chin and leveled me with his gaze. "Don't get smart with me. You don't want to fuck with my territorial side."

My bravado was now gone. I nodded.

That damn smirk was back, and then he turned and left me in the kitchen. I gripped the side of the island and took several deep breaths. I was wet and terrified at the same time. I didn't know if I wanted him to fuck me or if I wanted to run away from him.

Picking up the beers, I walked back into the living room and took each of them a beer. Gage was watching me when I walked back over and didn't sit in the seat beside him. I made my way over to Huck, who put his cigar back between his lips, then held out his hand for me. I took it as I eased down onto his lap.

Leaning back against his chest, I didn't look at the other two men in the room. I watched the television. Yes, I was being obedient. Huck had told me what to do, and I had done it. This kind of behavior should annoy me. Any sane woman who had self-respect would have told him no.

I was so damn needy to belong. His ordering me around aroused me. I wanted to make him happy. I liked it when he called me a good girl, and that right there was screwed up. When he moved his hand to my thigh, I held my breath. I had on shorts tonight, and I wished it were a dress.

Huck took the cigar from between his lips, and I felt his warm breath near my ear. I could smell the whiskey on his breath.

"Open," he said in my ear.

I glanced over to see the other two watching the television, then moved my right leg over to drape over his leg. His hand slid inside the leg of my shorts. The moment his fingers touched the soaked silk of my panties, he stopped.

"Go put on my shirt and nothing else," he ordered me in a low whisper.

I was not going to argue. Standing, I headed for the stairs, then stopped and quickly changed the laundry over before hurrying upstairs to change into the T-shirt he had given me to use my first night here. Taking off my panties and bra before slipping it on, I made my way back down to the living room. Huck's eyes locked on me when I entered, and the other two men didn't seem to notice me. When I reached Huck, I realized he had a blanket beside him.

He grabbed my waist and pulled me down onto his lap, then covered me up. Once the blanket was over me, he pulled the shirt up to my waist. Knowing he didn't want them to see me like this made my anger at him from earlier fade a little more. I didn't understand him, but I liked that he wasn't willing to share me. At least if he were willing, he wouldn't care that I had on no panties and they could see me if they tried.

Huck pulled my right leg over his leg and left me open. I leaned back and closed my eyes as he moved up the inside of my thigh. His fingertips barely brushing my skin. I bit down on my bottom lip to keep from making a noise when his fingers touched me. I realized that I was tender, and I jerked when his callous fingertip rubbed the entrance.

"Easy," he said low against my ear.

I barely nodded and opened my eyes to stare at the television. I couldn't focus on anything as I stared at the people running back and forth on the screen. Huck began to gently circle my clit, and I shivered, pressing against him.

I could feel the hard rigidness of his erection on my butt.

"You're so fucking wet that it's dripping down my fingers." His dirty words being said in a whisper against my ear only made it worse. "You're sore though," he added. "Right here."

Then, he slid a finger inside me, and I grabbed his arm with my hand. A low rumble of laughter in his chest vibrated against my back.

"I'll be gentle. Lie back and let me play," he told me.

Again, I did as I had been told. If he called me his good girl right now, I might orgasm. Although they couldn't see anything, I felt naughty, having Huck touch me like this with them in the same room. My hands fisted at my sides as Huck gently tortured me with his fingers while he smoked his cigar and watched the basketball game.

"Heat has got this one," Levi said, but I didn't look at him. I kept my eyes on the television.

"When this is over, I want to see what they're saying about tomorrow night's fight," Gage told him.

My breathing hitched, and I tried to calm down. I could not orgasm in this room. For starters, every orgasm Huck had given me, I had done that squirting thing, and second, I was loud. While this felt incredible and I didn't want him to stop, I was worried I wouldn't be able to control my orgasm.

Huck kept smoking, like watching television with his fingers buried in a woman's vagina was normal. If it wasn't for the heavy breathing I could hear in my ear, I would think he wasn't affected by this at all. A jolt of pleasure hit me, and I turned my head away from the others and closed my eyes tightly.

"Lift your ass," Huck whispered.

I did, and I felt him unzip his pants and jerk them down before he took my waist and pushed me back down. His erection was no longer inside his pants, but between my open folds. He had maneuvered that too smoothly. As if he was a pro. I didn't want to think about it. How many women he'd done this with. That was a bit of cold water in the face to calm me down.

Until he began to stroke himself between my legs. Making it rub against my clit and slide easily up and down with the lubrication of my arousal. I gasped when I felt the metal bar of his piercing hit my clit. Thankfully, the team Levi was rooting for did something good because he cheered and it drowned out my noise.

Huck's heavy breathing in my ear, along with what he was doing under the blanket, was too much. I laid my head back and closed my eyes. He was getting me worked up to the point that I no longer cared who was around to see or hear me.

"Are you gonna come?" His voice was a hoarse whisper in my ear.

"If you don't stop," I said breathlessly.

His hands grabbed my waist and picked me up, then turned me to face him. I straddled him and slowly eased down as he kept the blanket around us. His erection slid against me, and I rocked my hips to get friction. I wanted that bar on my clit again.

"Out." Huck's deep voice startled me as he turned to glare at the other two guys.

"Damn, I was hoping you'd forgotten we were here," Gage replied, and Huck tensed under me.

"NOW!" he shouted.

"We're going. We're going," Levi replied.

Huck didn't move until they were gone, and then his eyes swung back to mine. "Do what feels good," he told me.

I lifted my body up until the tip of his cock rubbed my swollen clit, then rubbed it back and forth. Needing more, I leaned forward until I felt him at my entrance. I sank down so that the tip was inside of me, and I rotated my hips.

Huck's hands went under the shirt and started squeezing my boobs and twisting my nipples. I let it go a little deeper, then rocked back and forth with it barely inside me. The sensation felt amazing. Huck said nothing. He kept his hands on my chest while I experimented, finding pleasure. I was afraid to let him sink fully inside of me. He was right; I was sore.

I started to bounce on about one-fourth of his length. Huck pulled the shirt up and over my head and held my waist while his eyes watched my breasts rise and fall with each move I made. I started going faster, feeling the buildup. The metal bar rubbed me, and I realized I might be in love with that piercing.

"That's it," Huck said. "Be a good girl and get yourself off on my cock."

The dirty talking ... yes, I needed the filthy words. I was close.

"I want to see you squirt all over my cock."

"Oh God, Huck," I moaned. "Oh, oh."

The surge was there. My body began to tremble, and I cried out his name some more like a chant before it burst free. Huck held me, keeping me from falling forward onto him.

"Fuck, that's hot," he growled.

I could feel the now-familiar release, and I knew that was what he was watching. I continued to jerk and cry out in his arms as the pleasure hit me several more times before it stopped. Gasping for air, I looked down and saw his soaked hard length. I guessed this was something that I was going to do and needed to get used to it.

"I got the chair wet," I said.

"I don't give a fuck." He picked me up and placed me in front of him.

"You didn't get off." I pointed out the obvious as he stood up.

"Not yet, but I'm about to. Bend over and put your hands on the table. I'm going to come all over this juicy ass."

Oh my. Okay. Obeying him excited me. Huck palmed my butt cheeks with one hand while he stroked his cock with the other. He grabbed a side and made it jiggle, then groaned. He continued to slap it just hard enough for the extra fat back there to bounce. I watched him over my shoulder as he pumped himself harder. His slaps on my butt got more forceful.

I realized I was getting turned on again. I felt each slap of his hand between my legs. I wiggled my butt this time, needing him to hit it again.

"That's it, baby," he groaned. "Shake it like that."

I did as he had said, and he began jerking faster. His mouth opened slightly as he kept his gaze locked on my butt. Every time I gave it a shake, he made a noise.

"Fuuuuck. Oh fuck, yes," he growled, and then he let out a shout as strings of white semen shot out onto my butt.

He stood over it, pumping himself, watching his release coat me. When he was done, his gaze moved to mine. I was breathing hard too. Completely turned on by what I'd just watched.

He scooped some of his release up with his finger, then shoved it between my legs and made a pleased sound in his chest. I let him continue his playing until he was done. When I finally stood back up, he lowered his head and kissed me hard. I wrapped my arms around his neck and sank into him. I loved the way he felt against me.

"Downstairs," he said to me, breaking the kiss.

I remembered the bedding. "I'm not finished with the bedding. It's in the laundry."

"Don't fucking care." His hand slapped my cum-covered ass. "Downstairs."

Chapter TWENTY-TWO

TRINITY

The fact that I woke up in time to get breakfast cooked was a miracle. Although Huck and I hadn't had sex again last night, we'd done many other things. He didn't move when I got out of bed to go start breakfast. I caught myself smiling while thinking about all we had done, but would have to remind myself that I had to keep my feelings out of it. No attachments. I wasn't worried that I'd fall in love with him. I still didn't think I had that in me.

Trying to make up for not cooking the guys dinner, I made sure to make everyone's favorite. Gage and Levi liked it when I made a large breakfast, but Huck always scowled. I was torn between doing what I normally did to make the majority happy or pleasing Huck.

He was the one who had stressed that this was just fucking. I had to remember that, and making decisions with that in mind meant I was making a big breakfast. It was what I would have done before we had sex. The only thing that I struggled with was, I liked when I pleased him and he praised me. The *good girl* thing was a weakness I had to work on. If I didn't, this would be more difficult when it ended, but then I had to accept I would feel something for him. He was my first. Emotional attachments came with that. Right?

Gage walked in, grinning as he inhaled deeply. "Smells so fucking good," he said as he grabbed a plate I had set on the end of the island. He surveyed the food I had laid out, then nodded his head approvingly. "You didn't let me down."

I was again thankful I'd woken up on my own this morning and not overslept.

"Food!" Levi called out as he entered the kitchen. "God, I love waking up here."

At least I made them happy. I tried not to think about Huck's reaction. I wasn't even sure how Huck would treat me today. Would I get the hot or the cold Huck?

"Listen," Levi said to me.

I looked at him with a serious expression.

"The Huck thing, when that stops—and it will—we want you here. Don't go getting any ideas about leaving."

I needed that reminder. The one about it ending. I had been telling myself the same thing, but having someone else confirm that this was a brief sexual thing with Huck kept me from getting my head somewhere it didn't need to be.

I nodded. "Thanks."

"I second that," Gage said as he walked to the table with his food.

Now, if I wasn't so nervous about Huck's reaction to my breakfast buffet, things would be fine. I picked up a piece of bacon and ate it.

"There's a fight on pay-per-view tonight," Gage said from his spot at the table. "If I ask real nice, would you make one of those killer spreads of food for it?"

I finished chewing and swallowed. "Of course. That's my job. You don't have to ask real nice, but I appreciate it."

The door from downstairs opened and closed. I walked over to get a cup down for Huck and pour him some coffee just so I had something to do other than look at him.

"If you bitch about the food, I will take you out back and kick your ass," Gage said before Huck could say anything.

"It'll be two against one," Levi added.

I wished they'd be quiet and not make a big deal out of it. He might not even have said anything if they hadn't pointed it out. Forcing a smile, I turned around with his cup. He was scanning the food. I waited on him to look at me. When he finally did, he wasn't scowling, but he wasn't smiling either. He simply gave me a nod and picked up a plate. Not the warmest reception, but I hadn't expected him to come up to me and touch me or anything. This was sex, not affection.

Keeping the two separate would be hard. Affection was something I had craved most of my life, but was too afraid to get close enough to anyone who might give it to me. Until Hayes.

Huck put the same amount of food on his plate he always did. Three pieces of bacon, two biscuits, cheese grits, and scrambled eggs. Sometimes, he got a cinnamon roll, but today, he didn't. When he finished filling his plate, I held out the cup of coffee for him. He took it without a word and went to the table.

This was a typical morning. Nothing different. Except my feelings were struggling.

Thank you, mind-blowing orgasms, for screwing me up.

Huck asked Gage about some transaction with a man I didn't know. They fell into shop talk, and I put a few things on a plate, filled a cup of coffee, then made my way out to the back patio. It was warm already, but then it was late spring in

Florida which was summer weather for the rest of the country. I tucked my legs under me and ate my second piece of bacon.

After cleaning today, I had to prepare for tonight, so that would keep me busy. I looked out over the pool and wondered if they'd use this area out here too. They hadn't yet, but the warmer it got in the evenings, there was a possibility. I needed to ask Gage. If they were going to swim, then the towels needed restocking, and the outside bar needed to have ice. I should probably do an inventory on the liquor for out here too.

I finished my meal and stood up to go get things started. Huck was walking out the back door as I turned. Being alone with him after all we'd done last night made me suddenly feel shy. Something about the light of day and reality.

"I'm heading to the shop, and then I'm needed at the ranch. I might not make it back for the fight tonight," he said, not moving to get closer to me.

"Okay," I replied, holding my empty plate and cup.

He studied me for a minute. "You're good then?"

No, Huck. Not even close.

I nodded. "I'm fine."

"All right," he replied, then turned and went back into the house.

That was painful. I could admit it. Really painful. But I could get over it. Think about other things. Not Huck.

I followed him inside the house and went to the sink and began putting away leftovers and cleaning up the mess from making breakfast. When I finished, I made a grocery list of items I needed. Gage walked into the kitchen while I was writing it all down.

"You good?" he asked me.

I clenched my teeth. Were they all going to ask me that? No, I wasn't good. Stop asking me.

I nodded, then took the list and held it out to him. "I need these things for tonight. Are you planning on opening up the pool area? If so, we need to check the liquor cabinet. You might need to pick some more up along with beer for the bar out there."

Gage took the list and tucked it into his pocket. "Yeah, we'll have the lights on out back. Might as well use the pool. It's time to start enjoying it. I'll just grab everything, and if we don't need it, then it'll get used eventually."

"Okay. Great," I replied with a false smile and turned to head for the cleaning closet to get out what I needed to start.

"He's my friend, and I'd kill for him. But you're family now too. If you need anything, let me know."

Gage's words should have warmed me, but they only drove home the point that last night had been a onetime thing.

"Thanks," I said, glancing back for only a moment before leaving the kitchen.

The day went by quickly. Cleaning had taken me several hours, and then preparing the pool area had taken another two hours. Once that was finished, I had the groceries I needed, thanks to Gage, and I threw myself into preparing food.

Levi and Gage both stopped by the kitchen to taste something I'd finished. Huck never came back, but then he had told me he probably wouldn't. I didn't think about it too much. Just every other five seconds. I was going to torture myself if I didn't stop it.

"This looks fucking incredible," Gage said, coming back in to look things over before people started to arrive.

I smiled, happy he was pleased. I'd needed a distraction today, and thankfully, this had provided it.

"Go get ready. Put on a swimsuit. You don't like watching the fight, but you've worked all day. You need to enjoy the pool," he told me.

My first thought was no. Huck had said I couldn't wear a bikini in front of anyone. But that had been before. Before we'd had sex. Before he'd gotten it out of his system. Not to mention, he wasn't even going to be here.

"You're frowning," Gage pointed out.

I shrugged. "Not sure if I am supposed to wear a swimsuit."

He raised his eyebrows. "Because of Huck?"

I didn't reply, but I knew the look on my face said it all.

"He's not your keeper. Wear what the fuck you want."

He was right. I wasn't Huck's. He wasn't here.

"Okay," I agreed.

Gage grinned and popped one of my homemade tortilla chips into his mouth. "Thatta girl," he said.

Walking up to the bedroom, I hoped I was doing the right thing.

Chapter TWENTY-THREE

HUCK

Breaking this damn mustang in ninety-degree weather was fucking hell. I wiped my forehead with my arm and cursed, walking back toward the stables. Why the fuck did Blaise want a freaking mustang anyway? We were in the thoroughbred business.

Maddy was walking out of the stables when I reached the entrance. She shielded her eyes from the sun and looked up at me.

"You look like you've had fun," she said sarcastically.

"Fucking blast," I replied.

She laughed. "I saw a little of it. There is no way I'd get on a horse like that."

She was getting better on the back of a horse, but she had her favorites that she trusted. Blaise had given up on trying to get her to ride any of the others.

"I enjoyed having Trinity at the house. Anytime she wants a change of scenery, send her my way," Maddy said. "Cree has asked for her twice today."

I nodded. "Okay." I didn't want to talk about Trinity. I was currently coming up with shit to do just to stay away from her.

"Be nice to her. She didn't tell me much, but, well, she has gone through some bad stuff. I don't know details, but I…" She paused, and I could see her struggling with something. "Please don't tell her I told you this and don't mention it to anyone else. But when I went out to the shed to take her a towel, she was curled up in a ball on the floor…rocking…and I don't think she was there mentally. It was as if she were someplace else. I don't know how to explain it, but it was heartbreaking. She's been damaged in the past. Go easy on her."

What the fuck? I stood there, trying to picture what Maddy had described and I couldn't.

Maddy patted my arm. "Hayes would have wanted her taken care of. Don't hold things against her. Whatever she's done, she probably had to." She gave me one last smile, then headed for her car.

I didn't move while I attempted to wrap my head around this. When I finally moved again, I didn't go into the stables. I headed for the Escalade. Guess I'd be going back for the fight after all.

There was shit Trinity hadn't told me. Maddy wasn't one to exaggerate. She also didn't make shit up.

What the fuck had Trinity left out?

For the first time since I had opened my eyes this morning and shut down where Trinity was concerned, I let myself think about her. I'd reached for her before fully waking up, and the pang of disappointment when I realized she was gone bothered me. I shouldn't have felt anything. It felt too much like an attachment. By the time I had made my way upstairs, I'd managed to get control of my head. There would be no thinking about Trinity.

Walking into the kitchen and seeing the ridiculous amount of food on the island had helped. If Trinity had emotional attachments to me after my taking her virginity, then she'd have tried to please me. She hadn't. She'd made the food the others wanted. I should have been relieved. No, I had been relieved. She wasn't acting like a clingy female over a night of hot sex.

Dammit all to hell. My fucking cock began to harden, thinking about it. Jesus, her ass was what poetry was written about. I needed some more to get her out of my system. The sex was too damn good to get over it after one night. I just needed to make sure she didn't get it confused with anything more.

I'd managed not to think about this or Trinity for most of the day. Maddy had blown that to shit with what she told me. Why the fuck hadn't she told me sooner? If Trinity had been rocking on the damn floor, then she had trauma. Mental shit, and me fucking the hell out of her wasn't going to end well. If I'd known this before yesterday, then I wouldn't have fucked her. The idea of missing out on that though seemed downright tragic.

Fact remained that Trinity had some crap going on in her head, and now, I'd gone and fucked her. I wasn't sure how I could fix this. Going home and carrying her to my room to fuck her all night was definitely not what she needed.

"FUCK!" I slammed my hand down on the steering wheel.

Why did the hottest fuck I'd ever had have to come with all these complications?

I pulled past the security gate, and the cars outside were lined up. More than usual. I pulled into the garage and headed inside to go find Trinity and ask her what the hell had happened in the shed. Well, maybe not like that exactly. I'd need to be gentler and not shove my dick in her.

What if she was *fatal attraction* mental? What the fuck would I do with that? I didn't know what kind of screwed up she was. I had gone and taken her damn virginity, and she might snap on me. I thought about her tits while she had gotten off on my cock last night and the way she had sounded. Maybe I could live with fatal attraction. If I got more of that.

I might be the one who was mental.

The house was loud when I walked in the back door. It wasn't time for the fight yet, but everyone had gotten here early. I needed to go wash the dirt and sweat off my body and change before I looked for Trinity. A few people called out to me, and I nodded but kept walking. I smelled like a horse.

Stepping into the kitchen, I scanned it for Trinity, but she wasn't in there. Her food was though. She'd gone all out. Gage was probably fucking thrilled. I started to head to the stairs when I paused and noticed the pool was all lit up and people were outside too. I hadn't known the guys were making it a pool party.

Levi walked by with two drinks in his hands, and I started to turn until I saw him stop. Her back was to me, but I knew that hair. Even if I couldn't see much else since she was sitting on the side of the pool. My eyes fell to her waist, then the flare of her hips.

Motherfucker.

Stalking to the door, I shoved it open. Levi leaned closer to say something to her, and she laughed. Swear to God, she laughed. First Trev and now Levi making her fucking laugh. I was almost to them when Gage stepped in front of me, blocking my way.

"Move, or this is gonna get ugly," I said through clenched teeth.

"She worked her ass off all day. I told her to go get on a bathing suit and come have some fun," Gage said, not backing down.

"Did you tell Levi to fucking drool all over her?" I snarled, not taking my eyes off the two of them.

"No. Levi is pretending. You know, like you did with her. To keep the others off. Don't see the problem here."

My hands fisted at my sides. "Because every horny bastard here is looking at her in that fucking bikini."

Gage held up his hands. "So? She's hot. They're not touching her."

My gaze swung to his, and I took a step toward him. Motherfucker raised his eyebrows and didn't move. We both knew which one of us was the most dangerous. His crazy ass. The ones who didn't fear death were the ones who feared nothing.

"She's mine." The words came out of my mouth before I could stop them.

"Really? Since when? This morning, you acted like you barely knew her."

He was pushing me, and the son of a bitch was doing it on purpose.

"Gage," I warned, "this is not your business."

He took a step closer to me, bumping his chest against mine. "What if I want to make it my business?"

"Huck?"

Trinity's voice was the only thing that stopped me from taking the first swing. My blood was boiling, and I'd never once wanted to hurt Gage. Until now.

I swung my gaze to her. She was wearing a hot-pink bikini that covered fucking nothing. I hadn't even seen the back with her standing up yet, but I already knew that sweet ass was on display. Gina and her slutty-ass swimsuits.

"Go to my room," I barked at her.

She stiffened, and I pointed toward the door.

"Go on back and drink your cocktail, sweetheart," Gage said, walking over to her.

"If you touch her, I swear to God," I growled.

Gage grinned at me. "You sound jealous, Huck. You've always shared with us. Right, Levi?"

Levi didn't say a word. I realized then that the entire place had gone silent. My gaze went back to Trinity. She was staring at me as if I terrified her. That wasn't my intention, but right now, this was me barely hanging on. I couldn't be any calmer.

"Go on back to the pool," Gage said to her gently.

That was when I moved. I was going to fucking kill him.

"HUCK! NO!" Trinity stepped in front of Gage and put her hand on my chest. "I'll go downstairs. But come with me."

I looked down at her, and those big brown eyes were pleading with me silently. Mental trauma. She had mental trauma. I had planned on talking to her about it. Instead, I had lost my damn mind, and she was the one calming me down. Who looked motherfucking mental now?

I nodded my head once, and she slipped her hand into mine. Gage's fucking smile made me want to shatter his pearly-white teeth with my fist. I glared at him. He'd gone too far.

"Please." Trinity pulled on my arm.

I turned back to her, and she started walking. I went with her, doing my best to calm the fucking monster in my head down. Then, she stepped in front of me and opened the door. Her perfect round ass had a goddamn thong up it. I snapped. I grabbed her arm and hauled her through the kitchen and down the hall and jerked open my door. Once I had her on the stairs, I slammed the door and locked it, then pressed her back against the wall.

"Your fucking ass is completely uncovered," I said through my teeth.

She looked pale. I needed to calm down. I was scaring her. She had trauma and shit. Fuck me, I had trauma. She'd shown her ass to every fucker out there.

"I didn't think you'd care," she whispered, her eyes wide.

I grabbed one of her asscheeks in my hand and squeezed. "You didn't think I'd care if you showed those fuckers your ass?"

She shook her head, still looking completely terrified. Jesus Christ, I was losing my damn mind. I reached for her bottoms and ripped them off her. She squealed, and that only seemed to make this insanity taking over me worse. I grabbed the ties of her top and undid it, then tossed it until she was naked.

I smelled like a horse's ass, but I didn't care. She'd shown her body to everyone. I yanked my shirt over my head, then unbuttoned my jeans and jerked them down until my dick was free. Reaching down, I grabbed her left leg and wrapped it around my back before I plunged into her.

She cried out and arched her back. Her tight pussy squeezed my cock. I hadn't checked to see if she was ready. My crazed need had taken over. Thankfully, she'd been ready.

"What made you so fucking wet?" I growled.

It couldn't have been me. All I'd done was scare the shit out of her. I was going to kill whoever had been the cause of it.

"You," she breathed.

"Liar. You've looked terrified of me since you saw me outside." I shoved myself deeper, trying to mark this cunt like I owned it.

"I know. But it's still you," she panted.

That was not the thing to say to a crazy man.

"Are you telling me you got wet for me when I was scaring you?"

She nodded.

Fuck, she was mental. I grabbed her ass with both my hands and started fucking her. There was no taking a shower first or even getting down the stairs. I had to fill this pussy with my cum. Make sure she knew who it belonged to. Not fucking Gage or Levi.

She was moaning and clawing at my arms.

"You love my cock, don't you?"

She nodded her head. Her eyes locked on mine.

"Listen to me," I said as I thrust into her hard. "I took this pussy. Me. Not fucking Levi and not Gage. I did. I took it. Do you understand me?"

She nodded again. "Yes."

"Do you want their cocks, Trinity? Is that it?"

She shook her head. "No."

"Whose cock do you want, baby?" I asked, feeling my balls tighten as I pounded into her.

"Yours. I want yours. Please."

"That's right," I cooed, leaning down to kiss her neck. "My cock. This pussy gets fucked by me. I make it feel good. I eat it, and I fuck it."

She cried out my name and grabbed my arms.

"Come on my dick, baby," I whispered and squeezed her ass tighter. "Be a good girl and wet my fucking dick."

Her body convulsed against me, and she whimpered as the gush I was becoming addicted to came out in two hard squirts. As she trembled in my arms, my release began to pump out of me as I continued fucking her. My teeth sank into the soft skin of her neck, and my body jerked as I filled her with my cum.

She was limp in my arms when I finally stopped, and I sank down to the step beneath me, holding her in my arms.

Her naked body pressed against me as she laid her head on my chest and sighed contentedly.

I hadn't thought it could get better with her, but it did. Every time, I seemed to fucking come harder. What was I going to do with her? I was coming in her like a damn idiot. She wasn't on the pill, and apparently, my dick was running the show. Not my head.

I closed my eyes and pressed a kiss to the top of her head.

"We need to get you on birth control," I said. "Because I'm not going to be able to wear a condom with you. It's too far gone."

She shifted and looked up at me. "What's too far gone?"

I wasn't sure how to word this because, in the long run, I wasn't the man for her. But until I could fuck her out of my system, I wasn't letting her go. I'd figure out what her trauma was and help her or get her help.

"Best way to say this is, right now, your pussy owns me." It wasn't poetic or romantic, but it was the blunt truth.

A small smile tugged at her lips, and then she giggled. Hearing her and seeing the laughter in her eyes made me feel warm in my chest or some shit.

I smirked. "That's funny?"

She nodded. "Yes."

God, she was fucking too cute to also be the hottest piece of ass I'd ever fucked.

"Why is that?"

She sat up and draped her arms over my shoulders. "I just opened up my pussy for business yesterday, and now, you're claiming it owns you. That's a pretty powerful pussy."

Hearing her talk about her fucking cunt and use the word *pussy* made my dick twitch back to life. Motherfucker, she was going to kill me.

I reached up and cupped the side of her face. "It's a real fucking powerful pussy," I replied, then kissed her. Simply because I wanted to, and damn if that wasn't a problem.

Chapter TWENTY-FOUR

TRINITY

The next morning, when the guys arrived in the kitchen, was my test. I had spent the past hour talking to myself about not expecting much from Huck. If I was going to do this, then I couldn't be hurt every morning.

Gage had his plate full and was eating when Huck walked into the room. I knew it was him without looking. I had some chemical thing happening in my body when it came to Huck. When he was near, I felt it like an electric pulse. However, I didn't turn to look at him. Instead, I began washing the larger pots in the sink.

When his large hand slid around my waist to my stomach, I sucked in a breath.

"Good morning," he whispered in my ear.

Hadn't prepared for this. My heart felt all fluttery and weird.

"Good morning," I replied, glancing back to look at him.

Our eyes locked and then his hand fell away, and he walked over to the island to get food. I, however, needed a moment to get ahold of myself. He made me feel weak just that easily. The man was lethal, and I couldn't protect myself by staying away from him. I craved him.

"Blaise needs me at the ranch. Won't be coming into the shop today," Gage said.

"We're good. Caught up for the most part. He gonna get you on that damn mustang too?"

"Fuck no."

Huck chuckled. I loved the sound of his laugh.

"Ray-Ray called already. Said you weren't answering your phone. She wants to know if she needs to run to the office supply store for that list of shit you left on the counter," Gage said.

I tensed at the mention of Ray-Ray. In all our new and exciting sex, I had chosen to forget Huck's other sexual activities. One being the gorgeous redhead who worked for him and sucked his cock. I hadn't sucked his cock yet. Would he get her to do that today?

Sure, I'd been jealous before, but this was a new level of jealousy I hadn't experienced. It felt like ice crystals slicing me in the gut. I took a deep breath, then scrubbed the pan in the soap water harder than necessary.

"I'll call her," Huck replied.

And ice crystals in my chest. They were causing havoc there too.

"She also asked if she needed to get a dress for the party at the big house on Friday night. Said you mentioned it last week."

Silence. As in you could hear a pin drop. The pot in my hand slipped and clanged in the sink. I went to reach for it, but those ice crystals were wrapping around my neck at the moment, and I wasn't sure if I was going to be able to breathe soon. I turned and left the kitchen.

I walked up the stairs, needing to get the hell away from Huck and the reminder that he fucked me like an animal but did the same to other women too. Opening the door to the bedroom I hadn't slept in since before going to Maddy's, I took a deep breath and told myself to get over it, then turned to close the door.

Huck's hand flat against the door stopped me. I hadn't heard him follow me. I stared at him, then spun around and headed for the bathroom. He was not who I wanted to look at right now.

"Trinity, stop," he barked at me.

Maybe it was the raging jealousy that had overtaken me, or perhaps I had just been pushed too far, but I spun around and glared at him. "You stop! I didn't ask you to follow me in here."

The heat in his eyes flared, and I didn't care if I was making him angry.

"What the fuck was that down there?" he asked, narrowing his eyes at me.

I let out a hard, bitter laugh. "Oh, I don't know. Maybe it was me hearing that your secretary-slash-cocksucker is going to a party with you!" I yelled. Yes, I was yelling. Who was I? I didn't yell at men. I rarely yelled at anyone.

"We fuck, Trinity. That's what we do. You know that. I made it clear. Not once did I say we were an item or exclusive."

No, he hadn't. He had just said *I* was to be exclusive.

"Really? Hmm, so I can go fuck someone else? Gage maybe? I didn't realize that the things you say when you're fucking me don't count. So, excuse me. I misunderstood. I am on the same page now. You can go."

I turned and stalked into the bathroom, but Huck's chest was pressing against my back, forcing me into the room before I could even get past the doorway.

I spun around and shoved at his chest, which was dumb because that never did anything.

"GET OUT!" I shouted.

He reached behind him and slammed the bathroom door.

"You want another dick?" he asked, his voice a low growl. "Is that it? Mine isn't enough now? I broke you in, and now, you want to fucking play?"

My chest burned. My throat burned. I closed my eyes tightly and wondered if this was the moment I would cry. Had he pushed me to tears? After eight years?

"I am making a point," I said quietly.

Then, I opened my eyes to look up at him. No tears. Not even wetness. He hadn't managed it. I felt some strength from that.

"Don't tell me that my pussy belongs to you and expect me to just obey you if your dick is going to be shoved in another woman's mouth. Or anywhere for that matter. I understand this is just sex. I accept it. But if this is just sex, then my pussy is mine, and I'll do with it what I fucking please."

Huck's nostrils flared as he glared at me. I didn't look away. I wasn't scared of him. He thought he could bully me, but he had no idea the shit I had survived. This was only hurting me because I cared about him. I felt things for him. And I didn't want anyone but him to touch me. So, yes, maybe my pussy was his, but damn if I'd let him know it.

"Okay," he bit out.

I frowned. "What does that mean? Okay?"

He backed me up until my butt hit the sink and caged me in with his hands placed on each side of me. Lowering his head, he looked me in the eye. He smelled so good. God, why did he have to smell so good? Why did this have to be the man to make me feel?

"Until we are done, that pussy is mine, and I won't stick my dick anywhere but in you."

I had not expected that. I stared at him. Not sure if I believed him. This was Huck we were talking about. He liked to fuck. Ray-Ray was at work with him every day. She could break him down.

"What?" he asked.

I tilted my head to the side and shrugged. "Not sure I believe you."

His eyebrows drew together in a frown. "Are you fucking kidding me?"

I shook my head. "I've seen Ray-Ray. She made sure to let me know that she takes care of your cock daily. You work with her every day. You expect me to believe if she unzips your jeans and gets on her knees to suck your cock, you're going to turn that down?"

Huck shoved his hand between my legs forcefully and squeezed my thigh. "Yeah, I do. Because since I ate your pussy in that garden shed, I've not had another woman. I can't even get fucking hard for anyone else."

He looked so angry when he said it that I believed him. Maybe I had a portion of control over him the way he had over me. I hadn't thought that was even possible.

"Then, why are you taking Ray-Ray to a party? She looks better on your arm? Is that it?"

He grinned then and shook his head. "What is with this jealousy and fucking sassy mouth, Trinity?"

I crossed my arms over my chest. "I don't like it either. Believe me, I didn't ask for it."

He said nothing for a moment, and I wished he'd take his hand away from my thigh. It was too close to my pussy, and I was getting freaking wet. Damn him.

"You need to check it. This will end eventually. Don't start acting like a jealous girlfriend."

I raised my eyebrows and leaned closer to him. "Then, you don't act like a jealous boyfriend," I whispered.

He pulled his hand away from me and stood up. "You're right. We both need to remember it's just sex. Nothing more."

I nodded, although the ice crystals were now jabbing me in the chest.

He turned to leave and paused when he opened the door. I thought he'd say more, but he didn't. I stood there as he walked out and left.

Once I no longer heard his footsteps, I dropped my head into my hands and groaned. Being the vulnerable one in the sexlationship sucked. Yes, I had made that word up, but I didn't know what else to call what we were doing.

Chapter TWENTY-FIVE

TRINITY

Trying not to think about Ray-Ray with Huck all day and what Huck's last comment had been before he walked out of the bathroom this morning meant I was focused on deep-cleaning things. I had even gone down to Huck's bedroom and taken the bedding to wash again. My thoughts kept going from, *When can I leave this place and get my life back?* to, *How will I leave this place and let Huck go?* Stupid sex. It messed everything up.

I was in the kitchen when the chime I'd finally figured out meant someone had come through the security gate went off. It was time for the guys to be coming home. They rarely arrived at the same time unless they were working together. I'd learned to have dinner ready by seven. They would eat when they were ready.

The door to the garage opened, and I expected it to be Gage. He was always hungry and normally the first to arrive to all meals. However, Huck walked in alone with a shopping bag in one hand and a box in the other. My gaze dropped to the bag, and although I had never shopped at designer stores, I could tell that bag was from somewhere expensive. It had a fancy look to it.

He lifted the bag and set it on the counter, then laid the long white box down beside it.

"Here," he said.

I looked from the bag and box back to him. "What?" I asked.

I realized Huck looked uncomfortable. It was a strange look for him. I was curious now.

He waved his hand at the items on the counter. "This. Take it upstairs. Maddy sent it."

Why was Maddy sending me things?

I shook my head, confused. "I don't understand."

Huck walked around the counter and closed the distance between us, then grabbed my chin between his thumb and finger. "You were right. I don't want you fucking anyone else, and I don't want you going anywhere with someone else. Until we've got this out of our systems, then it's exclusive. And that's your dress, shoes, and jewelry for the party at the ranch on Friday night."

Butterflies—wild, crazy, fluttering butterflies—were inside my stomach and chest. That was all it took for him to make me forgive everything. I was too easy.

"Ray-Ray has been transferred to another shop. She's not going to be at mine anymore."

I stared at him, wanting to throw my arms around him and bury my face in his neck. I wouldn't dare do it, but I wanted to. I had expected him to forget what I'd said this morning. Not for him to do this.

"Trinity," he said.

"Yes?"

"Are you done with dinner?"

"Yes."

He grabbed my hips and spun me around. "To my room. I need to fuck."

My body tingled with anticipation. I looked back at him over my shoulder. "Before we do that, I want to do something else."

He frowned. "What?"

Smiling, I licked my bottom lip. "Suck your cock."

"Fucking hell, you're gonna kill me. Go. Now. Before I shove you to your knees right here."

The rest of the week, I spent my nights in Huck's bed. If I let myself, I could pretend this was forever, that the happiness I was feeling wouldn't end. However, I tried hard to keep reminding myself that Huck would tire of me soon. These things I felt for him, I couldn't help. I was attached even though he'd told me not to be. I craved affection from him, and that was bad. I'd been deprived of affection and attachments my entire life. The little affection I'd gotten from Hayes was nothing compared to what I received from Huck. Although Hayes had loved me. That was something I couldn't make sense of.

Tonight, I would see Maddy again, and I hoped we'd get a moment alone. She was the only female friend I had to talk to. The cocktail party at the big house was Garrett's celebration victory for all the wins that Hughes Farm had walked away with at the Kentucky Derby.

The dress, shoes, and jewelry she'd chosen for me had taken my breath away. I'd never worn anything like this in my life. Thankfully, Maddy had a good eye for size. The dress fit perfectly. It wasn't too revealing, but I felt sexy in it. The pink satin material shimmered in the light. It wasn't low-cut exactly, but my boobs didn't cover up easily. The back was bare, except for the thin crisscross straps. I hadn't been sure I was going to be able to walk in the heels, but surprisingly, I had done just fine when I tested them out.

Looking at myself one last time in the mirror, I touched the necklace. That was my only concern. That this was real. The diamonds weren't big, but it was still a lot of diamonds. I didn't want to consider what it was worth if they were real.

I had never spent much time styling my hair. I had used a curling iron I'd found in the bathroom closet, but that was it. It was going to have to hang down. This was the best I could do. Although I knew that I simply wanted to please Huck, I was also aware that it was silly. Sure, I was going as his date, but this wasn't the kind of date that led to something more. It would lead to us having sex tonight. That was it. I was just thankful it was me going with him and not Ray-Ray.

A cocktail party with wealthy, powerful people at the home of a Mafia boss. I laughed at my reflection. What a crazy turn my life had taken. I tucked my phone and lip gloss into a small silver purse I'd found in the closet.

My nerves began to multiply among themselves as I walked down the stairs and toward the voices in the living room. Huck, Gage, Levi, and I were riding to the ranch together. When I'd asked Gage and Levi about their dates, both had smiled and informed me they'd let me know before the night was over. Which meant they intended to find a female at the party and leave with her. That would have been Huck's plan, too, if it wasn't for me. I shoved that thought aside, not wanting to think about it. Not right now.

I didn't speak when I entered the room. Simply because I couldn't. Huck was in a tuxedo. There was nothing that could have prepared me for that sight. I felt breathless, just looking at him. Gage and Levi were also in tuxedos, and they looked nice too. Gage was wearing a cowboy hat with his, which made me smile. They were all attractive men. Huck, however, stood out. His presence commanded attention.

Gage noticed me first, and the appreciative gleam in his eyes made me want to sigh in relief.

"Damn," he drawled.

It was then that Huck looked from his phone, and his gaze locked on me.

I saw his jaw clench as his eyes traveled down my body. I held my breath when his eyes finally met mine again. I licked my lips nervously. He needed to say something. Anything.

"Holy shit," Levi said, walking up behind him.

I didn't look away from Huck. I needed his reassurance. It was pathetic, but I did. Unfortunately, he was the only man whose opinion I cared about.

Finally, he stepped toward me and held out his hand. "Ready?" he asked.

The disappointment sank like a lead weight in my stomach. I walked over to him and took his hand. I still held on to a shred of hope that he would say something. We all walked to the garage. Gage in front, us, then Levi. No one said anything, and the silence was deafening.

I started thinking about my reflection in the mirror. I'd thought I looked nice. Maybe even pretty. The dress had given me confidence. Huck hadn't been impressed though. Or maybe he just didn't do compliments.

Gage climbed into the driver's seat, and Levi went over to sit in the passenger seat. Huck opened the back door and held my hand, helping me up in the heels I was wearing. I sat down and slid over, leaving plenty of room for him. Also because I needed some space. My self-esteem had taken a bit of a blow, and I needed to nurse it for a moment before walking into this land of the wealthy.

Huck didn't leave space between us when he climbed in. His leg was pressed against mine, and he rested his hand on my thigh. I stared down at it, then glanced up at him. Why couldn't I just ask him what he thought of the dress? Or how I looked? We might just be having sex, but I could still ask him what he thought. I wanted to tell him how handsome he was, but I couldn't seem to get the words out. I inhaled the hint of spice and cigar. It made me want to crawl in his lap and bury my face in his neck.

I didn't do that, of course, but I fantasized about it while I stared out the window. His hand tightened on my leg as we pulled through the security gate and onto the road.

Gage and Levi were discussing someone I didn't know who would be there tonight. Garrett didn't trust him, and they were to keep their eyes on him. They made a joke about a silencer, but Huck said nothing. He continued to hold on to my thigh with a firm grip. As if I were going to jump out of the moving vehicle.

I stared at his hand on my thigh, and for the life of me, I couldn't think of a way to ask him what he thought of my dress or how I looked. Everything sounded like I was begging for approval, and I was not going to do that. I might plead with him when he was inside of me, but that was different.

Gage asked Huck something about a deal, and Huck said it would be finalized on Monday. Other than that, nothing else was discussed. When we pulled under the entrance to Hughes Farm, I gasped. Twinkling white lights were everywhere. I sat up and looked out the front window, taking in everything. The entire mansion was lit up. It was breathtaking. Smiling, I glanced back at Huck and found him watching me.

"It looks magical," I said.

He only nodded, but his gaze stayed locked on mine.

Gage pulled the car to a stop in front of the house, and a man opened his door. I realized this was a valet parking situation when Huck stepped out and held his hand out to me. Outside of the car, it was even more incredible. Huck placed his hand on the small of my back as we walked up the path of fairy lights to the front door. I wasn't sure if I'd ever experience anything like this again, so I took in every detail.

"Does he always go all out like this?" I asked Huck.

"Hughes goes all out for everything," was his response, and then he took my hand and tucked it in the crook of his arm as we climbed the stairs.

"The guests tonight, do they all know what he is … what you all are?" I asked.

The entire group went silent. Huck stared at me. Was that something I wasn't supposed to ask?

"What do you mean?" he asked me.

I shrugged. "Exactly what I asked. Do they all know Garrett is the boss and you're"—I waved a hand toward them—"the Mafia?"

"Shit," Gage muttered under his breath.

Huck's hand fisted. "You been snooping, Trinity?" His tone was hard.

I realized then that he had never told me. "No. Maddy told me when I stayed with her. I live with y'all. Even if she hadn't, don't you think I would have figured it out eventually?"

Huck's hand relaxed, and he nodded. "I wasn't aware Maddy had spoken to you about it."

The front door swung open, and we walked inside. This was my first time inside the mansion, and in awe, I paused for a moment. Marble floor and a massive staircase that curled around, going up more than one floor. The chandelier that hung in the entrance was opulent.

"Mr. Kingston," the man at the door greeted Huck, then turned to the others as they entered.

Huck walked us under the chandelier and through a large arched doorway. We made another turn and then went down a few steps before walking out the two open double doors leading out onto a terrace that overlooked an elaborate garden. There wasn't a tree or bush that wasn't twinkling. Music played as people mingled with drinks in their hands.

To the right was a dance floor, and a live band sat off to the left of it. Tuxedo-clad men in cowboy hats and boots and beautiful women draped in expensive jewelry filled the area, making me feel more out of place than I had ever felt in my life.

An older man with a white beard raised his hand in greeting when he saw Huck. "Just the man I wanted to see. Garrett doesn't share you, and I need help with a problem thoroughbred that has excellent bloodlines."

Huck led us over to the older man, who was standing with a younger woman. The woman was currently ogling Huck. She was gorgeous and sophisticated. Her blonde hair was styled in an upswept hairdo, leaving her neck and shoulders bare. Her lean body allowed her to wear the kind of dress I could never get away with. It was so low-cut in the front that it almost went to her navel. She had no worries about her boobs breaking free. They were small and perky. Must be nice.

"Judas," Huck replied with a nod of his head. "I'd be happy to help, but you know Garrett must agree."

Judas chuckled as if that were funny. "Of course," he agreed, and then his eyes went to me. "Who is this stunning beauty?"

"Trinity Bennett," he said. "Trinity, this is Judas Aiken and his wife, Iris. They're old family friends of the Hugheses'."

Oh, wow, this man could be her father, and they were married.

"I'm shocked to see you with a date," Iris piped in with a smirk on her red lips. "You normally leave with a couple on your arms."

Neither Huck nor Judas responded to that comment.

Judas looked back to Huck. "I hear you're breaking a mustang for Blaise."

I tried to stay focused on the conversation. I knew very little about horses, so it was hard to follow. Another lady walked up, and Iris began talking to her. I could feel their gazes on me and hear their hushed tones. Even with the dress, shoes, and jewelry Maddy had sent me, it was clear I didn't fit into this world. I should have tried harder to do something with my hair.

"Let's go get a drink," Huck said to me, and I realized he was done talking to Judas.

Relieved that was over, I went with him to the bar that was set up under a tree with pink blooms.

Huck ordered for us, and I was thankful I hadn't had to tell him something I wanted. When he handed me a glass of champagne, I quickly took a drink, hoping to calm my nerves. I felt him watching me, and I met his gaze.

"Liquid courage," I said with a smile.

The corner of his lips curled up as he took the glass with dark amber liquid in it from the bartender. "This isn't my thing either. Part of the business though," he said, then took a drink.

"Is Garrett married to a woman half his age?" I asked, wondering if that was a thing among these men. I didn't see one older lady in attendance, but there were plenty of older men.

Huck chuckled. "Currently, Garrett isn't married. He's had a few wives over the years. Trev and Blaise don't have the same mother. But Garrett doesn't exactly look old. He might be forty-eight years old, but he could pass for late thirties. Even if he wasn't wealthy and powerful, women would be attracted to him. The Hugheses have good genes."

I wondered how many ex-wives Garrett Hughes had. I couldn't imagine being married to a man like him was easy. My thoughts went to Maddy and Cree. I hoped that her future wasn't going to be similar.

"The boys stayed with their dad then? They didn't go with their mothers?"

Huck took a drink. "Males born into the family don't leave their fathers. They're the next generation. Females often go with their moms, but even when divorce happens, they are still guarded."

Guarded? What did that mean exactly? I started to ask, but I stopped myself. I hadn't witnessed Blaise with Maddy, but she seemed secure in her marriage. I couldn't imagine a man not wanting her. Did she fear losing Cree if that day came?

"What about Hayes?" I asked. He'd left the family.

Huck tensed at the mention of his brother, and I instantly wished I hadn't brought it up.

"Our parents were dead. Different situation," he said. Huck nodded his head toward two men. "Garrett needs me. Walk around, explore. I'll find you later."

He was leaving me alone? I opened my mouth, but Huck was already striding away.

It was clear which one was Garrett Hughes. It wasn't the fact that he was very handsome. As in movie-star attractive. That aside, power seemed to radiate from him. It was as if his mere presence demanded respect. Was Blaise like that? Trev definitely was not. He was easy to be around. He made me laugh. Nothing about Trev Hughes was like the man Huck was now speaking to.

Garrett turned to walk back toward the house, and Huck followed him, along with the other man. I felt lost. Glancing around, looking for a familiar face, I took several more sips of my drink.

"We've not been introduced," a male voice said to my right.

I spun around, startled to see a very clean-cut, tattoo-free, shaven blond man smiling at me. He had no rough edges, much like Trev. He could have been a former frat boy. Privilege and money oozed from him.

"Uh, no, we haven't," I replied, forcing a smile.

He held out his hand. "Jasper Dillard," he said. "Hughes Farm boards our thoroughbred horses."

I slipped my hand into his. "Trinity Bennett," I replied.

"Are you just here as a date? Or do you have a connection to the Hughes family?" he asked.

We shook hands, and I pulled mine free, although he'd tried to hold it a moment longer than was necessary.

"A date," I replied, not sure how to explain how I was connected to the family. Did I say my fiancé had been a Kingston or that I cooked and cleaned for three of Garrett's men or that I was fucking Huck Kingston? Yeah, I wasn't going to get into any of that.

"Huck, correct? I saw you with him when you arrived. You're hard to miss." Jasper was flirting.

"Yes," I replied and took another sip of my champagne.

"Since it seems he's occupied, would you do me the honor of a dance?"

Oh crap. What did I do here? Was I supposed to accept this or turn him down?

A hand touched my waist, and I turned my head, expecting to see Huck, but instead, Trev stood there with his charming smile aimed at Jasper.

"I've been looking for you," he said to me. "I see you've met Jasper."

Jasper's gaze was now on Trev, and I could see the confusion in his expression. I'd arrived with Huck, but now, Trev was acting as if I belonged with him.

"Yes, she was alone, and I hated to see a beautiful woman standing all by herself," Jasper replied.

Trev looked at me and winked. "She's not alone, I promise. It was good to see you, Jasper. Have some of the punch. It's got an extra kick," Trev said. Then, with his hand on my back, he led me away from Jasper.

"Punch? Is there really punch here?" I asked. This did not seem like the type of event that would have punch.

"Fuck no," Trev replied with a smirk. "Jasper thinks he's more important than he is. His father is new money. Bought into an internet business that ended up exploding about six years ago. They purchased some thoroughbreds from us and pretend to know what the fuck they are doing on the track. They're also not in the realm of the know when it comes to the family. To them, we are a successful racehorse farm. Nothing more."

Interesting. I would have thought everyone here knew.

"Where are you taking me?" I asked Trev as we walked away from the main party.

The veranda wrapped around the massive home, and soon, we were out of the twinkling lights.

"To the better party," he said, leaning down near my ear.

"Better party?" I asked, curious.

A waterfall was the first thing I noticed, but as we got closer, I realized the waterfall was the focal point of a pool. Not just any pool, but one that belonged on some tropical island resort. There was music playing back here, too, but it was over a speaker system, and it was current hits. I looked around and noticed this was a younger crowd. They were dressed just as elegantly, and there was a bar set up back here too. Along with servers walking around with fancy finger foods on their trays.

"That shit back there is torture. I show face throughout the party to keep my father happy, but he allows me to hold my own party back here. Many of them have parents at the stuffy shit that you were being forced to endure, but some are just my friends."

Huck wouldn't know where to find me back here. I didn't want to go back to the other party alone, but I was torn. What if he returned and I wasn't there?

"As much fun as this seems, I should probably go back to the other party. Huck went inside with your father, but when he returns and can't find me ..." I shrugged.

Trev smirked. "Teach his ass right to leave you to the likes of Jasper fucking Dillard."

"Maybe, but your dad is his boss," I pointed out.

He rolled his eyes and sighed. "Fine. I'll go back with you if you want me to. Protect you from the Jaspers until Huck returns."

He had at least fifty guests back here. It would be selfish of me to ask that of him, although it would make it so much easier on me.

I shook my head. "No, that's okay. I'll be fine. Thank you though. I wish I could stay."

Trev leaned down and pressed a kiss to my cheek. "I'll check on you later," he assured me.

I turned and headed back toward the path we'd taken. For a moment, I was alone and could prepare myself to walk back into the intimidating crowd. Hopefully, Huck was back, and I wouldn't be expected to mingle alone. Maybe Maddy had arrived by now. That would make this enjoyable.

Turning the corner back into the world of twinkling lights and live music, I scanned the crowd for a familiar face. My champagne glass was empty, and I started for the bar when a server walked by with a tray of filled flutes. I exchanged my empty one for a new one, then took a sip while watching the intimidating strangers.

"It is you. When I saw you earlier, I thought my eyes were playing tricks on me. Now, tell me how the fuck you managed to get invited to a party like this one?"

There were moments in life that surprised you. Some were good. Some were painful. Then, there were others that reached inside you and twisted until you couldn't breathe. It was a level of horror that was hard to put into words.

The latter was one of those moments. Bile rose in my throat, and I had to grip the flute in my hands to keep from dropping it. I was unable to move. If I turned my head even slightly, I'd see him. I was afraid of my reaction if I had to look at that face. For six months, I'd lived in that house, and he'd never come around. My father's death and Hayes's death, I'd escaped his return. Tabitha loved to tell people he was unable to be there because he was currently in Guatemala or Honduras with a medical mission's team. When, in truth, Roy Hayley had never once done anything for someone else out of the goodness of his heart. Vile people didn't go on mission trips.

"What? No hello for your brother?" he asked.

"Why are you here?" I asked through clenched teeth, refusing to look at the monster in my nightmares.

The evil in his laugh made me cringe. "Because I know the right people. Make the connections. With a face like mine, you can work your way into anywhere."

I wanted to throw up all the champagne in my stomach. Preferably on his feet.

"The real question is, how did you get into an event such as this? I can't imagine after the death of your minister fiancé that you stepped up in the world."

I looked around, needing to find someone. Anyone to get me out of here. I should have stayed with Trev. Why was he here? Roy wasn't wealthy. He had barely finished college.

His fingers wrapped around my arm, and panic began to claw at me with talons I knew would eventually pull me under. I had to escape. I had to get away. I felt my throat closing, as if he were literally choking me as I stood here.

I moved quickly, jerking my arm from his hold, and then turned and ran for the entrance into the house. I didn't care if anyone saw me. Nothing mattered but finding somewhere safe to hide. The glass in my hand slipped, and I heard it shatter, but I didn't stop. I ran inside the Hugheses' mansion, and without knowing where I was going, I turned down a hallway, hoping a bathroom appeared—or any room I could lock myself in.

I turned into the first room on my left and closed the door, locking it behind me. Books surrounded me. Ceiling to floor on all four walls. A library. I tried to find a focal point and focus on it. I couldn't let the panic take me. I had to stay alert. I heard myself gasping and felt the burning in my lungs as I fought the phantom hands around my throat.

Breathe, Trinity. Breathe, I told myself.

I began to pace. The grip on my throat dug in deeper. It wasn't going to stop.

My legs buckled under me, and I kicked off the heels and pulled my knees to my chin, wrapping my arms around my legs. This was the only way I could find comfort. Closing my eyes, I began to rock.

Block it out. Block it all out.

It would end soon. Soon. It would end soon.

Chapter TWENTY-SIX

HUCK

"It's Trinity. You need to come with me." The look on Gage's face was a mixture most didn't see and live to tell about it. Something was very fucking bad.

"What happened?" I asked as I walked out of Garrett's office.

"I don't fucking know, but there's a son of a bitch who might have seen his last sunrise."

Frustration over not getting more information and seeing the rage in Gage's eyes was quickly turning to fear. Where the fuck was Trinity?

"She ran in the house. I can't find her," Gage said, turning and looking down the hallway as if the answer would appear.

I pulled my phone from my coat pocket and clicked the app that tracked her. I'd put it on her phone before I gave it back to her the day we took her.

"This way," I said, stalking past Gage.

My heart was fucking slamming against my chest. I'd left her out there for maybe forty minutes. What the fuck could have happened?

"Who was she with?" I asked as I continued toward the library.

"I don't know him. I haven't asked yet. I've been looking for her. But his fucking face is memorized."

My entire body tensed up. Someone had fucked with what belonged to me. Gage wasn't killing anyone. That was my fucking job.

I grabbed the doorknob to the library and turned. It was locked. Fuck! I pounded my fist on the door.

"Trinity!" I called out.

No answer.

I tried again.

Nothing.

"Don't rip the door off. Where's Garrett? Or Ms. Jimmie?" Gage asked.

I didn't fucking know. Garrett had left me in his office to look over some footage from a security camera. I had no clue where he'd gone after. I pounded on the door again, calling her name.

"Lord, what a racket," Ms. Jimmie, the Hugheses' cook and house manager, was walking toward us with a key ring in her hand. "Step aside, boy. I'll open it up. Don't know why it's locked."

She rattled the keys while she found the correct one, then slid it inside. When the door swung open, she stepped back. "Leave it unlocked when you leave, boys," she said. I pushed by her, and my eyes scanned the dark room until they landed on Trinity.

FUCK!

I rushed over to the corner where she was rocking on the floor. Her knees tucked under her chin and her eyes closed tightly. She was muttering something, but I couldn't understand what she was saying.

"Jesus Christ," Gage said behind me.

"Trinity, look at me, baby," I said as gently as I could.

She kept rocking. I battled with what to do. What was happening? She clearly hadn't heard me. This was what Maddy had seen. This shit was not okay. What horrific trauma would cause this?

I cupped her face with my hand. "Trinity, please, baby. Open your eyes and look at me."

She paused her rocking a moment, and the muttering stopped, but her eyes stayed tightly closed.

I brushed my thumb over her cheek. "It's me. Open your eyes. You're okay. I'm here."

She sucked in air as if she was struggling to breathe. What the fuck was happening now? I'd never felt so helpless in my life.

"She's choking." Gage sounded panicked. "Why the fuck is she choking?"

I didn't know!

"Trinity, you're okay. You can breathe, baby. Please take a deep breath." It was all I could do to keep my voice calm.

She gasped loudly and let out a cry. That was it. I couldn't handle any more of this. I pulled her into my arms and carried her to the leather sofa. I sat down, cradling her, and she started breathing normally again. Her hands had released her knees, and I watched as her eyelashes fluttered open. When her eyes met mine, she froze for a moment, then threw her arms around my neck, clinging to me as if her life depended on it. A loud, heart-wrenching sob shook her body. It was followed by another. I'd never heard anyone cry like this.

Knowing something had hurt her so badly that it caused this kind of reaction was fucking unbearable.

Someone was going to die a very brutal death. I didn't know who yet, but I would. I held her tightly, whispering in her ear. Promising her that she was okay. I had her. No one could get to her. I wouldn't let anything happen to her. She continued to sob, ripping me to fucking shreds with each pitiful wail.

I ran my hand down her hair and pressed kisses to the side of her head. I wasn't just consoling her, I realized. I was consoling me too. This shit wasn't happening again. Whatever the fuck I had to do to fix this, I would do it.

Gage was standing in front of the door, which he'd closed behind us, with his arms crossed over his chest, looking ready to murder the entire guest list. His jaw ticced as he stood there. He didn't say anything, but he didn't have to. If he felt even half of what I did right now, I understood.

My mind was reeling over who at this party could have caused this. I'd never even seen her tear up before. Not once, and women fucking cried. But not Trinity. She was sobbing now, and her hold on me was a death grip. I didn't loosen my hold on her. For the moment, I wasn't sure if I was going to be able to ever let go of her. I wanted to fix this. Make sure this never happened again. I couldn't stand the thought of it.

Her sobs began to ease, and they became small hiccups. I wasn't letting go of her. I couldn't and keep my sanity. I kissed her cheek, then leaned back to look at her face. Her eyes were swollen and red-rimmed. She looked so damn broken.

"I'm sorry," she whispered.

If she'd taken a sword and shoved it through my heart, it would have hurt less than hearing her say those two words.

I rested my forehead against hers. "Please, Trinity. Don't say that. Ever. I don't want to ever hear you apologize for anything the rest of my life. I don't think I can handle it."

She sniffled. "I made a scene. I broke a glass," she said softly.

"I don't fucking care. All I care about is that you're okay," I told her.

I reached up and held her face in my hands. "Who was he? I don't need why. I don't need an explanation. I need a name. That's all. Nothing more."

The fear in her eyes was only going to make his death more violent. Had my brother known about this? Had he seen her like this? If he'd known, wouldn't he have contacted me? He might not have taken lives, but I fucking did.

"He's here," she whispered. "I don't know why."

"His name," I repeated as firmly as I could without scaring her.

"Roy … Hayley."

The stepbrother. Motherfucker!

The library door opened, and I knew that within thirty minutes, Roy Hayley would be tied up in the cells underground until I arrived. Gage had been waiting for a name. He had it.

I pressed a kiss to her lips, then pulled her back against my chest and held her. Until I had her safely back in my bed, I wasn't letting go of her.

Chapter TWENTY-SEVEN

TRINITY

Eight years. It had been eight years since I'd cried. Not even a tear. Nothing. I'd go to my dark place to survive the horror, but no tears ever came. When I finally snapped out of it, I was always numb and dry-eyed. I tried to cry so many times, but I never could. It always felt like there was a wall inside that blocked out any deep emotion. I'd accepted it was probably why I couldn't fall in love. The wall protected me. It surrounded me. It was my strength.

When I'd opened my eyes, Huck had been there. His eyes full of concern, his words soothing. Something shattered. It felt like every emotion I'd held back for so long broke free and came roaring back to life. All the pain, hurt, heartache, anguish, sorrow, loss, regret—it all flooded me at once. Without meaning to, he had taken down my wall, then held me while my heart and head accepted the return of all I'd kept out.

If he hadn't been there to hold me, I wasn't sure I could have survived the onslaught. Once my sobs had finally subsided, I'd felt exhausted yet free.

Huck carried me to the car, held me in his lap the entire ride home, and then carried me down to his room. Since I'd opened my eyes and pulled myself out of the dark place, he'd been holding me. His arms had to be tired, but I had been reluctant to let go of the security that he provided. Levi had driven us home but left again after we got out of the Escalade.

I felt guilty for being the reason Huck had left the party early. At least the other two were staying there. I'd not even gotten a chance to see Maddy and thank her for the dress, shoes, and jewelry.

Why had Roy been there? I cringed, thinking about his touch on my arm.

I tightened my hold on Huck without thinking. He sat down on his bed with me. I started to tell him to let me down, but he lowered his mouth and kissed me. His tongue slid across my bottom lip, and I opened, feeling needy for a taste of him. He'd been distant earlier, and I craved this connection. It was a reassurance that I didn't need to get confused with permanency. But tonight, affection helped pull me back from my past.

His hand slid up my side until it covered my right breast. I arched into his touch. If he touched me, it would wash away all the dirty that came with memories of my past. His thumb brushed back and forth over my nipple. I turned toward him and pulled up my skirt so I could straddle his lap. His hands moved around to cup my bottom, and he paused when he felt bare skin. I couldn't wear panties with this dress.

"Trinity." His voice was hoarse.

"Hmm?" I replied, pressing a kiss to the side of his mouth.

"Why aren't you wearing panties?"

"Because you could see my panty line in this dress."

He squeezed my butt cheeks and groaned. "I was just going to kiss you, baby. You've been through it tonight. We don't need to fuck. Let me put you in one of my shirts and hold you until you fall asleep."

I slid forward until I could feel his erection between my legs. "Or you could fuck me until I pass out," I suggested.

His grip on my bottom tightened. "I'm real wound up right now. A lot of shit in my head. Seeing you like that has me wired. You need gentle. I can hold you gently. Can't let myself get carried away."

I leaned back and looked at him. "You're worried you'll fuck me too hard?"

His jaw clenched, and he nodded. I tried not to smile. I called it *fuck* or *fucking* because it turned him on when I said the word.

"Maybe I need to be fucked hard. Maybe having your hands all over me will take away the bad stuff. Make me think of only you."

The flash of hunger in his eyes was different somehow. It made me shiver. Was it territorial or possessive? What was the cause of it?

When he didn't move, I pulled my dress up enough so that he could see me, and I slid my hand down to play with my clit. His eyes followed me, and his body jerked when my finger slid in between my folds.

"You sure you want this tonight?" His voice was deeper.

I bit my bottom lip and nodded. I needed it. I needed to just remember him. When I slept, I wanted it to be Huck that I saw. He could wash away all the nightmares.

His hand went to the zipper on the back of my dress, and he slid it down. Then, he pulled it up over my head. I raised my arms so he could take it off. His eyes went to my boobs, and I let my arms down slowly. I watched him as his hands covered my breasts and held them.

"You were naked under that dress tonight," he said in a reverent tone.

I shivered.

"You were already the most beautiful woman at the fucking party. I was struggling with not touching you the way I wanted to. If I'd known you had nothing on under this dress, I'd have taken you to that damn library and fucked you."

He'd thought I was beautiful. Why that made me tear up, I didn't know. I'd just cried for the first time in eight years. I hoped I wasn't going to start crying about everything. My heart felt tight as I looked at him.

He lowered his head but kept his eyes locked on mine while he began to lick and suck on my breasts. My hands threaded through his hair as I watched him. Something had changed. I couldn't explain it, but there was this pull inside of me. A desperation of sorts to be near him. Almost as if I couldn't survive without being as close to him as I could get.

I began to shove off his tuxedo coat. I wanted his chest bare, our skin touching. He stopped what he was doing and helped me get the coat and his shirt off his body. I splayed my hands over his bare chest and soaked in the warmth of his skin. I loved how he felt, how he looked. Leaning down, I licked his tight, flat nipple, and he made a noise low in his throat. Switching to the other one, I did the same. The urge to lick his entire chest began to take over me, and I started licking and kissing the taut skin that stretched over his muscles.

"Baby, you've got about five more seconds of this," he growled.

Frantically, I kissed the spot over his heart and then licked at the tribal tattoo there. In one swift move, Huck had me on my back underneath him as he began to unzip his pants. His eyes locked on mine. I lowered my gaze, wanting to see him when he was free of his bottoms. Tonight, he had on black boxer briefs. When he pulled those down and his erection sprang free, I realized I loved that too. The metal bar taunted me as he moved over my body.

He took my right leg and spread me open. "As much as I want to eat that pussy, I need inside you. Can't wait."

I bent my knees up as he held his cock in his grip, then ran it along my wet entrance. He groaned as he sank inside me, grabbing my hips and jerking me forward until he hit that spot I knew would send me over the edge.

I watched his face as he pumped inside of me, loving how he looked. The way his mouth would open slightly and his eyelids lowered. I could see the pleasure in his expression, and knowing it was my body that was doing that to him made my heart soar.

"Does it hurt like this?" he asked me, looking down at me with a feral gleam in his eyes.

"A little," I admitted, "but I want it harder."

He let out an animalistic sound and started slamming into me with more force. "This it? Is this what you want? You want my dick to stretch that tight little pussy?"

I nodded, panting and grabbing at the quilt underneath us for support.

"Rub your clit," he ordered.

I let go of the quilt and began to massage it the way I would if I were alone.

"That's the prettiest fucking pussy I've ever seen."

That made me rub harder. I loved the way he talked to me during sex. His words alone could send me into an orgasm. I wondered if we could try that sometime.

He pulled out of me then and grabbed my hips and flipped me over. "Hands and knees, baby."

We hadn't done this position before. I hurried to obey, and he grabbed my hips again and then shoved inside of me. It was deeper than it had ever been, and I hadn't thought that was possible. He began to thrust in and out of me.

"FUCK! I'm not gonna last long like this. Your fucking ass is bouncing."

I was close. I started pushing back when he thrust forward. The spiral into bliss was coming. I'd never needed it as much as I did in this moment. My pussy was throbbing, and I squirmed against him.

"I know I said I was gonna stop coming in you until we got you the shot, but I lied. I want to coat you with my fucking cum. Pump you so full of me that you leak for days."

It was with those words that pleasure rippled through my body, and I cried out his name.

His shout followed, and I could feel the pulse of his fluid gush inside of me. Another orgasm washed over me, and I moaned as my body shook.

When it finally eased, I sank down onto the mattress, and Huck moved off the bed. He was only gone a moment before he was back, wiping up my thighs and legs, then the quilt beneath me. Once he finished, he climbed on the bed and pulled my back against his chest.

"You didn't clean yourself," I whispered.

"Not ready to wipe your juices off me just yet," he whispered, then kissed below my ear. "Sleep. I'm here."

Chapter TWENTY-EIGHT

HUCK

Maddy was sleeping on the sofa in my room in case Trinity woke up. Blaise was at the house while the girls slept downstairs, and Ms. Jimmie was keeping Cree. Levi and Gage were standing in the cellars located under the ranch.

I'd spent the drive over here remembering how Trinity had looked in that library. How her sobs had destroyed me. The fantastic sex hadn't removed the need for revenge. It might have heightened it. Being inside Trinity only made me want to possess her more. Instead of fucking her out of my system, it seemed she was locking me down every time I sank inside her tight cunt.

I slammed through the last steel door and closed it behind me. The man currently hanging by his hands in the middle of the concrete room hadn't been touched. Gage had sworn to me he'd refrain from doing anything. I wanted this. However, Gage had tied him up painfully enough that he was groaning through the gag in his mouth. His toes barely grazed the floor.

The small trickle of blood running down his arms from the locks on his wrists had him crying like a fucking baby.

I walked up to him and pulled the gag off. "Who are you?" I barked at him, already knowing who the fuck he was.

"You've got the wrong guy. I don't know you. I came with a woman I'd met at a bar last week. I'm an accountant—"

"YOUR FUCKING NAME," I cut him off.

"Roy Hayley. I don't even live around here. I live in Pensacola. I was in town on business and met this woman."

I held out my hand to Gage, who placed the knife I needed in it. We'd done this show many times before. But never had I done it with this much rage and hate. It had always been business. Never personal. It took on a whole new meaning when it was personal.

I held the blade against his cheek as he whimpered. "Unless I ask you a fucking question, don't talk."

"Okay," he whispered, holding still, afraid he'd get cut if he moved.

I wanted to laugh. The bastard was worried about me slicing his cheek. He had no idea. But first, I was getting answers. I ran the knife down to his chin, leaving a bloody trail as I went. He let out a long wail. Jesus, he was a pussy. The men we normally had down here wouldn't make a fucking sound until we removed a finger or an ear. The tongue also got a reaction.

"How do you know Trinity?" I asked him.

"That's what this is about? Trinity? What did that bitch tell you?"

Typically, I had control. I could pace myself. I let them beg and plead. That wasn't the case when someone called my woman a bitch. I was in his face, seething, as I buried the knife in his limp dick. He screamed as I twisted it. The screams continued while I pulled the knife out and wiped the blood on his pants leg.

"Let's try this again. How do you know Trinity?"

His eyes were wide, and the understanding that he wasn't going to walk out of here alive was starting to sink in. "She's … she's … my step … step … sister," he panted through his pain.

"The Tabitha bitch is your mother then," I said.

"My mom raised her. Whatever she told you is a lie," he started.

Gage let out a laugh as I took my knife and buried it in his thigh. Another agonized scream tore from his chest as he began to tremble.

I turned and looked at Levi and Gage. Levi was sitting on a chair with his ankle propped on his knee and his arms crossed over his chest. Gage was grinning like the crazed psychopath he was while watching.

"He's not very bright," I said to them.

"Nope," Levi replied.

"Those are the best ones," Gage said.

I turned back to Roy. "You get one warning because it is fucking clear you need it. I'm going to ask you some more questions, and at any time you lie or you degrade or say anything negative about Trinity, I'll take one of your fingers. Do you understand me?"

He nodded. Blood and tears streaked his face.

"When he says take one of your fingers, he means he will cut it off. Just clarifying because you appear to be a dumbass," Gage called out.

I smirked. "Now, what did you do to Trinity in the past that would cause her to get so upset at your mere appearance that she'd run away from you?"

He blinked, and snot bubbles came out of his nose. He started to shake his head, and I moved to go to him. Finger number one was going. He seemed to understand that.

"No, wait. I-I was her older brother. We didn't get along," he stammered out.

I reached up and held his right hand while he begged and cried. I took his pinkie. The man could wail like a damn baby. He was loud. Holding his pinkie, I showed it to him. Then, he threw up. I tossed the finger down to lie on top of his vomit. When he was finished puking and muttering, I slapped his face.

"SHUT UP!"

He quieted down.

"Now, let's try this again. What did you do to Trinity?"

He gasped and choked as the blood from where I'd taken his finger poured down his arm. "You're gonna kill me anyway," he sobbed.

"Think of it as a cleansing of the soul," Gage suggested.

I could hear Levi's chuckle.

"Who are you? Why are you doing this?"

I could ignore him. I could take another finger. Cause more pain, but I wanted him to die knowing why he was dying. Who I was. I walked up and pressed the knife under his chin.

"I'm the lucky son of a bitch who has her in my bed. I fucked her sweet pussy and tucked her in before I came to deal with your worthless ass. That's who the fuck I am."

He gasped, and more fucking snot bubbles came out. "So, she got herself hooked up with psychos. She was just engaged to a minister. He died."

I pushed the knife harder until it broke the skin under his chin. "The minister was my brother. And we're the fucking Mafia."

His eyes rounded, and he choked. I moved back from him.

"I'm getting bored with this bullshit. Tell me what the fuck you did to my woman when she was growing up." I'd just called her my woman. It wasn't lost on me, and I knew it wasn't lost on Gage and Levi. I heard Gage clear his throat, but I ignored it. Yeah, I'd fucking said it.

"Mom didn't let her eat," he said in between gasps. "She called her fat and wrapped up her boobs because she said they were fat. She went without meals a lot, and if she got caught eating anything without permission, she was punished."

Yeah, Tabitha was next. I was seething as I stared at him.

"How was she punished?" I asked through clenched teeth.

"Closet in the basement. Mom locked her in there. Would tie her hands up and gag her, then leave her there for days at a time. She'd ..." He swallowed and closed his eyes. "She'd end up using the bathroom on herself."

I walked over and grabbed a metal pole we used for beating, picked it up, and roared as I began to hit the wall over and over again. I had to do something, or I was going to combust. That fucker had to stay alive long enough for me to get it all out of him, but I wasn't sure I could handle it. Dropping the pole, I stalked back over to him. Inches from his blood and snot-covered face.

"What else?"

"Mom said she had demons in her, and that was why she had big boobs at eleven. She started her period early, too, and Mom was convinced that was a sign of the Devil. Then, at thirteen—" He stopped. "Look, I didn't live there. I was eight years older than her. We never lived in the house together. Mom married her dad the summer I went off to college. I just visited on holidays."

I held the knife to his ear. "But it wasn't your mother she ran from tonight."

"Please, no. Please," he sobbed. "You're gonna kill me either way," he moaned.

I nodded. "Fuck yeah, I am. But you can die quickly, or we can prolong it. I can take you one small slice at a time until you bleed out. Pieces are easier to dispose of."

"Oh God," he cried out.

"God doesn't give a fuck about you," I spit at him. "Tell me what you did, or I'll take this ear."

"Probably a better look for him. He's got fucked up ears," Gage said from behind me.

Roy let out a strangled moan. "I was twenty-one and horny. Her body was developed for thirteen. More than most girls I knew. Mom kept her locked away when I was there, but when she would leave …" He closed his eyes. "Just go ahead and kill me."

"I know you didn't rape her because *my* dick took her virginity. What did you do?"

It took every ounce of control I had not to reach up and just break his fucking neck. She had been thirteen, and he'd used the word *horny*. Fucking hell!

I heard Gage whisper, "Fuck," under his breath.

I hadn't told them about her being a virgin. It wasn't their damn business. But I wanted them to know. I had taken that pussy, and it was mine now.

"When Mom left, I'd wait until she snuck out of her room to get something to eat. Then, I'd corner her and force her to take off the bandage wrap Mom kept wrapped around her boobs so I could see them."

"HOW did you make her?"

He swallowed hard, and blood from the cut under his chin ran down his neck. "I pushed her down." He paused. "Kicked her," he groaned, "until she was hurt and couldn't move."

My entire body was shaking. I had to get this out of him before I unleashed the fury burning through my chest.

"You knocked her unconscious?"

He sobbed. "No. I … I just kicked her. Cracked her ribs, bruised her, knocked the breath out of her." He cried out even though I hadn't touched him.

"And?" I bit out, not sure I could handle any more.

"I … I … was horny. She had … her boobs were big. I was a kid."

I took a step toward him, and he let out a wail.

"I masturbated on her!" he shouted. "I would shoot it on her boobs and sometimes her face. Once, I opened her mouth, and … I'd never seen boobs like hers. I was just a ki—"

The knife slit his throat, and I watched as blood gurgled out of his mouth. His eyes went wide as he choked on his own blood. The life went out of his eyes.

Then, I threw my head back and yelled at the top of my lungs while rage pounded in my veins.

I'd killed the fucker without thinking. I wanted him to suffer more. But I snapped. The image in my head of my Trinity hurt and unable to fucking move while that sick son of a bitch masturbated on her was too much. I'd wanted it to end. Him to fucking stop. I couldn't take it anymore.

"I wanted a slice at him," Gage sighed. "Sick fucker. I hope there's a hell he can burn in."

Chapter TWENTY-NINE

TRINITY

Huck's warm body was behind me when I opened my eyes. His arm was around my waist, and the smell of spice surrounded me. I inhaled deeply and snuggled closer. Closing my eyes again, I started to relax when they snapped back open. I had to make breakfast. I'd slept so hard that I had no idea what time it was. Huck was still asleep, so that was a good sign. My internal clock was pretty accurate.

I started to ease out of his hold when his arm locked down tight on me, and he pulled me back against him, making a grunting sound. Smiling, I tilted my head back to see he was still asleep—or at least partly. I waited a minute, then tried again to ease out from under his arm, but this time, he rolled onto his back and brought me with him until part of my body lay across him.

His eyes met mine then. The sleepy look with his half-hooded gaze was sexy. I wanted to stay down here with him, but just because I was screwing him didn't mean I was free from my jobs.

"I have to go make breakfast," I reminded him, then placed a kiss on his chest.

"Not this morning," he mumbled. "Staying your ass in this bed with me."

Laughing, I reached up and touched his face. I loved his face. He might possibly have the best face on the planet.

"Gage and Levi will be upset. They need to be fed."

"They're not here," he replied, then pushed me back and hovered over me. He lowered his head and kissed my collarbone, then my neck. "You're staying right here with me all fucking day," he whispered in my ear.

I shivered. That sounded wonderful.

"You don't have to work today?" I asked.

"Gage and Levi are going into the shop for me today."

"So, we are going to do what in bed all day?"

He ran his hand down my side and then over my thigh to slip it between my legs. "I'm going to eat my breakfast first. After I get enough of this sweet pussy in my mouth, we're going to fuck."

My pussy clenched. "All day?"

"Mmm, we'll rest some. I want to fuck you in the shower. I want to keep my dick buried in you after we come and just hold you."

I bit my bottom lip. "I know you've pulled out a lot, but there have been many times you didn't."

He bent his head and placed a kiss on my nipple. "I'm not gonna lie. The more I think about my baby growing inside you, the more I want it. Makes me fucking hard to think about it."

I froze and stared up at him. "What?"

I was not ready to be a mother. I hadn't had a mother. I wasn't sure I could be a good one. And he didn't know yet about my other stuff. Sure, he'd seen me at my worst yesterday, but when he found out why, he would probably be worried about my ability to be a good mother.

"That brain is spinning," he whispered, pressing a kiss on the corner of my mouth.

"It's just … we can't. I mean, there's a lot about my past that you don't know. And a baby is a big deal. It means commitment, and I am not letting you take my baby and kick me out when you're tired of me."

Huck grabbed my wrists and pinned them above my head as his body covered mine. "I don't think a man can be any more committed to a pussy as I am to yours."

He was grinning like this was funny. It was not funny. It was serious. I could be pregnant now. I'd been happily fucking away, not worrying about it. But what if I was?

"Real commitment. Not fucking." I frowned, wishing he'd take this seriously.

Huck pushed my legs open with his knee, then settled his cock at my entrance. "You're already fucking wet. Such a good girl," he said as he slid into me slowly.

This was unfair. He was trying to distract me with sex.

"Huck," I breathed. "We need to discuss this. Pull out, okay?"

"Mmm, but I want my girl's cunt to be full of my cum all day," he whispered as he slid almost out of me, then pushed back as deep as he could go.

A moan escaped me, and for a minute, I forgot what it was we were talking about.

"My pussy," he said with a harder thrust. "No other dick is ever getting near this pussy."

He grunted as his pace began to pick up. I pulled my knees up and cried out his name as he sank into me. The metal bar rubbed inside of me.

"I love that fucking piercing," I moaned.

He chuckled against my neck. "My Prince Albert?"

"What?" I panted.

"The piercing is called a Prince Albert," he explained.

Then, he began to do something with his hips that made it rub the one spot over and over. Every part of my body began to tremble.

"That feel good?" he asked.

I couldn't make words at the moment. I just nodded and moved my hips with his as he teased and rubbed the same spot deep inside me. My nails dug into his biceps, and I was pretty sure I was crying or pleading. The climax that pierced through me was earth-shattering. The gush between my legs was more than usual.

Huck shouted my name and shot his release inside of me. For the moment, I was experiencing bliss and did not care. I wanted to keep him here forever. His mouth covered mine, and his tongue swept against mine slowly. I held on to him, using my mouth and my body to say the words I couldn't.

When he broke our kiss, he kept his face close to mine. His warm breath heated my skin as he continued to slowly pump inside of me. Even though we'd both reached our orgasm.

"I'll get you birth control," he said against my cheek. "But even if I've not put a baby in you yet, you're still mine. You're not leaving me, Trinity. I'll fucking chain you to my bed and eat your pussy three times a day. I won't let you go."

Tears stung my eyes. It was so odd to feel that again. I buried my face in his shoulder to hide my emotion. I didn't want him to think I was making this about more than just sex. He'd made that clear. But when he tore down my emotional walls, he did something else too. He'd given me back my ability to love. Something I'd thought was broken in me. Maybe it had been, but Huck had healed it.

"Do you want to leave me?" he asked, stilling his slow thrust inside me.

I shook my head and gulped.

"I can feel your tears on my skin, sweetheart, and right now, I'm not in a headspace to see you cry. So, I'm gonna need to know why."

I took a deep breath. "I'm scared." There. That was the best I could do.

He didn't want to know that I was crying because I was in love with him. Telling Huck Kingston I was in love with him would be a sure way to get kicked out of his bed.

"Of what? I'll fix it."

I smiled at that response. He thought he could fix everything.

"Losing this," I admitted.

"My dick?"

I laughed. "No, and yes."

He kissed my neck. "I swear to you that you own my cock. Completely own it. Your cunt has ruined me. That is not something you need to fear. If you need proof, give me five more minutes, and we'll start round two."

I shook my head. "You'll get tired of me."

He moved off me then and turned me on my side, forcing me to look at him. His thumb brushed the tears off my face as he scowled. "What do I need to do to assure you that won't ever happen? Fuck, Trinity, I've never brought a woman to my bed. I've never fucked the same one more than a handful of times, and that list is small. I don't eat pussy. I get my dick sucked. But I can't seem to get enough of yours. Walking into that party last night with you on my arm, I felt like a motherfucking king. You will have to kill me to get away from me."

He looked so fierce as he said all those things. It wasn't love. But it was something. It was more than just screwing.

Maybe I could love enough for both of us. If he wanted me this much, then that was enough.

I nodded. "But no babies. Okay? Not for a long time."

He smirked. "Okay. But if I've put one in you already, that shit is done."

I didn't want to worry about that. Not today. "We should be careful from now on."

He frowned and cupped his hand over my pussy. A finger slid inside, and he groaned. "But, fuck, I love feeling my cum up in you."

I laughed. "We will go get me the shot."

He leaned forward and kissed me softly on the lips.

"Never claimed anyone before," he whispered. "Never will again."

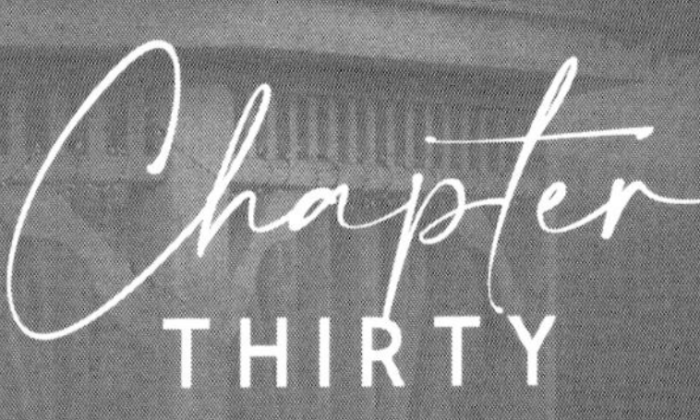

Chapter THIRTY

TRINITY

I'd placed the cinnamon rolls on the island with the rest of the breakfast when Huck walked into the kitchen. I had butterflies in my stomach, my heart had that funny feeling, and the smile on my face was unavoidable. I was in love.

He didn't look at the food, but his eyes held mine as he walked toward me. I fought the urge to throw myself in his arms. Sure, we had spent yesterday in bed, in the shower, in bed again, in a bubble bath, on the sofa—you get the picture—but I never knew when Huck wasn't going to turn cold.

"Don't like waking up and you not being there," he said when he reached me. His hand gripped my waist and tugged me against him. "I want you in my bed when I open my eyes."

I tilted my head back to look up at him. "I have a job."

He scowled down at me. "I need to change that."

I shook my head. "No. Gage and Levi expect breakfast when they get up."

Huck lowered his head until his mouth was inches from mine. "I don't give a fuck. I want you in my arms when I wake up."

I put my hands on his chest. "Huck, what are we doing?"

He kissed the side of my mouth. "I'm currently trying to grope you."

I laughed and shook my head. "No. I mean …" I paused.

This was nice. No, it was wonderful. Did I really want to press him to put a name to it? Yesterday, he'd been different. He had said things to me and promised me this was long-term.

"I'm just here for the food. Please carry on." Gage's voice stopped me from having to decide what I was going to say.

I smiled and started to move out of Huck's arms, but he held me tightly, not letting me go.

"You made their damn breakfast," he said, lowering his mouth to my neck to kiss it.

"Aren't you hungry?" I asked him.

"Very, but what I want is between your legs."

"Get a room," Levi said, then yawned as he walked into the kitchen.

"Shut up. Let them go at it. I like watching," Gage told him, making me blush.

Huck glared at him over my head, which only made him laugh.

"We got that thing to handle today. Either fuck her or eat."

Huck nodded, and his hold on me loosened. "Eat with me," he said.

I followed him to the island and put the blueberry pancakes and a piece of bacon on my plate, then walked over to sit at the table. Gage pushed the maple syrup in my direction. I reached for it as Huck sat down beside me. His plate was loaded this morning. He never ate that much. I didn't say anything though. I loved knowing he liked eating my food.

Gage was looking at me as he chewed his food. I met his gaze, and he glanced at Huck a moment, then back at me.

"Trinity, you never talk about your parents," he said.

Huck turned his head to look at Gage. I saw a silent conversation they seemed to have with their eyes. What was this about?

"Uh, well, my mom died, giving birth to me. My dad died of a heart attack ten, well, almost eleven months ago," I told him.

He leaned back in his chair with his cup of coffee. "Your dad ever remarry?"

Tabitha was not someone I wanted to talk about. Especially after last night.

"Yes. When I was ten."

Huck slid his hand over my thigh and held it there.

Gage's gaze turned serious. "You don't like her."

"No."

"Why?"

Huck's hand squeezed my leg, but he didn't tell Gage to stop asking questions. I wasn't sure why he was asking, and it seemed strange, as if they'd discussed this before doing it.

"She was mean. She didn't like me," I told him.

I didn't want to talk about this. My chest felt tight, and I put my hand over Huck's.

"No more," Huck said to Gage.

Gage nodded and set his cup down.

Huck turned his hand over and threaded his fingers through mine. It wasn't much, but that simple connection made the tension ease, and I was able to eat the rest of my breakfast. He didn't let my hand go until we were both done.

"You okay?" he asked me when I put my fork down.

I nodded.

He leaned down and pressed a kiss to my lips. "Much as I want to go back downstairs with you, I got shit that needs to be handled."

"I know," I replied.

He let my hand go and stood up. "You want to go to the ranch today? Visit Maddy?" he asked me.

"I don't want to bother her while she's working."

"It's Saturday, baby. She and Cree are probably having a day by the pool. If I can get you a decent bathing suit, I'll take you over and let you have some woman time. Could be we don't get back until late tonight. I'd rather you be there than here alone."

That sounded nice. "Okay, sure."

Chapter THIRTY-ONE

HUCK

It smelled like mothballs and cheap floral perfume as I stood over Tabitha Bennett as she slept in her king-size bed alone. I wondered if she had realized Roy was missing yet or if they spoke often enough for her to be concerned. Didn't matter either way.

Hitting women wasn't something I did. My dad always told me that even if a female drove you fucking crazy, to be easy and just set them free. Tabitha wasn't a woman. She was a monster. One that had haunted Trinity for too damn long.

I slapped her face, then shoved the gag in her mouth, enjoying the wide-eyed look as she woke up. Her muffled scream made me laugh. Grabbing her arm, I yanked her up, then shoved her face-first into the pillow in order to tie her wrists together. I made sure to do it tight enough that the blood flow was cut off. She kicked and bucked, screaming into the damn gag.

When I had her restrained, I grabbed her arm and jerked her up until she was standing.

"Walk with me, Tabitha. I have a story to tell you," I said as I pushed her forward toward the hallway.

Gage was leaning against the wall with his arms crossed over his chest.

"Gage, this is Tabitha. Tabitha, this is Gage. And you remember me, right? We met at my brother's funeral."

Gage smirked, and she started twisted and jerking against me as if she was going to get free.

"Keep it up, and I'll let Gage slap you across the face."

She stilled and glared at me.

"Now, like I was saying, I've got a little story for you. We were killing some traitorous bastards, and Gage put a gun to a woman's head, but I stopped him because I recognized the ass. You see, Trinity has a world-class ass. If I could write a song, I'd write one about it. I didn't want my dead brother's fiancée killed, so we took her with us. Joke was on me though because I got addicted to her pussy. Sweetest fucking cunt I've ever had, and her tits, goddamn, they're incredible."

Tabitha was making noises again, and I slammed her face against the wall.

"Shut up. You're interrupting me. I'm telling you a fucking story, Trinity owned me with that pussy, but dammit if I didn't start getting obsessed with her smile, her laugh, the way she walked, those big eyes. Took her having a traumatic meltdown for me to realize that I'd fucking kill for her. And that leads me to why we are here."

I pulled her back from the wall and started walking again, pushing her as we went.

"Last night, Roy was a wealth of information. Of course, I had to cut off his pinkie, his dick, slice up his face, and a few other minor jabs of my knife to get it all out of him. Once he was done telling me all your sins and his own, he got off lucky. I just slit his throat. It could have been much worse."

I looked down at Tabitha, and she had gone pale. I laughed as we walked to the stairs. I shoved her forward until she had to either walk down the stairs or fall face-first.

"My dad made sure to raise me to respect women. He had never met you, and I realize that, but it's still deeply ingrained in me. You won't be hung up and sliced to pieces like Roy. Instead, this closet, where my woman was tortured during her childhood, is where you're headed."

Levi opened the door for me, and I threw Tabitha inside. She sat there, staring up at us. I could see the hatred in her eyes. Not even a fucking tear. Levi began to tie her feet up, and she fought against it, but it didn't bother him. Once he was done, he walked over and tied her gag on with a rope so she couldn't get it out.

"When you get to hell, tell Roy I said hi," I told her before Levi closed and bolted the door.

Turning, I headed back up the stairs with Levi behind me. Gage was at the top, and he led the way as we headed for the back door we'd broken into. None of us said anything as we left. The absence of any proof Trinity had lived in that house spoke volumes. Family photos of Tabitha, Roy, and Benjamin, but nothing with Trinity's face in it. The room that must have been hers was a sewing room full of old women's crafts and shit. The room Roy had used had his pictures on the wall. High school trophies, diplomas, it was all there.

We headed back through the woods until we made it to the place we had left the SUV. Gage climbed into the driver's seat, and I took the passenger seat. I wasn't in the state of mind to drive. My fucking chest hurt from seeing that place. Knowing what she'd gone through, living there. I hated everything about that house.

Although we were almost a mile away, we could hear the explosion. I sighed and leaned back in my seat. That shit was done.

"Bye-bye, Tabitha." Gage chuckled.

He was one messed up son of a bitch.

Chapter THIRTY-TWO

TRINITY

I listened to the voice mail again. Hayes's grandmother, telling me that if there was anything I needed or something she could do for me and Roy to let her know. She'd called Roy, but he hadn't returned her calls. She hoped we knew how much they loved Tabitha.

I stared at my phone, trying to understand what this was about. Did I call her? She expected me to know what she was talking about. I searched the internet for Tabitha's name and read the first thing that popped up.

Fire, explosion, gas leak … nothing left. I looked at the date—two days ago. Tabitha had died in an explosion caused by a gas leak. The house and everything in it had burned to the ground.

I didn't feel anything. Should I?

The garage door opened and closed. I slipped my phone in my pocket. It was Gage. He stopped and studied me. Normally, I was never sitting in the living room when they returned in the evenings. I was sure it appeared odd now. The television wasn't on. Just me, alone in the living room, sitting there.

"You good?" he asked.

I nodded. I was fine.

"Dinner is ready," I told him.

His gaze searched my face again before he walked on through to the kitchen.

Huck hadn't texted me all day. That wasn't like him. Today must have been a busy one. I stood up and decided to go get a shower. I didn't know how late he would be. It was already after seven.

My thoughts kept going back to the fact that Tabitha was dead. It was strange. Seeing Roy, then this, when I'd gone over half a year, barely thinking of them. I was sure Hayes would be disappointed in my thoughts. He'd have wanted me to feel something. Oddly enough, what I felt was relief. The house with all those terrible memories that haunted me was gone. Did it mean I was human that I felt this way, or did this merely justify Tabitha's belief that I was evil?

After my shower, I curled up in the middle of Huck's bed and closed my eyes. The next time I opened them, I knew I had been asleep, but I didn't know for how long. Sitting up, I looked around for any sign that Huck had come home. When I didn't see anything, I got off the bed and checked my phone. It was after twelve in the morning. No text or call from Huck.

Are you okay? I texted him.

I waited several minutes and no response. I was now officially worried. Pulling on a pair of shorts with Huck's shirt I'd been asleep in, I headed for the stairs. Didn't he know that I would worry? I knew that he did dangerous things. Not coming home or explaining why was concerning.

When I reached the main floor of the house, I heard voices. Feeling somewhat relieved, I followed the sound. It was coming from the living room. Gage and Levi were talking, but I didn't hear Huck. I heard Gage say my name, and I stopped before walking in so they couldn't see me.

Gage lowered his voice. "I don't know what to tell her if she asks. He hung up the fucking phone. Maybe he texted her."

"Do you think he's with her?" Levi asked.

"He's drunk. It's not like him." Gage paused. "I don't know."

"Why would he get drunk?"

"Fuck if I know."

"Blaise will know. Huck tells him shit."

"If I've got to go down to Devil's tonight, I'm gonna be pissed," Gage grunted.

"Liam will handle it if he has to."

"Can't believe he went to fucking Devil's."

"What? Since Liam bought it, the strippers have gotten way better. It's kind of like family, right? Liam's Cree's grandfather, too, you know."

Gage muttered a curse.

"I'm going to bed. He's going through something, apparently," Levi said, then yawned.

"What do you think Trinity is going to do if she finds this shit out? If he calls her drunk with 'Pour Some Sugar on Me' playing in the background and whatever female he's with talking, it's gonna be ugly."

I stepped back, then turned and walked quietly away. I felt as if I'd been punched in the gut. When I reached the steps leading upstairs, I walked up them and back to the room I'd been given here. Tears burned my eyes. Not just because Huck had chosen to go to a strip club and get drunk, but also because he'd felt he needed to. This was what I'd known would happen.

My reaction to seeing Roy had probably been the turning point for him. He had acted different since that night. As if his head was somewhere else. Could I blame him? Even though he'd been sweet and held me, the more time he had to think about it, he had to have questioned a future with me. I hadn't told him what Roy had done to me as a teenager. He didn't know the abuse I'd suffered from Tabitha and Roy. I didn't think telling him about it would help. He would just see how completely damaged I was.

Closing the bedroom door behind me, I wiped the tears from my face and looked around the room. Perhaps it was time I left. He was getting drunk because of me. The weight of dealing with this and us was getting to him. I didn't know where to go or how to go anywhere. There was one person I thought I could trust, but I might be wrong there too. It was my only option.

I took the time to pack up the things that were actually mine, then climbed in bed in hopes that I could get some sleep. I would call Maddy first thing in the morning. Either she would understand and help me or she'd tell Blaise, who would tell Huck. But if Huck was ready to end things, then perhaps he'd be relieved I was leaving.

Every hour that passed, I silently cried and stared at the ceiling. I had heard Gage and Levi go to their rooms and close their doors hours ago. I kept my phone beside me, waiting on something from Huck. I hadn't known my heart could hurt like this. But then I had never been in love. I should have known once he saw me at my worst, he'd change his mind. How could someone like me be a good mother? It was clear he wanted kids.

Tabitha was dead. That house was gone. But the horror that had marked me there didn't leave. The things that had happened in those walls had left its imprint on my soul. It was cracked.

When the sunlight began to fill the room, I stood up and began to get ready. My body working on autopilot. Poor Huck. He'd had no idea when he started this with me how messed up I was. He didn't want to face me with it. Tell me the truth about his feelings. I was naive to believe that sex meant more. I'd even started to think we had a bond that was stronger than my demons. My heart had been the liar, or maybe that was just me.

Once I was dressed and my bag was zipped up, I called the only person who might possibly help me.

I made the cinnamon rolls with extra icing, the way Gage liked them, and was sure to make extra biscuits with sausage gravy for Levi. Huck had never said that anything I made was his favorite, and I wasn't sure if he had come home last night or not. But just in case, I made his usual choices. Gage walked into the kitchen as I was washing up the dirty pots and pans.

"My favorite way to wake up," Gage said, but I didn't turn to look at him. I was afraid I'd cry.

"Extra icing on the cinnamon rolls," I replied as lightly as I could.

He groaned.

"Huck still asleep?" Gage asked, but I could hear the note of uncertainty in his voice. He was feeling me out. Trying to see what I knew. If Huck had contacted me.

"We both know Huck didn't come back last night," I replied.

The chime went off and I closed my eyes in relief. Maddy was here.

I could hear Gage's chair legs as he pushed the chair back and stood up. He was checking the cameras to see who had just driven through the gate. I walked into the living room and picked up my bag. Gage was standing in the doorway, frowning at me when I turned around.

"You leaving us?" he asked, looking at my duffel bag. "That why Maddy is pulling up outside? Did Huck tell you to go?" His tone took on a hard edge. Like he was angry.

"He didn't have to," I replied. "And he shouldn't have to."

Gage took a step into the room. "What the fuck does that mean?"

I would not cry. I would not cry.

"It means that I heard you and Levi last night. I know about Huck and where he was." I shrugged. "He's had enough. You saw me the other night. I'm messed up, and that won't ever go away. The things …" I stopped. There was no point in telling Gage this. "I've just got a lot of twisted shit in my head. Huck saw it, and he doesn't want to hurt me."

Gage ran a hand over his head. "Trinity, I swear to you, that is not what last night was. Something else is going on with him. It's not you."

The front doorbell rang, and I wanted to hug Gage. This was goodbye. I wished Levi were down here too. But it was time to go. Prolonging it would make it worse.

"Goodbye, Gage," I said with a teary smile, then walked to the front door.

I heard his footsteps behind me, and I knew he was going to stop me. Maddy, however, was here, and she had said she understood. I opened the door, feeling as if my heart was going to shatter when I walked away from here.

Her gaze met mine, and she gave me a sad smile. "You sure?" she asked.

I nodded.

"Okay then."

I stepped outside, but Gage was at the door, keeping me from closing it.

"You talked to Blaise before you came over here?" he asked, looking past me to Maddy.

She raised her eyebrows at his question. "I'm sorry, Gage, but when did I start answering to you?"

He crossed his arms over his chest. "If anyone knows what's going on with Huck, it's Blaise. I'm just asking if he knows Trinity is leaving."

"He does. I don't keep things from my husband. Besides, he tracks my every move. Remember?" she replied with an annoyed frown.

Gage muttered a curse. "Okay then." Then, his gaze shifted back to me. "But you're wrong. I swear to you that Huck hasn't changed his mind about you because of that night. If anything, he's only gotten more possessive and protective. When he finds out you're gone, he's going to lose his shit."

I didn't respond because arguing with him would do neither of us any good. I wanted to be gone by the time Huck came home. Seeing him would be more than I could take.

"Let's go," Maddy said to me.

I started down the steps, passing her as I walked down to her silver SUV.

"Where's she gonna go? We don't even know if it's fucking safe for her," Gage called out.

"To the only other people I know who can keep her safe," she replied.

I hadn't discussed that with her. I had planned on having her take me to a cheap hotel.

"Oh, fucking hell," Gage replied.

I didn't wait for him to say more. I got in the car and closed the door. In all the times I had been alone, not once had I felt as completely lost as I did right now.

Chapter THIRTY-THREE

HUCK

I had one text from Trinity last night, and I hadn't been in the right state of mind to respond. She was going to be upset, and I knew it. But after yesterday, I'd needed distance to process things. Rage because I hadn't been around enough to figure it out had snowballed into too fucking many emotions for me to handle. I couldn't talk about it. So, I'd gone to Devil's, where I knew I wouldn't cross paths with anyone in the family, and found a dark corner, drinking until the pain was numb.

Opening the door to the house, I found comfort in the smell of Trinity's cooking. I'd talk to her about it, but not right away. First, I needed to take her to my bed and forget it all. I'd woken up on Liam's office couch this morning, wanting to see her face. Knowing it would make this easier.

When I stepped into the living room, Gage sat in my chair with a glass of whiskey. It was ten in the morning. He glared at me and poured the rest of the contents of his glass down his throat. Levi walked into the room, and when he saw me, he just shook his head. Was this because I'd called Gage drunk last night? I hadn't wanted Trinity to hear me like that, but I'd known I had to let them know I was alive.

"Dude, where have you been?" Levi asked.

"Sleeping off last night," I replied, walking past both of them on my way to the kitchen. Right now, I needed Trinity.

"She's gone," Gage called out behind me.

I froze. I'd heard his words, but they weren't registering. What the fuck did that mean?

"Left an hour ago with Maddy," Levi added.

Trinity was with Maddy. Had she left to come get me?

I turned back to them. "Where are they going? Did you tell her where I was at? I didn't see them when I left."

Gage was still looking at me like he wanted to plant his fist in my face. What the hell was wrong with him? This couldn't be about his breakfast. Trinity had cooked. I could smell it.

"Afraid she wasn't looking for you. She was leaving you." Levi might as well have wrapped a rope around my throat and pulled it.

"What the fuck did you say?" I asked, thinking this was bullshit.

They thought this was funny. My head was not in a good place, and I didn't need their fucking jokes. I needed Trinity.

"You didn't come home. Didn't call or text your woman. Were out drunk at a strip club. SHE FUCKING LEFT!" Gage stood up, his angry glare leveled on me. "What the hell were you thinking?"

This didn't make sense. Why would she go to Maddy's if she was leaving me? She was upset. If she was leaving me, she wouldn't have gone to the ranch.

"She went to Maddy's. That's not leaving me. She's hurt because she doesn't understand. I'll go fucking fix it."

"Sure. Take your ass right on over there. I said she left you. She's not there."

My heart started pounding as hard as my fucking head.

"Where is she?" I asked through clenched teeth. "And how the fuck did she know I was at Devil's last night?"

Gage glanced at Levi, then back at me. "She overheard us talking last night. We thought she was asleep downstairs."

"FUCK!" I roared. "AND YOU DIDN'T THINK TO CALL ME?!"

Gage threw his arms in the air. "I fucking called you. Levi called you. YOU WEREN'T ANSWERING!"

I pulled out my phone and then went to the tracker I kept on her. It said *Unavailable.* I refreshed and tried again. Un-fucking-available.

Panic was starting to take over. I stared at it as I ran my hand through my hair, then pulled at my hair as I tried to figure out how to find her. Blaise. If Maddy had taken her, Blaise would know where.

"What the fuck was Blaise thinking?" I growled, then pressed his number.

"You done with whatever shit messed you up?" Blaise asked when he answered on the first ring.

"Where is she?" I clipped out.

"My wife likes Trinity. You're the closest friend I have. You're family. Which is why when Madeline asked me why you'd gotten drunk at the club last night and I didn't have an answer, I let her go get Trinity. You want to tell me what the fuck you were doing?"

My hand clenched at my side. "I will. But it's better to show you. Just please tell me where she is."

"I spoke with Madeline. Trinity isn't mad at you. That's not why she left," Blaise said.

"Then, why the fuck did she leave me?" I growled.

"She thinks you want out."

"Why the fuck would she think that? I was gone one night. One goddamn night. Where is she at, Blaise?"

He sighed. "She was determined to go. Madeline took her to the only person she knew who could keep her safe if she wasn't with us."

"FUCK!" I shouted. "Please tell me they just went to Devil's. She's not headed to Miami." I was already stalking back to the garage door.

"Devil's. Liam's apartment."

I had just fucking been there. Slamming the door behind me, I didn't say anything to Gage or Levi. They'd let her leave. Sure, it was Maddy who had taken her, but still. They could have said something to make her stay.

What was this shit about her thinking I wanted out? Had she missed the fact that I was fucking obsessed with her? How was that not clear?

As I reached the Escalade, the garage door opened up. I didn't look back at whichever fucker it was. Neither of them had stopped her. Once I had her back here, where she belonged, then I'd listen to their reasons and possibly forgive them.

"I told her you were gonna lose your shit. That the night at the party hadn't changed your mind. But it's time you fucking admit it to yourself and tell her that you love her. If she had known that, she wouldn't have left." Gage's voice stopped me.

I gripped the handle on the Escalade. Was that what this was? I loved her? How the fuck would he know what love was?

I jerked open the door and turned to look at him before I got inside. "How do you know I'm in love? You don't know what fucking love is. What you had wasn't love. It was obsession and it had been toxic as fuck."

But was he right? I would kill anyone who stood in my way of getting her back. The idea of her leaving me felt like my chest was being ripped open. The only time I felt fucking settled was when she was with me. Her smile fixed any shit that was wrong.

"Maybe it was toxic but if you feel anything like I did then I know how it fucking owns you. Makes you weak. Hurts like a bitch," Gage said before stepping back inside and closing the door.

Fuck me. I'd fallen in love with Trinity.

Chapter THIRTY-FOUR

TRINITY

Maddy wouldn't stay with me all day. I knew that, but I was thankful she was still here. I didn't know these people, and right now, I didn't want to be alone.

Had I made the wrong decision? Would Huck hate me for leaving? Was my heart going to always feel as if it had been destroyed?

I dropped my head into my hands and sighed. I missed him. If I had stayed even if he was done with me, at least I would still get to see him. But would I have been able to deal with that kind of agony … having him there, but not being able to touch him?

"If you want to come to my house, you can. Or Garrett's house even," Maddy said across from me.

I shook my head. Huck wouldn't want that.

The door to the apartment we were in opened, and Liam, Maddy's father, walked in with a frown on his face. Liam owned a strip club—or his motorcycle club did. They owned several, she'd said. Most in Miami. She had brought me to Devil's, his club in Ocala, where Huck had been last night. Liam had an apartment above the club.

"We got company," he said, looking at Maddy, then shifting his gaze to me. "And he's real close to taking out some of my men. I told him to give me five minutes before he hurt someone."

Maddy sighed, then reached over and took my hand. "I expected this. Even though I turned the tracker on your phone off, I figured he'd find you. They always do. You can't run from the family."

"Tracker?" I asked, confused.

Maddy nodded. "Yes. When I checked your phone, it had the same tracker on it that Blaise keeps on mine. Which means you're important to Huck. Before you get mad, know that I've been in your shoes. And if it wasn't for that tracker, I'd be dead."

I swallowed nervously. "Huck is here?" I asked, then lifted my gaze to Liam.

"And raising fucking hell. What's it gonna be? You don't want him up here, we will do our best to stop him, but I can't promise you we can," he told me.

He was here and upset.

I stood up. "I didn't know he'd look for me. I'm sorry. Yes, he can come up, or I can just go down. I don't want to cause problems for you."

Liam chuckled. "I'll send him up. Fucker's got the territorial gleam in his eye I've seen on Blaise, and I don't want to stir that nest again." He walked back out the door, closing it behind him.

I looked down at Maddy, who was grinning.

"Long story. I'll share it with you sometime. Do you want me to stay? Or do you want to be alone?"

There were things I needed to say to him, and having someone else hear that would be difficult.

"Alone is better."

She nodded, then stood up. "It's terrifying to love a man like him, but I promise you, it's worth it."

She didn't understand. Loving him was easy; it was losing him that was killing me.

"Thanks for all you've done to help me. I've enjoyed getting to know you." I felt myself get choked up again.

Maddy stepped forward and hugged me. "Huck came here, which means our friendship is just beginning." When she let me go, she winked at me, then headed for the door.

It swung open before she got there, and Huck filled the doorway. His gaze shot past her and locked on me. Just the sight of him made my chest swell. I wanted to keep him, and the fact that I wasn't going to get to was shattering me.

Huck started toward me in long strides, looking so fierce that I worried that maybe I should have had Maddy stay. Was he mad because I'd had his boss's wife help me leave? That might have been a mistake.

"Fucking hell, Trinity," he said as he reached me and pulled me against him. I could hear his heart beating fast as his arms tightened around me. "Don't ever leave me again."

My hands gripped his shirt, and I buried my face against him, wanting to soak him in. He smelled like whiskey and cigarette smoke. But thankfully, I didn't smell another woman's perfume. Maddy hadn't taken me into the club downstairs, and I hadn't wanted to see it. Even knowing he'd been here last night, possibly with another woman, I wanted to hold on to him and never let go.

Did love make you this crazy? Shouldn't I pound on his chest and tell him how much it'd hurt that he'd ignored my text and been here, watching other women strip? Yes, I should. And I was going to, if I could stop clinging to him.

"Why did you leave me?" he asked. His voice was strung tight, like he was in pain.

"Because you wanted to be with other women. I thought that meant we were done," I said against his chest, not looking up at him.

"What? Trinity, look at me."

I took a deep, calming breath, then did as he'd asked.

His hands cupped my face. "Baby, I don't even see other women. You fucked me up. I just see you. Just want you."

The lump in my throat was getting thicker. "But you were here last night."

He nodded. "In a dark corner, alone, drinking, not facing the stage. No women."

God, how I wanted to believe him. If this wasn't a dream and he was really saying these things, then I wanted them to be true more than I wanted my next breath.

"I heard Gage and Levi last night. Gage heard a woman in the background when you were on the phone."

He groaned. "That was one of the waitresses. Yes, I ordered drinks, but that's it." He brushed his thumb over my cheek. "I couldn't pick her out of a lineup. I don't even know her name. I wasn't here because of you or us. I … I was sent something, and it was hard. Real fucking hard, and I had … have a lot of shit to work through, and that's going to take me a while. My head was in a bad place last night."

He looked pained, as if it hurt to even think about what had upset him. I looked into his cornflower-blue eyes and wished I could make whatever was hurting him go away.

"Why didn't you tell me?"

"I'm going to, but it was too raw yesterday. I've made some mistakes in life, but not like this. Not this brutal. Forgiving myself might never be something I can do."

I put my hands over his and leaned into him. "You have me. I lo—" I stopped, realizing that I was about to tell this man I loved him. Not a good idea.

He inhaled sharply. "Not yet," he said through clenched teeth. "Don't finish that sentence."

The way just a few words could crush me when they came from this man. I nodded, feeling as if he'd just shaken me, reminding me that loving him was not part of the deal. But it was unfair that he thought he could control my heart when not even I could control it.

"Jesus, baby, stop looking at me like that." His voice was strained. "Sit down. I was going to wait until we were home, but you need to see this." Then, he let out a defeated sigh. "And after you see this, if you still want to finish that sentence …" He trailed off.

I walked over to the sofa and sat down on the closest end to me, keeping my eyes on Huck. The muscles in his neck flexed as he reached into his pocket and pulled out a folded piece of paper. His eyes looked like they held a world of suffering in his gaze. I wanted to make it go away. Hold him and tell him I loved him. Tell him how loving him had changed me. How he'd given me something I hadn't known I was missing.

Huck stepped over to me and held the paper out to me. "Read it."

Confused, I reached for it and unfolded it slowly. Part of me wanted to understand what was wrong with him, and the other part wasn't sure I could bear it if this was causing him such torment.

When I opened the folded paper, the first thing I realized was that it was a letter, but it was the second thing that knocked the wind out of my chest. This was Hayes's writing. My eyes shot back up to him.

He pointed at the letter. "Read it."

Huck,

Hey, big brother. I'm going to start this by apologizing. For everything you're going through, for my being weak, and for not being the brother you deserved. I was never like you, but I wanted to be. I wanted your strength, fearlessness, loyalty. When I looked at you, I saw Dad, and I loved you and hated you for it. I wanted to see Dad when I looked in the mirror, but that was never going to happen. I wasn't like Dad. That was all you.

Maybe if I'd chosen your life, left home, and become a part of the legacy our father had left behind, I'd have found acceptance. I could have been me. Not the version I pretended. Not the guy everyone thought I was. But again, I was weak. I wasn't fearless. I wasn't you. I had demons no one could ever see.

Understand that choosing to take my life wasn't an easy one.

Horror gripped me, and my eyes shot up to lock with Huck's. My vision blurred as I looked at him. Emotion clogged my throat. Had I just read that wrong?

"What?" I whispered.

Something wasn't right. Hayes had died of a brain aneurysm. Not suicide. Hayes wouldn't have done that.

"Finish," he replied softly.

I could see the agony in his expression. This was real. I placed a hand on my chest as the pain seared through me.

It was a selfish one. I didn't want to face the truth. I'd chosen to be a minister because it had seemed safe. Surely, if I served God and taught the scripture, he'd fix me. Right?

Wrong.

It hadn't worked. No amount of reading the scripture, praying, serving the church fixed me. I never changed. I pretended. I was so good at it, but every day, I died a little more inside.

I'm gay.

I've known it since I was about ten years old. Maybe earlier. At first, I thought it was because girls made me nervous, but the older I got, I knew that wasn't the case at all. I dated girls, but even kissing them was difficult for me.

I met Mark my first year in college. With him, I could be myself. I might have been happy, but my need to please our grandparents kept me from being honest not only with myself, but with everyone else too. Because of my refusal to be who I was, I lost Mark. He gave me an ultimatum, and I didn't choose him. I chose the church. The lies. The world I had built for myself. The facade.

Anyway, I struggled for a while alone, but then a woman walked into my life who needed saving too. She had her own set of demons. The first time I saw her in the congregation, she was detached. The brokenness in her gaze was one I recognized. I felt what she so openly let others see. Needing someone who didn't have it all figured out. She was as lost as I was, so I befriended her. That would be another one of my sins.

Trinity Bennett wasn't broken. She was hurt in ways that went deep. Her need to be loved, to feel wanted, and for affection tugged at my heart. For a moment, I thought I could save her, and in doing so, it would make my life okay. I realized soon though that she wasn't weak. Not like me. She didn't pretend. She accepted her life and didn't try to be someone she wasn't.

As I'm sure you'll hear, if you haven't by now, I proposed to her, and she said yes. I knew she wasn't in love with me, but like me, she wanted something she couldn't have so badly—to be wanted and accepted. I thought for a moment that I could give us that. But the more she pressed to get closer to me, the more I put up a wall. Hurting her was the last thing I wanted to do, and the thought of leaving her alone again was the one thing that made me question if I should go through with this. But again, I was selfish.

I know you can find her. Do it for me. I shouldn't get to ask you anything, and I know that, but please watch over her. She's got darkness that is even more powerful than mine. She needs what I couldn't give her. She needs to be cherished. She needs a safe place where she belongs. She needs a man to love her. That man wasn't me, and I'm not asking you to be that man. I know you're not cut out for that. She just needs protecting, and you can protect her better than anyone I know.

I'm sorry for a lot of things. Not coming around to see you more. Not telling you the truth, for leaving without saying goodbye. But in this life, I had the best brother a guy could ask for. I was always proud of how tough you were. How you chose who you wanted to be and didn't ask anyone's opinion. Just please try to understand.

This is all I know to do. This is my freedom.

I love you.

Live this life for both of us.

Hayes

"Oh God," I whispered.

Disbelief gripped me. The words I had just read were written in Hayes's handwriting. It was so familiar to me that I had even heard his voice in my head as I read it. I could feel his personality within the words. But so much confused me.

Where had this letter come from? Why had everyone been told his death was a brain aneurysm? How had I not realized this? I'd been close to Hayes. I should have seen it. Should have known he was struggling. He had needed someone, and I could have helped him.

Huck stood with his eyes closed as he hung his head. "I wasn't around. I didn't check on him enough. I didn't make time to get close to him. If I'd just put aside my disdain for our mother's parents and taken time for my brother, I would have seen it. I could have been there. I could have stopped him."

The agony in Huck's voice gripped me. He was blaming himself.

"But I did see him every day. For six months, we were together, and I missed it. He was hurting, and I … I was so consumed with my mistakes, the shadows from my past, that I didn't see he needed someone," I said to him, standing up. "If you are blaming yourself, stop. I was there, Huck, and I let him down. Not you."

He shook his head as he lifted his eyes to meet mine. "He was my baby brother. When our parents died, I swore I would protect him. I went to live with those people because he needed me. It was my job, my responsibility, and I failed."

Taking a step toward him, I reached out my hand and placed it on his arm. "Did you read the words in this letter? He wasn't blaming you. This is why he wrote it. So you would know why. Not so you could put this on yourself."

Huck ran a hand over his head and sighed heavily. "It arrived in my post office box yesterday. I don't know who sent it. Whoever he had left it with was supposed to have sent it at his death. They had known he was going to do this. I have to know who knew. The minister and his wife must not be above lies. I guess suicide is a worse evil than lying about the cause of your grandson's death. That sickens me. They were fucking embarrassed and lied about it."

I wasn't going to make excuses for them. He was right. They preached against sin when they had so many in their closet.

I wrapped my arms around him and held him. I couldn't make his pain go away, but I could comfort him. I had only known Hayes for six months. He was Huck's brother. The grief was going to stay with him for a long time. I pressed my face to his chest, wishing I had the right words for both of us.

"It's like losing him all over again." His deep voice was laced with sorrow.

"I'm sorry I wasn't home when you got there. I can't promise insecurities will ever go away," I whispered. "If I'd had any idea you were hurting, I'd have come to find you. Not left you."

We stood there for several moments, saying nothing. There were times in life that words only filled a voice and served no purpose. This was one of those.

"Trinity," he said, breaking the silence.

"Yes?"

"Never fucking leave me again."

Chapter THIRTY-FIVE

HUCK

You didn't truly heal from loss. I knew that all too well. When I'd lost my parents, they'd left me Hayes. He hadn't been taken. It was what had gotten me through my darkest times and my grief.

As I lay in my bed with Trinity asleep in my arms, the words in Hayes's letter kept replaying over in my head. I couldn't help but think that he had known once I saw her, was around her, that I would want her.

He had made it sound like she would need me, but fuck if it wasn't the other way around. Hayes had left me Trinity. I had always believed we were born, we lived, we died. Dust to dust. Made sense. No faith in supernatural beings or powers. I dealt with facts.

Until now.

Sometimes, things happened that couldn't be explained. My walking into that house and finding her six months after my brother's death couldn't have just been a coincidence.

Or fucking luck. The more I tossed it around in my head, I couldn't help but think my brother had had a hand in it. That he was watching over both of us, even after he was gone. Which meant my facts might be bullshit after all.

I looked down at Trinity's head on my chest. Just having her made the bad shit easier to accept. Knowing that she was mine, I could deal with the pain, regret, loss. My little brother had known somehow that she was for me. He had also known if he told me that in a letter, I'd send someone else to watch over her.

My arm tightened around her body. "I love you," I whispered, knowing she was asleep but needing to fucking admit it anyway.

She moved then, and her head tilted back until those almond-shaped eyes met mine. The room was dark, but I could see the different emotions flickering within those depths. Earlier today, she'd almost told me the same thing, and I stopped her. Then, I lied about why. The truth was, I hadn't wanted the first time I heard her say those words to be tarnished by the grief that the letter had caused.

I had also wanted to say it first.

"Did . . ." She paused, then blinked a couple of times. "Did I dream that?"

A smile tugged at the corner of my lips. Damn, she was cute.

"What exactly?" I asked, although I knew what she was asking me.

A frown wrinkled her forehead, and she dropped her eyes, then moved her head back to where it had been. "Nothing," she whispered.

I rolled her onto her back and held myself above her. "Oh no, you don't," I told her as I leaned down to press a kiss to the corner of her full lips.

"I was dreaming," she said, then lifted her head just enough to kiss my lips.

"Hmm," I replied as I pulled her bottom lip between my teeth. "Tell me what you were dreaming then."

She made a sexy little sound and arched her body toward mine. "Nothing."

I trailed kisses over to her ear. "That stings, baby," I whispered in her ear.

She tensed, and her body went still beneath me. "What?"

I leaned up enough to look down at her and ran my knuckles down her cheek and over her mouth. "I tell you that I love you, and you call it nothing."

Her eyes went wide, and then she wrapped her small hands around my wrists. "I wasn't dreaming?"

I slid my knee between her legs and pushed them open. "No," I replied, reaching down to hook her left leg over my arm before sinking inside of her slick opening. "Not fucking dreaming."

Her hips lifted to meet my thrusts as she cried out.

"The only pussy I want." My voice was thick with need as I pulled back and then filled her again. "You're mine."

"I was going to," she panted and then moaned, "tell you."

I slammed into her harder. "I want to hear it while my dick is deep inside you."

"OH!" Her nails bit into my arms. Turned me on every damn time.

I pushed her thighs open wider and drove into that sweet cunt, then held myself there. Our gazes locked, and her pussy clenched me.

"I love you."

Just hearing her say it turned me into a desperate man. I reached down and ran my knuckles against her jaw. She was perfect.

My fingers dug into her right thigh that I was holding as I pumped into her tight heat. She rolled her hips underneath me. Nothing had ever felt better than being inside her.

"You own me," I told her as my balls drew tight and I felt myself getting closer. "Come on my dick, baby," I urged her, brushing my thumb over her swollen clit.

As if I could control her orgasms on demand, she cried out my name and began to tremble beneath me. The warm gush soaked my cock and balls, sending me shouting her name as my body jerked, emptying my release inside of her. Marking her. Knowing the only man she'd ever have inside her was me.

The last jolt of pleasure rocked me, and I held her hips so that we stayed connected.

"I fucking love you." My voice was hoarse from the shouting.

The shy, sated smile that came over her face made me feel like I owned the damn world.

TRINITY
THREE MONTHS LATER

The summer was almost over, but no one let Florida know that. Even with the umbrella shading me somewhat, it was hot as I lay out on the lounge chair by the pool. Huck had returned last night after being gone for business for three days, and we had slept very little. When we were apart, he came back, wanting me to the point of exhaustion. Not that I was complaining. I loved nights like that.

My eyes kept wanting to close, and I started to drift off to sleep when a touch on my bare stomach startled me. My eyes opened, and Huck was sitting beside me, running the back of his finger from under my breast to the top of my bottoms. He was home earlier than I'd expected.

"Hey," I said as his gaze moved from my stomach to meet my face.

"Did you put on sunblock?" he asked me.

"Yes, sir."

He smirked. "That's the kind of shit that gets you fucked."

"Wearing sunblock?"

He slid his hand inside the front of my bottoms. "Calling me sir."

I laughed and opened my legs for him.

He cupped my pussy, but didn't do anything more.

"Before I get distracted," he said, "we need to talk."

The serious way he had said it had me scooting back and sitting up. "About?"

"Something important."

These past few months, we had grown closer. He'd faced his grandparents with their lie about Hayes's death. His grandmother cried so pitifully that I truly felt sorry for her. It had been clear she was haunted by her grandson's suicide. There would be no family get-togethers for Huck and his grandparents though. I wasn't sure he'd ever forgive them. Even after his grandmother had admitted to being the one who had mailed him the letter.

There were times I would let my old fears in and worry that he would tire of me or realize he wasn't in love with me. But somehow, he always knew when I was struggling with my insecurities and did all he could to reassure me. Which only made me love him more.

The Huck who had run hot and cold only ran hot now. When I wanted to touch him, I no longer held back, for fear of being denied or unwanted. I went with him to the shop several days a week. He was teaching me to ride horses at the ranch. For once in my life, I felt like I belonged. I had a home. It was wherever Huck was.

When he didn't say anything more, I realized he was waiting on me to say something.

"Okay," I said, clasping my hands in my lap.

"I'm working on how to begin," he replied.

I felt a sick knot in my stomach.

"That doesn't sound good," I whispered.

His eyebrows drew together in a frown. "I guess it depends."

I bit my bottom lip. "You're scaring me."

"Baby, when are you going to stop expecting the worst?"

I wasn't sure that day would ever come. "I don't know. You just look serious."

He grabbed my leg and tugged me closer to him. "Do you remember when I told you that if you tried to leave me, I'd tie you to my fucking bed?"

I smiled and nodded.

"Last night, when you cried my name and came on my dick, what did I say?"

"That I fucking owned you," I replied, feeling the heat in my cheeks.

He nodded, then ran his hand up my leg. "It's not smart. Loving me," he whispered. "But damn if I'm gonna let you stop."

"Loving you is out of my control, but it's the best thing that's ever happened to me."

"I'm not a good man."

I smiled at that. "You're right," I agreed. "You're a bad man. But that turns me on."

He chuckled. "Is that so?"

"Yep. But I'm messed up in the head."

He reached up and brushed his thumb over my bottom lip. "You're perfect."

I wasn't, but if he wanted to think so, I would not argue.

"You'll never know just how fucking dark I am. If you knew the shit I've done, that I do, you wouldn't love me."

I wrapped my hand around his arm. "You're wrong."

He closed his eyes. "What if I told you that I've tortured people for revenge?"

I was sure he'd done more than that. "They must have done something very bad."

He laughed and pressed a kiss to my lips. "You love me, no matter what?"

I nodded. "Yes."

"Fuck," he groaned and pulled me into his lap and buried his head in my chest as I straddled him. "I'm possessive, dangerously so. Although I didn't know that until you."

I ran my hands over his head. "I've noticed."

"If anyone touched you, I'd kill them," he said, lifting his head to look at me.

I saw it in his eyes. Something I had wondered about. I had told him about his grandmother's call, telling me Tabitha was dead. We hadn't spoken any more about it, and oddly, no one had called me again to discuss it. But I still thought about it at times.

"If you want to tell me that you already have, don't," I whispered. "Because I think I've known for a while."

He was quiet as his eyes stayed on mine.

"Huck?"

"Yeah?"

"Is that all you need to tell me? Just about all the murders you could possibly commit in the future if someone breathes in my direction? Trust me, I'm aware. I recently checked to see if there was an obituary or missing person post for Jonathon Kilgore."

I already knew about Roy being a missing person. I didn't say that though.

"Do you want there to be?" he asked me.

"NO! I absolutely do not!"

A slow grin spread across his face, and when Huck smiled, it made everything that had ever been wrong in my life okay. The past no longer mattered. Just this. Us.

"I'm so fucking in love with you that I can't concentrate if I don't know where you are and what the hell you're doing. I've even wondered if *love* is a strong enough word for this shit you've done to me."

I brushed his cheek with my thumb. "Yeah, that's hot," I told him.

His big hands grabbed my thighs and jerked me closer until our chests touched. The hard ridge of his erection pressed against my pussy, and I rocked against it just a little.

"Don't. Not yet. I gotta finish," he groaned.

"Okay."

"I'll never let you go. You're not ready now, and I understand that. I'm not ready to share you yet anyway, but one day, I want to knock you up. I want you to be the mother of my kids. My life has dark shit that I will never let touch you, but I can't live it without you."

My eyes stung with unshed tears as I looked at him.

"I was gonna do this on one knee, but you went and pressed that sweet pussy on my dick. I'm sure as fuck not moving you."

One knee …

I stopped breathing.

Huck took my left hand in his much larger one, then kissed my fingers. When the cool touch of metal brushed against my skin, my gaze dropped from his to the diamond ring he was sliding on my finger. It was a large princess cut white diamond with a twist of smaller diamonds. I stared at it, unable to believe what I was seeing.

"I want forever. I want you to have my last name. I want you." Huck's voice was thick with emotion.

I lifted my gaze to meet his. This beautiful, massive, possessive, dangerous man wanted to marry me. This wasn't something I had ever allowed myself to fantasize about. He never spoke of marriage.

"Say something," he whispered.

I looked back down at the ring. "Huck, I would have said yes to you with a ring from a gumball machine."

A low, deep laugh vibrated his chest. "Damn, I could have saved a lot of money."

I lifted my eyes to meet his and let the tears roll down my face.

His world scared me. This life wasn't always going to be easy. But as long as I was loved by this man, I could face anything.

Straight Fire Teaser...

Chapter ONE

SHILOH

I was a list-maker. I made lists about everything. I followed the lists, and I achieved my goals. It was why I always carried a notebook and pen with me. Using technology for my list-making didn't feel the same. Physically writing on paper was the only way the system worked for me.

My uncle Neil, Mom's older brother, glanced over at the notebook in my lap as he drove his truck to our appointment. He was nervous about where we were going, which, to be honest, intrigued me.

Working for my uncle was the only job I knew. He'd hired me eighteen months ago when I left my life in Boston and came to Ocala, Florida. My parents, especially my mother, were furious. She rarely called me, and the few times we had spoken, it had been harsh. I'd let her down by choosing a life she felt was beneath me. Getting up every day and going to my uncle's private practice gave me stability and purpose.

Most of my lists consisted of things to get done in the office. It was something she would never understand.

"A few important details we need to go over," Uncle Neil said, snapping me out of my thoughts. "I have your signed NDA and the other paperwork, but I want to make sure you understand the seriousness of the situation."

I turned to give him my full attention in hopes of assuring him I would be fine. This wasn't the first house call I'd made with him. Since Lynn, his former nurse, had gotten married and moved, I had been going with him to check on patients that he made house calls to. They were all wealthy people who couldn't be bothered with going to an actual hospital or doctor's office. I had found it was for privacy purposes with most of them. This patient, however, seemed to have a new level of privacy attached to them. I had never been required to sign an NDA before.

"This isn't a normal house. There are things you will see and hear that you will question. Don't. And when I say don't, I mean, DO NOT ask any questions, do not repeat anything you hear, do not use your cell phone while on the property, do not engage with any of them unless they ask you a question. You are to simply do what you're being paid to do. Take care of the patient. He will be difficult. He will be inappropriate, and honestly, if he wasn't in such bad shape, I wouldn't let you near him. Being as it is, he can't do much. There is a woman in the house. I've met her. She's very nice and kind. But do not make friends with her. She is Huck Kingston's fiancée, and he's very protective of her."

I nodded my head. This wasn't the first time he had given me this lecture since he'd called me this morning to let me know he had a job for me. It was obvious he was nervous about my being in this house. I had asked if they were famous, not that I cared. It was rare I knew or recognized anyone famous. They weren't famous. They were just powerful.

"I'll be fine. I promise."

He reached over and squeezed my hand. "I know you will. I just don't want anything bad to happen to you. These are dangerous people, and they are connected to a very powerful family."

"Yes, the Hugheses. They own a lot of stuff. Horses and things," I replied. I wasn't sure why that made them so important, but I'd heard my uncle mention them with reverence and respect more than once since I'd been working with him.

We stopped outside a large iron gate, and Uncle Neil pressed a code, then spoke his full name into a speaker. The gate slowly swung open. It was very secure and a bit over the top, but I didn't say that. Uncle Neil might turn around and take me back to the office if I said something negative.

"The patient has a punctured lung, three broken ribs, a leg cast due to the severity of his break, and what else?" I asked, wanting to make sure I remembered everything.

I had read over his chart that Uncle Neil had given me, but I wanted to make sure I'd missed nothing. The full leg cast was temporary and would be cut down below his knee in two weeks. That had been written at the bottom in red.

"Bruised ego and an anger issue," he replied with a frown. "That is the most important thing for you to remember."

I gave him a firm nod. "He's mean and angry. Got it."

Uncle Neil gave me another stern look. "I'll do the talking. You speak when required. I've been working for this family for over twenty years. I have a good relationship with them, and for the most part, I do trust them." He paused, then sighed. "Let's go meet the patient."

Uncle Neil had already done the surgery. This had all happened in the middle of the night, and I'd been woken up at five this morning with a phone call from him, telling me he had a patient and needed my assistance.

"He is sedated for now. That will give us enough time to introduce you to the others here and go over what you need to handle," he told me as we walked up the front steps to the house.

One of the large double doors opened when we reached the top step. A Viking-sized man filled the door with a scowl on his face. I paused because he was intimidating and slightly terrifying. That was one thing Uncle Neil hadn't mentioned.

"He's awake and bitching," the massive man said. "Can you shut him the fuck up?"

Uncle Neil chuckled and nodded his head. "I should have figured he'd be hard to sedate for long. Huck, this is my niece, Shiloh. She is my replacement for Lynn and understands the importance of your privacy."

Huck's gaze swung to me, and his scowl deepened. The way he was looking at me would make me believe he disliked me on sight. "Shiloh." He said my name as if he knew me and again wasn't a fan.

That caused me some concern because I knew that perhaps he did know me—or the me before. The me I didn't know myself. This had happened a few times since my return to Ocala, but not once had someone acted as if they didn't like me. I did, however, have a few reservations about the former Shiloh.

Uncle Neil cleared his throat. "Uh, yes." He glanced at me with a worried frown. It wasn't like I could answer this. "She's responsible and excellent at bedside care. Gage's personality will require someone who isn't easily upset. Shiloh works well in that department."

Huck continued to study me, as if waiting for me to say something. I smiled in return. If these people did their research, they'd find my picture and name on my uncle's website. He could have known who I was for that reason because if he knew the former me, he wasn't saying it. Finally, he stepped back to allow us to enter.

"I'll let Gage make this call," he said, still watching me with unease.

Uncle Neil went inside first, and I followed him. Curious as to why Huck didn't seem pleased with my being the nurse. I did hope Uncle Neil had noticed and would perhaps broach the subject.

"I'll take her upstairs and deal with the patient," Uncle Neil told him.

Huck was still scowling, but he simply gave a nod, then walked away.

Uncle Neil turned to me. "Ready?"

"Yep," I replied.

The tension in his shoulders and tight line of his mouth made it clear he had noticed Huck's odd behavior toward me. Why hadn't he said something? My uncle tried to shelter me from the life I used to have. It didn't bother me normally because I preferred to not have to ask questions. But if I was going to be in this house regularly, then I thought it needed to be addressed.

If they had known me before two years ago, then they needed to know that Shiloh Ellis no longer existed. I'd forgotten her life the moment I hit the black ice and crashed into the side of a mountain.

ACKNOWLEDGMENTS

Those who I couldn't have done this without:

Britt is always the first I mention because he makes it possible for me to close myself away and write for endless hours a day. Without him, I wouldn't get any sleep, and I doubt I could finish a book.

Emerson, for dealing with the fact that I must write some days and she can't have my full attention. I'll admit, there were several times she did not understand, and I might have told my six-year-old, "You're not making it in my acknowledgments this time!" to which she did not care.

My older children, who live in other states, were great about me not being able to answer their calls most of the time and waiting until I could get back to them. They still love me and understand this part of Mom's world.

My editor, Jovana Shirley at Unforeseen Editing, for always working with my crazy schedules and making my stories the best they can be.

My formatter, Melissa Stevens at The Illustrated Author. She makes my books beautiful inside. It's hands down the best formatting I've ever had in my books.

Beta readers, who come through every time: Annabelle Glines, Jerilyn Martinez, and Vicci Kaighan. I love y'all!

Damonza, for my book cover. This cover could not be hotter if it tried.

Abbi's Army, for being my support and cheering me on. I love y'all!

My readers, for allowing me to write books. Without you, this wouldn't be possible.

Printed in Great Britain
by Amazon